THE POORLY MADE
AND OTHER THINGS

Also by Sam Rebelein

Edenville

THE POORLY MADE AND OTHER THINGS

A STORY COLLECTION

SAM REBELEIN

WM

WILLIAM MORROW
An Imprint of HarperCollinsPublishers

Versions of these stories first appeared in the following publications:

"Hector Brim," *Planet Scumm*, Spring 2021; "My Name Is Ellie," *Bourbon Penn*, July 2019, also anthologized in Ellen Datlow's *Best Horror of the Year: Volume Twelve*, October 2020; "Wag," *Dark Moon Digest*, January 2017.

FIRST EDITION

Design by Diahann Sturge-Campbell
Art by Parrot Ivan/Shutterstock, Inc.
Map by Leah Carlson-Stanisic using art by Antipathique, Adobe Stock Images

Library of Congress Cataloging-in-Publication Data has been applied for.

ISBN 978-0-06-325229-5

24 25 26 27 28 LBC 5 4 3 2 1

For that timid young boy in Ohio who wanted
to tell stories and all other kids like him

I had hung my shaving glass by the window, and was just beginning to shave. Suddenly I felt a hand on my shoulder, and heard the Count's voice saying to me, "Good morning." I started, for it amazed me that I had not seen him, since the reflection of the glass covered the whole room behind me. In starting I had cut myself slightly. . . . I saw that the cut had bled a little, and the blood was trickling over my chin. I laid down the razor, turning as I did so half round to look for some sticking plaster. When the Count saw my face, his eyes blazed with a sort of demoniac fury, and he suddenly made a grab at my throat. I drew away, and his hand touched the string of beads which held the crucifix. It made an instant change in him, for the fury passed so quickly that I could hardly believe that it was ever there.

"Take care," he said, "take care how you cut yourself. It is more dangerous than you think in this country."

—JONATHAN HARKER'S JOURNAL, Bram Stoker's *Dracula*

CONTENTS

MAP OF
RENFIELD & BRADDOCK

Renfield County

Braddock County

The Billowhills

▲ Boldiven Lodge

▲ Mount Slake

Crumdugger
State Forest

Shembelwoods

Bent River

• Slake Hill

Billows Road

County Road 7

▲ Bartrick Prison

• Edenville

▲ Dome Lab

▲ Lillian Art
School

• Lillian

• Leaden Hollow

• Tinker's Falls

Bartrick Lake

• Bent

• Furrowkill
(Branson College)

Nettle River

• Bartrick Mill

▲ Bent Asylum

N

W   E

S

Deep Shembels

• Burnskidde

Billowhills

Clate River

Bent River

to the Taconic

THE POORLY MADE AND OTHER THINGS

From: Rachel Durwood <radurwood@bhs.org>
To: tom.durwood@gmail.com
Subject: The Stain

Dear Tom,

So I've been a really bad sis. I meant to email you *days* ago but I just . . . kept not doing it. That's lame of me, I know, but there it is. Sorry. Well, it's Friday—no school tomorrow—so I figured I'd have a drink and finally finish writing this fuckin thing. Idk why I've been so weird about it. But I had a drink, then I had three drinks, and now I'm sitting on the floor of my bedroom with no lights on, hittin Send. Sorry haha.

I know I sank into my own shit after Mom, and I'm sorry about that, too. I know I've been bad about reaching out these last few years, ever since you moved. I *know* I was supposed to be there. We were *supposed* to be there for each other. But it's been months since the funeral and not a word from me. What an asshole. Feel free to just write back, "Fuck you, Rachel." I deserve it. I've abandoned you. I'm sorry. But I hope you still read this. It's sort of an apology, but if I'm being honest, it's really me trying not to be lonely, all cooped up in my sweaty-ass apartment, watching the sun set over the Bent. I just wanted to say hi.

But apologies in advance because this "hi" is going to be *very* long and *very* rambly. Like, "thirteen emails in a row" rambly. Being a high school sub, you don't exactly communicate with a lot of adults, so it'll feel good to just get this shit off my chest. Bear with me, okay?

So I'm writing you now because I've just finished kind of a weird project. That's not an excuse or anything, but I've buried myself in this project the last couple weeks or so, and especially the last few nights. It's really been . . . eating all my time. I've *let* it eat all my time. And I wanted to write to someone who might understand how I've been feeling. How I've been *thinking* about Mom and home and . . . Obviously, I've been thinking about you. So here I am, sharing this weird-ass project/apology with you, hoping that, even if you hate me for making you feel alone again, maybe you'll still listen and understand.

I really hope you understand.

To start with, right after Mom died, I met someone online. He seemed nice. Some kind of doctor, from Lillian. Fancy, I know. I was scared and alone, and it was good to have someone to talk to. It'd been a while since I dated anyone, and . . . Idk.

Anyway, I went back to his place after our second date, and he had this *big* slab of Renfield wood hanging in his living room. Just . . . hanging there, over the mantel, with its weird stain. It made me feel cold all over. Like something was sliding over my bones, wrapping tight, squeezing the blood out of my limbs. This guy clearly thought it was cool, like he was showing off a Picasso or some shit. And when I asked him where he got it, he just gave me this horrible smile. So I was like, "You know what, I forgot my . . . thing in my car," and I got the *fuck* out of there. Figured he'd try to drink my blood or something. You never know.

Or maybe he was fine, and *I'm* the freak. An oversensitive asshole who pushes people away. Maybe it's both.

Maybe you just. Never. Know.

Either way, that night officially set me off on this project. And I've been obsessing over Renfield shit ever since. Not just the wood, but . . . everything.

You *remember* all the stories, right? Monsters and giants and kid-eaters and that guy in the tub? Of course you do. I say that like moving to the city made you forget about home. About good ole Renfield County. Well, maybe I'm nuts, but I think those stories answer . . . everything. I mean that, on top of all the *other* crazy-ass chaos here in Renfield County, I think Renfield provides a reason for Mom.

Did you need a reason for Mom? I did. I do. I really do.

So. I've been compiling all these anecdotes and articles and newspaper clippings into a kind of history report. I really have not slept the last few nights putting it all together, which I *know* is bad, I *know* you're gonna give me shit about that, but it all makes sense, I swear, so please just keep reading? I know correlation doesn't necessarily imply causation, and that's fair. Whatever. But I've been trying to lay it all out and see where Mom fits. A lot of this you already know, of course, growing up here. But it's been helping me to present it like this, all clear and linear. And I swear that, written out like this, it all makes sense. I swear it works through everything. *I'm* working through everything.

You'll see.

Also, not gonna lie, it's been kind of fun. I used to *love* history reports, in high school. So I've been digging through old police records, town archives . . . The ladies at the Edenville Library let you dig through a *surprising* amount of old shit if you're a teacher. Even just an uncertified sub. They were *thrilled* I was even talking to them. So, yeah, that's been a part of this, too. Just lonely ole me, in the library, with my old ladies, after dark. Havin a gas.

Fuck. That's not fair of me to say. I ignored you and hung out with strangers instead. I suck. I'm sorry.

Look, I know I don't deserve to ask you for anything right now, but please read all of this? It's not bullshit. It's about Mom. About *us*. So I *need* you to read this history report.

I need you to *see*:

Hundreds of years before the blood, the giant, Lawrence, and the damned, the Renfields were the first family to settle up here, far north in the New York woods. Because they were here first, the place was always known unofficially as Renfield County. Even when another family settled nearby, then a third, and then dozens. The land was always considered Renfield land.

Then came the morning of December 20, 1927, when the neighbors were the only ones left to clean up the blood. When there was so much of it, coating the stairs in a slick frozen sheet. It caked the floor of the kitchen, the foyer, the living room. A ragged red trail wound a route out the back door through the snow toward the barn—little Robert crawling away. Lawrence must have fired his shotgun from inside the house at Robert's back, just as the kid was shoving open the door. The force of the shot sent Robert flying forward, and blew half the door off its frame. Later, that back door hung loose off its upper hinge, the lower hinge all dented debris. Wood flakes scattered around, buckshot in the wall. As the neighbors cleaned, the back door squeaked shut in the wind, clapped, squeaked open again. Outside, they could see the impression in the snow where Robert had dragged himself away from the house, wounds steaming in the winter air. He only made it two or three yards before Lawrence caught up to him.

Robert Renfield was four when his dad walked up behind him and blew his skull apart into the snow.

HECTOR BRIM

When she'd been gone for seven days, Gil took an ax to her piano.

There'd been a small reception in his apartment after the funeral. Just Natalie's parents, his mother, a handful of friends, and a few neighbors, including Mrs. Preston down the hall. Gil did nothing the entire time but wish them all gone. They had no comfort to give. No reassurances of higher meaning or better places, which they did not believe in. It wasn't the kind of crowd they were, so it wasn't the kind of crowd Gil needed. Mrs. Preston was maybe the only exception. She'd once spoken to him in the elevator, convincingly and unsolicited, about reincarnated pets and the spirit realm. But Gil squirmed in her company. Even *her* words of sympathy and reassurances felt small and cold. She seemed to sense this, leaving the reception early, patting his arm, and telling him, "Knock on my door if anything comes up." There was something ominous about that. It made Gil squirm even more.

He finally managed to usher out everybody else, and as the door closed on Nat's parents, he heard her mother say, "Don't you think we should stay a bit longer?"

"No," her father said, gentle. "Honey, come on. He wants to be left alone."

The door shut on that. *Alone* vibrated throughout the apartment.

For a long time, Gil didn't move. Just stood there, still black-suited and formal, leaning against the door, needing to break something.

He turned. Gazed around at what had been their home. The tall ceilings, exposed brick. Paint they'd picked out together. Shelves filled with their books and photographs. And in the corner, those bone-and-black keys she'd hunched over with her long fingers, smiling as she played him the songs she wrote privately on lunch breaks.

"You could be a famous singer," he'd told her once.

"But then I wouldn't sing for *you*."

The ax was buried in the hallway closet. Why he'd brought it with him when they'd moved down to the city, he couldn't say. Maybe a part of him knew.

He loosened his tie. Rolled up his sleeves. Tore the closet door open. He knelt, began tossing old jackets over his shoulder. A tennis racket. Cobwebbed shoes. He dug the ax out of the dust. Hefted it back into the living room. And began hacking that piano to bits.

A long sliver of wood sliced at his cheek as pieces flew through the air. He felt the sting, but his entire stupid life stung now anyway, so what did it matter. He started with the keys, then moved sideways to the body. The jangling, springy chorus of snapping wires beat against his ears. He grinned, reveling in it. In the breakage of every-thing this once solid, formidable, smiling, perfect thing had been.

The ax crashed again and again.

A wire whipped across his bicep and he stopped. Stood panting above the wooden ruin, debris scattered across the floor. The ax hummed, frozen above his head. He felt himself pulse. Felt the leak down his arm, on his cheek.

The way the truck had hit her as she stepped unknowing off the curb, her arm had nearly cracked in half. Right along the bicep, right *there*. Feeling the wire now across that same spot, on his own arm, he was right back there, ax forgotten. Holding her as she went. Watching her arm twitch. Watching those long fingers go limp. The truck driver standing in the street, rocking back and forth on his heels. Retching. Weeping. Gil never heard his apologies. He just watched the arm twitch . . .

A sound. Soft, far-off. A kind of skittering slowly filled the apartment. Gil let the ax drop and clatter down out of his hand. He listened. Hundreds of insects, or tiny paws, scratching at the floor. Scrabbling across the wooden boards. A hollow, frantic scramble.

Gil frowned. Cocked his head. The noise grew louder. Louder. Began to roar throughout the room. But he couldn't tell what it was.

Someone was standing behind him.

He turned. He was alone. *Alone.* Of course he was. She was gone. But for a second, he'd *felt* someone. Felt a pocket of displaced air or . . . something. He couldn't explain it. He just felt watched.

The roar drowned this feeling out. His pulse, the leaks across his skin, quickened. He realized the noise was now joined by the coppery snaking whir of springs bouncing against each other. Gil turned again, looking around the room, starting to itch and sweat. What the hell *was* it? It sounded half-wooden, half . . . ivory. Sliding across the . . .

"Oh."

He looked down.

The debris of the piano was moving.

As he watched, it rolled itself across the floor and, slow but steady, wove itself into a wide, crooked heart.

Gil blinked at it. Then threw up.

* * *

Because Gil belonged to a group of skeptical, scoffing Manhattanite friends, he didn't really know what to do with . . . this. He didn't have the tools or the language to process the supernatural. And he knew that was probably why his wife had waited an entire week to show herself like this. Nat knew—she *must* have known—that she'd have to wait for a break. A moment when he'd actually believe what he was seeing. Some kind of rock bottom. Well, watching him hack at her piano with an ax was probably the best chance she'd get. Like Gil, she'd been a skeptic, so he *knew* she'd think like that. She'd think, *How can I really convince him?* That is . . . *if*. *If* she really were . . . haunting him.

If.

Gil sat on the couch, knees tucked tight under his chin. He stared at the floor, at the wet spot from the puke he'd mopped up, right in the center of the piano heart. He'd carefully left the heart untouched.

He dug the heels of his hands into his eyes. Shook his head. Laughed. Tried to pull himself together. Laughed again. Gave up. He figured whatever was happening, he might as well go all in. And if he was starting to go crazy, then fuck it, what the hell.

He cleared his throat. Looked around the room, feeling self-conscious. "Alright," he said. "Are . . ." He cleared his throat again. "Are you . . . here?"

There was a green and yellow light fixture in the hall. Something Natalie had brought down to the city, and loved.

It flickered on.

Gil began to cry.

A low rushing breathed down the hall. Gil held his breath. Sliding along the floor, around the corner, came a box of Kleenex. It slid to a halt just before the couch.

"Oh," he said.

* * *

By sunset, he'd cried everything out. He sat calm on the couch, knees still tight against himself. Sore now, after sitting folded like that for hours. Clutching a wad of sodden tissues, he peered down the hall to the light fixture. Not sure what else to do, he said, just sort of confirming, "You're really here."

The light blinked.

Heat flooded his chest. "I . . . I miss you."

The light flickered.

Gil sat up. He stretched his legs and his knees cracked. He wrung his hands, thinking.

"Are you . . . *mad* that I broke your piano?"

The light blinked twice.

Gil nodded. "Okay." He sniffed, ran a hand under his nose. "Okay."

He quickly figured out that he could ask Nat simple yes or no questions through the light. She'd blink once for yes, twice for no. As long as he kept the questions simple, she would answer.

Over the next three weeks, every chance he got, he'd speak with her. And, of course, told no one about it. Sometimes, she would float old pictures around to make him smile, or throw her jewelry across the room. Once, he'd felt a hand on his back. It made him jump and scream. But the hand wrapped around his shoulder, warm and safe. He melted into its company.

He sat under the hall light for hours every day. Talking, reminiscing, sometimes just staring. Silent. Trying not to ache.

Finally, he worked up the strength to ask the most terrifying question he could think of.

"Are you in pain?" Gil sat slumped against the wall. He stared up at the light. Waited for it to respond.

It didn't.

"Hey. Are you in *pain*?"

The light flickered.

She wasn't sure. She *might* be in pain. He could tell. Could feel it through the walls. Some kind of gnawing uncertainty. A looseness or unbalance. Something . . . off with her.

It was after another week of this—of talking and crying and clinging to her, of barely leaving his apartment just to be *near* her, even if it was just a flicker of who she was—that Gil finally decided she probably needed help.

Something echoed through his brain: *Knock on my door if anything comes up . . .*

Well. Something had definitely come up.

Even if she hadn't offered, Gil probably would have trusted Mrs. Preston more than any of his skeptic pals. Especially now that he'd isolated himself for weeks, barely answering their texts and calls. He and Mrs. Preston weren't friends. Not by any stretch of anything. They said hello to each other when they crossed paths in the lobby. In the elevator sometimes, they chatted politely about the weather, city life, reincarnated pets that one time, spirits rarely, and . . . well, they *had* chatted about Nat. Or with her, even, when she'd been there.

That hurt to think about.

Mrs. Preston was about eighty, a good fifty years older than Gil. He couldn't say what she did for a living, really, or call her voice to mind unless he thought hard about it for several seconds. She was just some (and he felt bad thinking this) generic, squat, sweet old lady in his mind. And he was pretty sure then, he realized (and this made him feel slightly better), that to *her*, he was just some generic, tall, handsome young guy. But if anyone would believe in ghosts speaking through light bulbs and piano shards, he felt like it'd be her. Her door stank of sage and mystery every time he walked by it. She had that . . . vibe. A weird energy of *knowing* things. And at the reception, it'd seemed like she'd definitely known. Or guessed.

So.

He stood in the outer hall. Peered down it at Mrs. Preston's front door. He worked his hands into his pockets. He glanced back at his own door, which felt like looking at Nat, now that she seemed to be in the very beams of his apartment. He looked away. Twisted his hands back and forth in his pockets. Dug his cheek into his shoulder, itching the old scab from the piano shard.

What exactly was he going to say to her? How *precisely* did he think she could help him? How could Mrs. Preston help Nat, furthermore? Did she need to "move on," whatever that meant? What if Mrs. Preston thought he was crazy? What if he . . . What if he *was*?

He shook that thought away. Useless at this point. He was in too deep.

He stood there. His hands twisted harder. Faster. The cheek scab itched. With each second, the hallway grew longer.

"Fuck it," he muttered. And he marched down the hall.

The whole thing came tumbling out in jagged starts and stops, almost as soon as she opened the door. He stammered his way through the explanation of the piano and the light. He skipped over some parts that seemed more insane than others. But he was also describing his wife's ghost inhabiting his apartment, so what sounded insane versus what *didn't* felt like kind of a toss-up. The more he talked, the more self-conscious he felt. As he spoke, his hands never left his pockets.

Mrs. Preston listened to the whole thing, face twitching between confusion, concern, and something else. She smiled at him as he rambled, babble coming out of him in one long stream.

"And I feel," he finished, at last, "that she's just . . . spaced out. Stretched. That her . . . I don't know, the spirit? Has just expanded into the whole place. Instead of being *in* her. And . . . well . . ."

He stopped. Something he'd said had made Mrs. Preston's eyes light up. They danced over him. He wasn't sure how to take that. Almost backed away from her.

She knew, he decided.

"It's funny you use that word," she said. "Expanded."

Gil shrugged. "It's how I feel. Er—"

"You think it's how *she* feels?"

"Of course," he said. "And, and confused. Lost. I know her, I can *feel* it." The words were more high-pitched, more desperate than he expected. His cheeks burned. *What am I* saying?

But Mrs. Preston just nodded. Grinned wide.

"One moment," she said.

She shuffled away into her apartment, leaving the door open. Gil stood there. His mind railed at him. Called him stupid, told him to go back to his cage and hide with the dead. What did he think he was doing here? Bothering an old, kind woman with his bullshit.

He was just about to stalk shamefully back down the hall when Mrs. Preston returned, still grinning. She held her hands tight to her chest. Whatever she was holding, Gil couldn't see it.

She leaned against the jamb. Sighed. Closed her eyes for a moment. Ran her thumbs in circles around the thing in her hands.

"My husband," she started. Stopped. Swallowed some sharp stab of tears. She tried again, voice stronger this time. "My husband. When he died, I didn't know what to do with myself."

Mr. Preston was a somewhat nebulous entity to Gil. From what he'd gathered, the man had died about two years before Gil and

Nat moved in. She'd mentioned him once or twice, but no more than a passing mention.

Gil stood a little straighter, alert.

"And, apparently," she continued, "he didn't know what to do either. Because he never left."

The bottom of Gil's stomach opened.

"I never knew," he said.

"Oh, yes," said Mrs. Preston. "His spirit was still with me. And in such pain . . . I knew *I* wasn't ready to move on. But I could feel *he* wasn't ready, either. *Because* of me. I could feel it through the walls. And whenever he made himself known, whether it was just a little sign or a feeling I got, I could tell that he was still there because he was worried I wouldn't be okay alone."

Gil's eyes flicked down to her hands.

"We were both hurting," she went on. "But then a friend gave me this."

Her fingers blossomed and revealed the thing she'd been hiding. A business card. She held it out to him, delicately, in both hands. To be offered, so ceremoniously, something so simple and secular made Gil suddenly uneasy. He gave her a dubious look. He removed a hand from his pocket, slow, and took the card from her. It was grimy, mostly blank. Looked almost homemade. Nothing on it but a number, in deep, black font. And a name. Gil turned it over, expecting more on the back. There wasn't any.

"I don't get it," he said.

"He helps people," said Mrs. Preston. Her eyebrows yanked themselves up and down, confidential. Her head trembled. As if passing on this knowledge excited but exhausted her. Drained her of some old burden.

Gil looked down again at the card. Its edges frayed. Dark brown spots. Passed between dozens of hands over dozens of years.

Just a number. And a name.

He tried to hand it back to her. "I don't need a therapist."

She shook her head, put her hands up, palms out. "No, no. You misunderstand. He isn't . . . He's a kind of healer."

The card lingered in the air between them. Once he realized he was stuck with it, Gil allowed himself to draw it back in. It felt heavier than it had a few seconds ago.

"He helped me understand," she explained, "that when people die, their spirits expand. Swell out of the body into the air. To be part of everything without being bound. That's the beauty of being *released* after death. But if they feel . . . unfinished, people get stuck. Halfway. They . . . echo back. These echoes aren't contained in bodies anymore, of course, so they become tethered to a specific place. Like your apartment. Sometimes an object, like a mirror. And they sort of . . . bounce around in there, in that loose, expanded state, instead of swelling into the air and being free. It's *hard*. But this man." She wagged a finger at the card. "He helps set them free. That's where my husband has gone now."

"Gone," said Gil. It was the only word that really stood out.

She nodded. "But gone where he's a *part* of everything, like he's supposed to be. Gone to . . . a better place."

"Ah-huh." Gil stared at the card. It grew heavier. "Well, thanks," he said. Immediately he hated himself for sounding disingenuous. "I mean, really. Thank you. I'll . . . I'll give him a try."

She grinned again. He tried not to look at her teeth, realizing just how gray they were. "Do. He *helps*. He'll help your wife find her way."

"Right. No, I appreciate it. I'll give you the card back after I call him?"

"Oh, no. I don't need it anymore. It's yours." With that, she waved, wished him good luck, and shut the door. A waft of incense puffed out after her. He coughed.

Gil remained for several seconds, until he heard the chain slide on the other side of the door, and he figured it was probably time to walk back down the hall. The entire way, he held the card out in front of his chest. Stiff. As if it were on fire.

Nothing there. Except a number. And a name.

When he got home, it took him ten nervous minutes, one hand holding the card, the other turning in his pocket, to finally take out his phone and dial the number.

It rang twice.

When the line connected, he heard a cough. The crack-rustle of moving leather. Then a voice. Low and thick, like the drone of a distant lawn mower: "Hector Brim. Help you."

Gil swallowed. This was not the voice he'd expected. It did not feel safe. It did not feel helpful. It felt, instead, like someone had stretched rubber bands across his limbs and now tugged them hard. He wanted to hang up, and curl in on himself.

"Hello," he managed. "My name is, uh, Gil. I have a, a problem."

"Most people do."

This threw him off. "It's . . . Ah-huh. Right. Well. I got this card from a friend. I . . . It's my wife. She—"

"When did she pass?"

Again, Gil was taken aback. The voice hadn't skipped a beat. No preamble. No explanations. The blank simplicity of the card made itself felt here, too. This man knew what he was about.

"About a month ago," he said.

"Recent."

A pause. Gil's grip on the phone tightened. He wasn't sure if he was supposed to say something or if the man on the other end was thinking. He pictured the voice out there, what its owner looked like. Saw him sitting in shadow, draped over an armchair in a corner somewhere. Nothing but stillness and dark. He realized how opposite this was of what he had expected and—

The voice broke in on him: "Your address?"

Numb, Gil could think of nothing else to do other than to give it to him.

"Mm. Been there before."

"Yes. Um. Mrs. Preston. She gave me your card."

"Not much for names."

Another pause. Gil winced.

"So," he said.

"Alright. Three hours work for you?"

"Three . . . Sorry, three hours from *now*?"

"Mm."

"I." Gil cleared his throat. "Yes. Sorry. Yes. That works."

"Be four hundred."

"Sorry, dollars?"

The line went dead.

Gil began to pace, heart and mind racing. Eventually, he landed on the couch in the living room. Tucked his knees up under his chin. Coiled himself there, tight and anxious. He wondered what he was supposed to do for three hours. Knew he would do nothing but sit.

Regret flooded him.

A better place . . . Christ, that's . . . What is that? What a fucking cliché. That might be all well and good for Mr. Preston, but whatever that "better place" was, Natalie would be *gone*. And suddenly, he wasn't so sure he wanted that. Even if it meant hurting her, he wanted her to stay. Because if she left, he'd be totally, completely *alone*.

He thought about asking the light in the hall for her opinion, but he was afraid to know the answer.

No. He knew. And he knew he knew. This was the right thing to do. He was just scared, that was all.

So he sat. Waiting. His entire body throbbing.

Finally, he got up and wrote a check to Hector Brim.

When Hector Brim was young, he moved to the city because he wanted to feel connected to everything. All the voices and echoes he could possibly hear. He'd brought with him his bag of Brim family tricks. The tricks were old, but new to him and exciting. For the most part. There had been a few that, for the several years his father trained him, passing on his inheritance, Hector had never really liked or understood.

For example, the brand.

"Doesn't it hurt?" Hector asked once, when he was nine.

"This tool is for angry, violent spirits," his father explained. "Ones beyond our help, and in need of control."

"But they're people, too."

"Everybody is people, too."

"So we should help *everybody*."

His father smiled. A limp, tired thing. "You can try. That's all this family *has* done, for nearly fifty years. Try . . . Come, let's keep practicing. Hold the brand to the light again. Your form needs improvement."

When Hector moved to the city, he rented a small apartment in Chinatown, and everything was magic. This was back when he was really helping people, and the irises of his eyes were sunlight on leaves. He looked through these bright green eyes at his new apartment, beaming. They shone as he thought of all those echoes, all the people there to help. All around him, in the tall glittering of the city.

It was a bright time. Being young.

But the more time he spent in that apartment—the more he listened to the radiator's metallic tattoo, the scurry of rat-feet on floorboards, the couple upstairs who fought and broke things, and the alley downstairs where people screamed at two a.m.— the smaller it felt. More cramped. More lonely.

Jobs poured in. Word of mouth. People desperate. Seeking closure. Seeking help. Seeking proof of Something More.

He kept doing it, dealing out his family tricks like candy. But the high lessened every time. For a while, he kept bringing the stones to the shore every time he used the box for a job. Kept dumping the stones into the brine and trying to feel good about it all. Trying. He even tried to feel good about the times he had to use the more violent tricks, like the brand.

But something held him back.

One day, before he brought the latest stone to the beach, Hector gazed out his one small window at the afternoon. He held the stone in his hand, soaking in its warmth and company, the voice inside. He always liked to sit with them like that. Just for a little while. The company was good, for what it was. The sun gleamed against all that glass stuck up in the sky. He tried to breathe it in. Feel less cramped. Tried to press his palm against the window and touch it all. All those people . . .

But the family tricks don't work that way.

His eyes landed on a face. Stuck inside another window, far across the way, gaping out at the same bleak cityscape. And seeing that, Hector realized that he wasn't connected to anything at all. He was in a cage. His palm against the bars. That face was in its own cage. And all across the city, there was nothing at all but cage upon cage upon cage. All alone. All clanking, scurrying, fighting, breaking, mugging, fucking, crying, dying. No trick could help or stop all that. He realized this, and something inside of him began to turn. Began to bend.

He never took that last stone to the beach.

Eventually, his entire world became nothing more than the warm-metal piss-stink of a life lived in a constrictive, concrete Hell.

And that was a very long time ago.

Gil opened the door. He had to take a step back and blink. Looking at Hector Brim gave him vertigo. The doorway swam a little, and it took him a moment to steady it. The man was well past six feet tall, looming a solid foot over Gil. He was old. Tufts of dirty-snow hair cotton-balled across his head. The vertigo came not from his height but from his body, which was cracked to one side. Head lilting toward his left shoulder, and the shoulder sagging outward. It was the bag in the man's left hand. It dragged an entire half of his body down toward the floor. A massive, black leather briefcase. Stuffed with what Gil assumed could only be bricks. The man's eyes made Gil dizzy, too. The irises were a deep moss. Overgrown and forgotten. The man's beige trench coat must have weighed a ton. And it was August.

The man spoke: "Gil?" That old lawn-mower groan.

"I am. Yes." Gil stuck out his hand. Hector Brim stared at it. Gil retracted.

"Come in," he said. "Mr. . . . ."

"Just Brim."

Brim had to duck under the doorway. He stepped into the room, feet heavy, echoing. Gil closed the door behind him. As soon as Brim entered the apartment, he locked his eyes on the ceiling. Grunted. Moved into the living room. The carcass of the piano was still in the corner, but Brim didn't even glance at it. He moved in slow circles around the room, gazing up at the ceiling. The bag thudded against his thigh, but he seemed not to mind. He'd done this hundreds of times before. Thousands, maybe. Gil could tell.

The room was silent except for the soft pound of the bag and the flutter of the trench coat. Gil stood awkwardly by the door. Shoved his hands into the pockets of his jeans. Should he say something? Brim didn't seem to mind the quiet, so Gil remained silent. Brim swung his head from side to side. It swung him into the hall, and his body followed it, as if the rest of his spine were only vaguely attached to his skull. *A broken rag doll*, Gil thought. He hesitated, then followed in Brim's wake. When he did, he found Brim standing in the middle of the hall, staring straight up. Straight into the light fixture.

"Jesus," Gil couldn't stop himself from muttering. "That's her."

"Seems like."

"I mean . . . You're the real deal. Aren't you?"

"Never heard anything to the contrary." Brim kept his eyes on the light.

Gil became immediately aware that Nat was hiding. That she was pointedly not making herself known. She didn't want to go. She wasn't ready to leave him. He could feel it. His hands turned in his pockets. Anxiety tugged at those rubber bands in his arms. He shuddered.

"Woman down the hall," said Brim.

"Um. Mrs. Preston."

Brim grimaced. "Names . . ."

Gil wasn't sure what he meant by that.

"She explain to you?" Brim asked. "About souls?"

"She said something about expansion? I mean, no, not really. I . . . Look—"

"Mm." Brim lurched back into the living room. He breezed

past Gil, pressing him against the wall. The bag almost rammed into Gil's knee as he passed. Again, Gil followed. He felt stupid following this man around *his* apartment, but he wasn't sure what else he was supposed to be doing.

"Souls," said Brim. He positioned himself in the middle of the living room, and Gil felt his blood go cold. Brim stood in the exact center of where the heart had been. Maybe Brim already knew that. That was probably the point.

In his pockets, Gil's hands churned.

"When our bodies release them," Brim continued, "they spiral out into the ether." He placed his briefcase on the floor. "Typically, they go elsewhere. Don't know much about *that*." He undid the zipper running along the top of the briefcase. Its lips yawned open. Gil could almost hear it sigh. "But if there is a lack of what you might call *closure*, the spirit remains. In a somewhat half-tethered, expanded state. Your wife, for instance." The bag looked like it was choking. It gasped for air. Jaw muscles stretched tight against whatever was lodged in its throat. Gil felt it, like a living thing. He stepped back. "Your wife has *expanded* out of her body and has sunk herself into the very beams of your home. It is, I'm sure, uncomfortable." Brim reached down into the gaping maw of the bag. It seemed to gag around his wrist. Gil took another step back. "What we do here is re-condense those souls. Bind them back into something more . . . solid." Brim pulled a box out of the bag's innards. He held it up and looked at it.

The box was an ancient thing. It had the same passed-down quality as Brim's card. Its sides shone black from decades of hands. The small brass latch had once glittered, and now bore the dull refraction of a dying fluorescent.

Brim placed the box on the floor next to the bag. He slid open the latch, lifted the lid, let it fall back. The empty box and the stuffed bag sat next to each other, yawning at the ceiling. Trying to swallow it whole.

"The box will accomplish that," Brim concluded. "It is a . . . powerful tool. My grandfather, Porter Brim, crafted this box when he was my age. He removed his own fingers as an offering, and used his stubs to carve this, from Renfield barnwood. Not that that means anything to you?" He gave Gil a questioning glance. Gil shook his head. "Mm. Thought not."

Brim ambled over to the couch. Sat down with a large rush of air. He sighed. The coat settled about him. He was still.

Gil stared at him. Almost a minute passed. Brim sat motionless, hands in his lap. Eyes blank. Gil shifted side to side. Part of him wanted to grab the ax again and hack the little box apart. Silence throbbed against his ears until, finally, he burst. "Sorry, I don't understand what's happening."

Brim jerked his shoulders. "Your wife will condense inside the box. I'll take her to a place where she can be free. She'll be ready in a minute or two."

"Yeah, sorry, I don't know what the fuck that means, though." Anger curled into Gil's voice. Brim stared at him, unmoved. Those old eyes, those twin moss-covered rocks, gaped out from their sockets.

Gil stepped forward. Took his hands out of his pockets. "Hey. What does that *mean*?"

Brim sighed again. Everything seemed hard to him. Everything a struggle. He seemed to drag himself through talking just like he dragged his body through space. "Look, don't bother asking how it works, because I don't know. Just that it does. The box draws souls inside itself. Once inside the box, they crystallize into stones. The stone reflects the true spirit of the person being condensed. Agate, pyrite, opal, amazonite, obsidian, red coral . . . Most people are quartzite." He shook his head. "You wouldn't *believe* how many people are quartzite."

"I don't give a shit about quartzite. I know my wife. I don't need to see her true whatever the fuck."

"Not about need. Happen anyway." The final word strained as Brim stood. He unbent himself from the couch and his joints cracked. He shuffled back to the box, continuing to crack and pop along the way. He towered above the ancient, wooden thing. Peered into it.

"Ah," he said. He stooped, reached inside.

Gil felt manic. Felt angry energy beating through his body like massive drums. He was restless and tired, and he wanted this man gone. He wanted his wife back. Wanted her to stay. Not *crystallized*. *Fuck* this.

He charged to the door, threw it open, and said, voice shaking, "You know what? This, this is done. I'm sorry. I don't want this."

Brim didn't move. He kept his hand in the box.

"Hey. Did you hear me? I—"

"Tiger's eye."

Gil blinked. "I'm sorry?"

"Tiger's eye." Brim held up a gleaming honey-colored stone, about the size of his thumb.

Gil swallowed. "Where . . . where did that come from? How did you get that? What is that?" His mind rejected it. This rock was not his wife.

Brim ignored him. "Tiger's eye is a good one. Your wife was very confident."

Gil shook his head. "Stop."

"She was grounded. Practical. Had an artistic streak."

"Please stop."

"She made you feel safe. Brought good luck."

"I said *stop*."

"Here."

Brim strode over to Gil. He held out the stone. Eels swarmed in Gil's stomach. He hesitated. Then gave Brim his hand. Brim placed the stone in Gil's palm. It was warm. Felt . . . full.

"Can you feel her?" Brim asked.

Gil's voice came from far away. "Yes."

"Can you hear her?"

His eyes burned. He didn't move his hand. He felt the warmth, the pulse of those ribbons of color. Tried to focus, and feel or hear anything else.

"No," he said. His voice caught in his throat.

"I can. She has a beautiful voice. Hearing her sing must have been very special."

Gil looked up. The man's face remained mossy and distant.

"What are you going to do with her?" Gil asked. "I mean, how does this help her? She's *in* there? Fucking . . . *in* there?"

"I'll take her to the beach. Many other stones. There, she can be with the ocean and the land and everything else. Free. Connected to the entire world."

"Oh," said Gil. He didn't take his eyes off the stone.

After a long time, Brim slid it from Gil's hand. "It's time."

Gil felt suddenly cold and empty.

"I can take her to the beach," he said, desperate. "Let me take her."

Brim shook his head. "There's another step."

"Can I at least wa—"

"It must be done alone. It's how the trick works."

Gil shrank. "Oh."

"Don't worry. She'll be fine. Think of it like spreading your ashes into the ocean."

"Ah-huh. I . . . I like that."

"Most people do."

These were the last words they exchanged. Brim slipped the stone into the breast pocket of his coat. With it, Gil felt like his soul slipped away, too. He opened his mouth. Nothing came. He closed it. Brim gathered up his bag, gagging it again with the box and sealing its lips with the old, bulging zipper. Gil watched, feeling empty. Not sure what else to do. He gave Brim the check. And the man was gone, thumping out the door with his bag. Quiet and somehow shameful, like he'd just broken Gil's heart. And Gil, just as ashamed, slumped back onto the couch. Coiled himself back up. The walls closed on him. The apartment was empty. Down to its very beams. For the first time since the funeral, he felt truly, irrevocably alone. An animal in a cage. He told himself that it was the right thing. That she would be alright. That *he* would be alright. He told himself everything was fine. Everything was good.

And then he wept.

Outside, lurching through the hall, Brim heard him. He smiled. He knew that feeling. And it was so delicious, letting it spread around him like a weed.

Hector Brim never went to the beach. Instead, he dragged himself along the subway, back to his hot, cramped apartment. The bag kept him lopsided, whacking against his leg as the subway moved. Sometimes he thought about not bringing it. Bringing just the box. He usually just needed the box. But you never know. If the woman had been stubborn, he'd have needed the lighter, the saw. Maybe even the brand. Best to be prepared.

Scraping down the street, bag thumping at him. August, and the trench coat made him sweat. Could take it off for once. But without the coat, he wouldn't have his father's echo, which was company, at least.

The echo kept asking *why*.

Rolled his shoulder back. Rolled the voice out of his mind. Didn't need the judgment. Just the company.

Back at his building, not as nice a place as Gil's. No tall ceilings. No elevator. Everything here warped, curling wood. The floor didn't reflect or clap as you walked on it. It screamed.

Key stuck in the lock. Door stuck on the jamb. AC broken, leaking on the floor.

The coat twitched. Called him back to the beach. Tried to remind him this wasn't what the family tricks were for.

Tried.

Hector took off the coat, and the echo vanished. He hung it on a hook by the door. Limped into the main room. Turned and stood before the large glass table. Perfect, unstained. Ancient. Passed down, like almost everything else here. And resting in its center, the massive glass bowl.

That was Hector's, and Hector's alone.

Hector dropped his bag on the floor. He stepped out of his loafers, nudged them against the wall. Gray-blue balls of hairy dust fluttered in his wake. He moved back down the hall, to the coat. Reached inside the pocket. As he brushed against the fabric, he heard the faint echo-cry of his father. Ignored it. Removed the chunk of tiger's eye from the pocket. Moved away. Returned to the table. The bowl.

He ran the warm stone between his fingers. Felt the woman in there. Heard her. He held her above the bowl for a moment. Listening. Watching. Feeling her through his fingers. She was attractive, willful, and he could feel her throwing herself around with the confidence that tiger's eyes usually indicated. She *did* have a beautiful voice. Probably wonderful to hear her sing. But it was even more beautiful to hear her scream. Beautiful to hear her trapped inside that tiny stone. Afraid. Confused. Beating her head against its sides, unable to understand the cell she'd been sucked into. Utterly alone. In the dark. Lost, hurting, scared, and, above all, stuck there for eternity.

He smiled.

He dropped her into the bowl.

She clattered down against hundreds of others. Brilliant colors flashed through the glass. Purple, blue, green, red, and orange. Bright white and pitch-black. Stones of every kind. Quartzite. There was a *lot* of quartzite.

Hector's fingers itched with excitement. He grinned, wide and wolfish. He let himself linger there, fingers twitching over the rim of the bowl, for as long as he could stand. This was the best part of his day. He savored it. Then plunged his hand inside. The roar was orgasmic. Thousands of voices, all howling, weeping. All sucked into the box against their will and beaten into rock. Locked in some cramped, intangible vessel, with nothing but four walls and a hard floor. Unable to feel or see beyond its bonds. They did not sleep. Did not hunger. Nothing to break the monotony except tears and the memory of light.

Hector closed his eyes. Lost himself in this cacophony, this chorus of suffering. His knees began to quake. He had to sit down. He kept one hand in the bowl, fingers hot against the screams of the many dead. He reached around blind for a chair with the other hand. Dragged it to himself. Dropped into it. Sighed. The euphoria, the ache, the *company* of this bowl. So good. Good to not feel *alone*.

He licked his lips. Swam his fingers around. The stones clicked and beat against each other. Voices faded and grew as he grazed against each new soul.

This, he thought. *This* was the true connection. The heart of everything human. Suffering. Shadow. Loneliness.

Somewhere in the back of his mind, his father's voice still begged. Told him, for the millionth time, that this was not why the tricks had been passed down. They were passed down to *help* people.

When you were young, Hector, you understood. So why this? *What happened?*

Who the hell knows, he answered, and shoved his father out of his skull.

His hand stopped. His thumb had landed against one piece in particular. Hector fished it out of the bowl. Held it above the rim. Looked at it. It was cold. Lifeless. He had to squeeze it hard to feel the soul inside. What a coincidence. Mr. Preston. Huddled deep into the rock. Closed in on himself in the corner of his cell. Silent and limp.

Hector remembered him now. Remembered how the man used to thrash. To beg. All quiet now. All empty-eyed and sad.

Sometimes this happened. Sometimes so much time had passed, and so much despair had been spent, that the souls inside the stones faded. Stopped crying or trying to escape or anything. They just . . . stopped. Sat down. Grew cold. And remained there. Staring at the walls. Miserable. Forever.

Hector understood. It happens.

He popped the stone into his mouth and ate it. Crunched Mr. Preston between his teeth, ground him into nothing, and swallowed him out of existence.

Whatever beauty there was in the world, Hector Brim never felt like he had been made privy to it. But at least he could try to make himself feel better.

Try.

He closed his eyes, and dove his hand back into the bowl.

Except for the sound of stones running between his fingers, the little apartment was silent. Upstairs, the couple still fought, after all this time. Down in the alley, a pregnant homeless girl vomited.

Everyone everywhere alone.

From: Rachel Durwood <radurwood@bhs.org>
To: tom.durwood@gmail.com
Re: The Stain

So Lawrence Renfield killed his entire family one morning five days before Christmas. Only took him three minutes to do it. Three. Isn't that insane? Do you think you could do all *this* in three minutes, Tom? Because I don't:

May, age sixteen, he killed in the upstairs bathroom. Shot her through the door, which we know because of the hole in the door and because of the splinters the doctor pulled out of her, along with all the buckshot. Henry, age eight, he killed in the living room, sitting in an armchair with a book. Lawrence shot him dead-on, pulverizing the book and punching a hole straight through Henry's stomach, through the back of the chair. The hole was so complete, so perfectly made, that police found shreds of book plastered to the wall behind the chair. Adelaide, Lawrence's wife, he killed in the kitchen. She was standing at the sink when he blew her face out the window. They found half an eye in the snow outside, apparently, but somebody pocketed it while they were investigating the scene, as a souvenir.

One of the Edenville Library ladies told me the eye showed up at a Halloween auction one year recently, but nobody believed it was the real deal. Except the guy who bought it, I guess.

Anyway, there were Adelaide, Henry, May, and Robert, of course. But there was also the baby girl, fresh and unnamed, whom Lawrence bludgeoned to bits in its crib with the butt of the gun.

From the way the blood splatter dried, police could read almost the entire story. They could tell Lawrence killed Adelaide first, *boom*, then he whirled around into the living room and *boom*, there went Henry. The shots must have alerted little Robert and May (I mean, *I'd* be fuckin alerted), and they hid in separate rooms on the second floor. When Lawrence trudged upstairs and killed May, Robert made a break for it. Lawrence chased him down the stairs, shot him in the back, and assumed him dead. The baby must have been screaming then, because Lawrence went back upstairs, beat her to death, and came back down to find Robert gone. Lawrence followed that deep red trail in the snow out the back door and came upon Robert crying by the barn. He placed the shotgun against the back of his son's head and pulled the trigger.

Three minutes, to do all that.

I can't decide if that's a lot of time. I think it'd take me longer. I *like* to think it'd take me longer. More than three minutes at least. That just . . . doesn't seem like enough time. I don't know. It's almost . . . impressive. Don't you think?

When he was done, Lawrence dragged the torn pulp of his son inside the barn. Gun in one hand, fistful of shirt in the other.

And *that*, of course, is where things get weird.

MY NAME IS ELLIE

My name is Ellie, and I like ceramic figurines.

Not the little angels or the ones based on paintings, but the ones that are just little people.

Which I know is not what most ten-year-olds are into, but I like them.

Which is something my mom says I picked up from my grandma.

Which is my mom's mom.

Which is funny because I also got my name from my grandma, whose name was Ellen.

Which, for a while, was pretty much the only thing I knew about my grandma, who died before I was born.

Which my dad once said, at a party when he was very drunk, is a good thing.

Which is because she scared him.

Which my mom said is only because my dad is "intimidated" by women who know things he doesn't.

Which she said is all women.

Which my dad said isn't true and she knows it, that's not why he was afraid of her, to which my mom said, "Shut up or I'll dip you in glaze and pose you myself."

Which I didn't really understand.

Intimidated isn't really a word I understand either.

Anyway.

One of the only other things I know about my grandma is that she lived in a large lonely house in the middle of the woods.

Which my mom says smelled very nice when it rained.

Which she says was one of her favorite things about living in that house when she was my age.

Which always makes me wish I'd gotten to meet my grandma and see her house.

Which is gone now.

Which is sad, because my mom says it was beautiful and had lots of stained glass and "gables."

Which sounds fancy even though I don't know what a gable is.

My mom says that Grandma's house was in the woods west of Lillian, across the river. That's where all the fancy people in Renfield live, up around Lillian. To get to her neighborhood, you had to drive over Bartrick Bridge, and go past the prison, which seems spooky except I think the prison is cool. *We* live in Bartrick Mill, but that's because we don't have as much money as Grandma did. Grandma's family earned a lot of money from lumber (which is a fancy word for *trees*), so she could afford to live by Lillian, in her nice house in the woods.

My mom says that Grandma's house was *surrounded* by pine trees, and the driveway wound up a *big* hill, and the air was always misty, so you couldn't see the tops of the trees on this hill, and the house was *so* high up that when you couldn't see the tops of the trees, it felt like you couldn't see the very top of the world itself.

Which my dad says is horseshit.

Which my mom says is a bad word, and whenever he says it, she makes him put a dollar in the jar on our counter.

Which my dad always does without grumbling.

Which my mom says is because he's actually very nice (and he is!), he just gets scared when she talks about my grandma, that's all.

Which Mom says is also kind of why Dad won't go in my bedroom at night, and why he sometimes won't even go in there by himself during the day.

Which can be annoying sometimes, if she asks him to go in there to get my laundry, to help her with the chores, or something.

But she also understands, because of all the ceramic figurines in my room.

Which he says he's never liked, ever since he met my grandma.

Which my mom says was in college, during a winter break.

Which was about a year after they'd started going out.

Which I think is gross to think about—my parents going out.

Anyway.

My mom says that my dad really liked Grandma's house, too, and that he even liked all the figurines at first.

Which was good, because Grandma Ellen had lots of them on the shelves all around her house.

My dad says there were hundreds. All standing around in suits and fine dresses, waving to each other or playing games or doing other simple poses. All over the house. On shelves, in cabinets, on the mantel, on tables, on the stairs, and just standing on the floor. At Christmastime, they hid three Christmas figurines in the house, all wearing Santa suits, and whoever found them got a candy cane.

Which my grandpa never approved of, because he thought candy was the devil, but that's one reason why my mom says I would have liked Grandma Ellen's house.

She also says I would have liked the house because everything was a dark, rich wood, and all the ceilings were carved into arches, and all the rooms echoed if you yelled, and you could stand in one corner and whisper to someone in another corner and they'd whisper back, and the wallpaper was very pretty, and there was a library filled with books (which sounds like heaven to me), and because there were people who lived inside of the walls.

Which my mom says she told my dad about before he visited for the first time.

Which she says she was really nervous about—even more than him meeting her parents.

Which she says is because she thought he might think she was crazy.

Which, my dad says, he did.

At first.

My dad says he thought the house was too big. He hated all the open space. He didn't like how lonely it was. And he says the "altitude" (which means it's very high up, which I said already) messed with his head and made him dizzy whenever he climbed the stairs. He didn't like looking out the windows at the trees and not knowing where the trees ended. He says the mist made him nervous.

Which my mom says is only because he doesn't have a "sense of mystery."

Which I understand, because my dad is always the one who plans everything and keeps track of stuff.

Which my mom calls "being grounded."

Which she likes about him.

But which she also says can be a bad thing, because it means you're not open to new and weird stuff.

Which is why my dad didn't believe her about the people in the walls, and why he still doesn't like all my figurines. He's just not open.

To which my dad says, "That's definitely one way to put it."

Which he says without looking at Mom or me.

My dad says he figured my mom was just hearing mice in the walls, or some other critters. He says she must have been scared sleeping as a little girl in a big, lonely house in the middle of the woods.

Which my mom says is wrong because the woods never bothered her, and the sounds she heard were definitely people sounds.

Which she says included things like laughter, utensils clicking against plates, bootsteps, teeth-brushing, and whispers.

Which she says would only happen at night, and only after everyone else was asleep.

That's when she'd hear them wake up.

Which she says sounded mostly normal—like people yawning and shuffling around and making coffee, and making that sleepy murmuring you hear people do in bed just after they wake up—except smaller.

Which she says is because they *were* much smaller—only about half a foot tall.

Which meant their days were shorter.

Which she says always started with them making tea.

Which she always thought was terrible because she could hear the kettle on the stove whistling, shrill and loud, through the wall, and it always made her ears ring.

Which was then followed by the gentler sounds of the people going about their day.

Reading the paper, playing games with each other, two meals, and a snack right before dawn, when they would go to sleep.

Which my mom says she heard every single night, for years, ever since she was a very little girl.

My dad says she told him this, and he thought she was kidding.

But then, he says, he heard it, too.

The first night he stayed at my grandma's, my mom fell asleep right away (forgetting about the people in the walls because she was so used to them), and my dad was left alone to listen to their sounds all night long, scared stiff.

He heard them make tea.

He heard them read the paper.

He heard them play chess.

He heard them laughing.

He heard them dancing.

And then, at dawn, he heard them pick one of their own and tear them apart limb by limb with their bare hands.

Which he's only told me once or twice, and both times it's made his hands shake.

He says he could hear all of it.

He says he *knows* it happened because he could hear, through the wall over the bed, the skin bursting and the joints ripping and the screams of the one chosen and the chant of the ones doing the killing.

Which went, "This is our choice. This is our choice. This is our choice."

Which my dad says he could hear coming from all over the wall.

Which he says must have been filled with hundreds, maybe thousands of people.

"This is our choice. This is our choice. This is our choice."

Which they said over and over as they did the "butchering," which my dad says is the only word for it.

Which he says was then followed by all the people in the walls, very formally, saying good night to one another.

Which was then followed by silence, as dawn slid through the window.

In the morning, Grandma Ellen smiled at him and asked him if he heard the people in the walls.

Which my mom said she'd forgotten about because she'd been so tired.

Which she said she was sorry about, because she'd meant to stay up with him so he wasn't scared.

My dad said he *did* hear, and did they know the people in the walls killed each other?

My dad says that this was the worst part because Mom and Grandma Ellen just laughed and told him that was normal. They'd always thought the people in the walls were just regular people, except that they were smaller and they made "sacrifices."

Well, some people make sacrifices all the time.

Which doesn't make them *bad*, just different.

Which my mom and grandma explained to Dad.

My grandpa said the people in the walls didn't have jobs, and called them "communists," but I don't know what that means.

My mom says none of this made my dad feel better.

My mom says he spent the rest of the day staring at the walls, jumping when anyone said his name.

My mom says she caught him scratching at a rip in the wallpaper once.

My mom says he didn't want to go to bed.

My mom says they lay together in the dark, talking, and she promised she'd stay up with him.

My mom says she feels bad about it, but she drifted off again, leaving him alone, staring at the ceiling.

My dad says he thought about shaking her awake, but something told him not to.

My dad says he didn't move a muscle all night.

My dad says he heard them again, and he could hear them so clearly that he could picture what was happening in his head, step by step, when they did the "butchering."

They'd chant, "This is our choice. This is our choice. This is our choice."

They'd tear and break and crush and twist and rip.

They'd press the sacrifice's eyes back into their sockets until the eyes popped, then they'd tape the mouth shut (he says he could hear the peal of the little duct tape).

They'd saw open the neck and then tape that shut, too, so the sacrifice bled into their own throat and drowned in it, and because their hands were already twisted off, they couldn't take off the tape so they'd just wriggle around like worms until they died.

Then the people in the walls all said good night to each other, very formally, and went to bed.

My mom says he didn't need to tell me that part.

My dad says it's the only part that matters.

Which always makes my mom angry.

Which makes my dad stop talking.

My dad says, at the time, he didn't know why they killed their own, how they chose the sacrifice, or what they did with the bodies.

Which he says he imagined simply piling up behind the walls, for years and years, slowly filling the house until the walls warped and small person parts began sliding out through cracks in the wallpaper.

Which he told my mom.

Which made her nervous because she was scared she might be scaring him away.

Which she tried not to do, by assuring him that the people in the walls just had a very different way of life.

Part of which must have been eating their own.

Which must have been where the bodies went.

Which she assured him was a good thing—it meant their society was "self-sustaining."

Which my dad says he asked my grandpa about.

Which my grandpa denied, because the small people sounded much too polite to eat their own, despite all that killing they did very regularly.

Which my grandpa almost said more about, but stopped himself.

Which made my dad *really* wonder where the bodies went.

Dad says he spent the whole next day sitting in a chair in the corner while Mom ran around the house, trying to find the Santa figurines.

Dad says she asked him to join her, but he couldn't.

Dad says he was too scared to even think.

A few days into the trip, he went looking for Grandma Ellen, who he found in the attic.

Which is where he found her kneeling by a small metal latch in the wall.

Which was about three inches tall, in the wall right by the floor.

Which he says she had open and was scooping something out of.

Which, when he got closer, he saw was parts.

Arms. Legs. Heads.

Small person parts.

Which made him want to throw up.

Which made my grandma get a chair and tell him to sit down.

Which he did, as he waited for her to get him a glass of water.

He stared at the small open door, and at the little basket of parts she'd been scooping (all the fingers and feet sticking out), until she came back.

Which she did, carrying a glass of water he was too scared to drink.

Which is when she explained about the limbs.

Which started, she said, when my mom was in middle school.

Grandma Ellen said that one day after my mom came home from school, she and my mom were wondering about the people in the walls and had wanted to know what they looked like.

"They seem so sweet," my grandma had said. "Saying good night so politely every night and making tea."

My mom, who, again, *hated* the sound of their little kettles, had only half agreed.

"But," she'd said, "I *do* think I'd like to meet them one day. Maybe peel apart the walls and look inside."

Which gave them both the same idea at the same time.

Which led to them tearing apart a wall in the kitchen that very minute, giggling and looking around inside with flashlights.

Which revealed hundreds upon hundreds of people, each about six inches tall, hanging from beams like bats, arms crossed over their chests, fast asleep. They were dressed very nicely, in vests and trousers and housedresses and pantsuits and gowns and tuxedos and all kinds of things. Even a monocle or two.

Which my mom thought was just *adorable*.

Which is why she took one.

Then they covered up the wall hole with cardboard, nailing it in place.

The person she took screamed and squealed and kicked and even bit. My mom tried to keep it in a glass jar, but it "suffocated" (which my dad says means "ran out of air"), so she had to get another one.

Which she did by peeling up the nails in the cardboard she'd patched the hole with, and plucking another person out of the wall as they slept.

Who, according to my grandma, she kept in a terrarium.

Which lasted a while, until the small person broke their head against the glass wall and killed themselves.

Which led to my mom taking another. And then another. And another. All of them killed themselves, or died by accident. One made a rope from her little pants and hung herself in the terrarium.

"Some people keep guinea pigs, or fish," my grandma explained to my dad. "They die all the time. It's not any different. Pets are hard."

But my grandma started feeling guilty that my mom couldn't keep any of them alive.

So she took the most recently dead one, fixed it up, dipped it in glaze, and baked it, turning the person into a little ceramic figurine. Keeping it locked in the same little position forever.

My grandma surprised her with the first one, and then dipped the next dead pet (which came a few days later) in the glaze, too, so the first would have a friend on the shelf. They posed them together on the mantel, my dad told me. Two little figures waving at each other. Then my grandma and mom started making figurines together, which became their favorite thing to do.

But the small people got tired of this. They got tired of losing people at random all the time. So every morning, they chose one of their own and served them up in the attic.

"Isn't that a hoot?" my grandma said to my dad, laughing.

He wanted to know why they killed each other so violently.

Grandma Ellen said the butchering was actually very helpful because it made turning the people into figurines much easier. This way, my mom and grandma didn't have to scoop out the blood or the eyes or try moving the limbs through "rigor mortis" (which is when a dead body gets too stiff to move). They just had a bunch of parts they could adjust however they wanted. The people in the walls did it to "appease" Mom and Grandma Ellen, which means "make them happy."

"They think we're gods," Grandma Ellen told my dad.

I asked my dad why he was never really into the figurines, and he gave me a strange look.

I asked him why he decided to stay with Mom if he didn't like them so much.

Which is when he told me that my mom told *him* that if he tried to leave, she'd sacrifice him to the giants.

"You're *my* choice," she told him.

He said that made him nervous.

I asked him if she meant she'd sacrifice him just like the small people did.

Which is when his eyes got really wide, and he said, "Yes, but Ellie—*everybody* is the small people."

"But we're not small," I told him.

"Yes, we are," he said.

"But we don't live in walls," I told him. "There aren't any giant people around."

"We *do* live in walls," he said.

He told me that every so often, the giants pick someone. They bring them up out of the wall, they fix them up, and dip them in ceramic. They pose them, make them however they want. Sometimes, if the giants are taking too many people, it's easier to sacrifice someone, or a couple someones. If someone's really old or really sick, we sacrifice them to the giants.

My dad says that's what happened to my grandpa.

My dad says he had Alzheimer's, which is when your brain rots before your body does.

My dad says he asked to go.

My dad says they all got together in the living room and cut him up. Dad couldn't do it, so he was the one who handled the duct tape.

Which he also almost couldn't do.

My mom popped the eyes, he says, and Grandma Ellen twisted off the hands.

Which he says is the worst thing he ever saw.

Which he says was only made worse by my mom and my grandma chanting as they worked.

"This is our choice. This is our choice. This is our choice."

He says he felt watched by the people in the walls. He says he felt their fingers wriggling at the boards, pushing their faces against the wallpaper and trying to see. He could feel hundreds of curious faces looking at him from all around the room.

He says once they'd butchered my grandpa, they got all the pieces in a basket and then hauled the basket outside, to the backyard.

He says they carried it farther, into the woods.

He says they got the basket on a rope and pulley attached to one of the trees.

He says they worked the rope and hiked the basket up the tree.

He says that after ten hard minutes of work, the basket disappeared into the mist.

He says that they could feel something tugging on the rope, up there, beyond where they could see, at the very top of the world.

He says that when they pulled the basket back down, it was empty.

Which is why, he told me, he went nuts and burned my grandma's house to the ground.

Which he says was terrible, because he had to make sure he didn't get caught, and because he could hear all the little voices in the walls screaming.

He says he could see their little hands flailing outside the wallpaper.

He says he could hear their bodies burning.

He says he could see them tumbling out of the walls as they died. Melting, bleeding, and popping like cooked sausages.

He says he felt bad that Grandma got trapped in the fire, too.

He says he doesn't feel *that* bad, though.

All of which he says I am never allowed to tell my mom.

Ever.

Ever.

Ever.

Which I told him I wouldn't.

Which is also why he doesn't like to go in my room.

He doesn't like to think about the figurines in there.

He doesn't like to think about where my mom keeps getting them.

He doesn't like to think about how I get one every year for my birthday, and how sometimes my mom will surprise me with one at random.

But my mom just says that's because he's not open to new experiences.

Because he's "grounded."

My mom says that when I hear our house settling at night, it's not the house at all.

She says it's the people in the walls.

Sometimes, I stay up and try to hear them.

Sometimes I listen very hard.

But I never hear anything.

My dad says this is because they're scared, and don't want to be heard.

My dad says they're scared of people like Mom, and Grandma, and me.

My mom says that's ridiculous, and Dad should be careful, or she'll sacrifice him to the giants, and feed his parts to them in a basket, which we'll haul all the way up a tree so someone larger than us can scoop them out of a latch in the attic.

Just like Grandpa.

Which my dad never says anything to.

Which makes my mom laugh, and then she ruffles his hair and says she loves him.

Sometimes, when he's drunk, my dad says Mom is cruel.

He says I shouldn't like the figurines she gives me.

But I think he's not thinking about it the right way.

I think Mom is right.

Plus, Mom gives me new figurines all the time now.

Mom says I'm almost the same age she was when she started making her own.

Mom says she's excited to show me how to make *my* own figurines.

Mom says, soon, she'll show me the hole in the attic where she gets the parts.

Mom says she'll show me how to use a knife, too, so I can help take care of Dad when he gets old and sick.

Mom says it's all like having a Mr. Potato Head, except you always have new ones to play with.

Which I'm excited for.

I like Mr. Potato Head.

And I like ceramic figurines.

From: Rachel Durwood <radurwood@bhs.org>
To: tom.durwood@gmail.com
Re: The Stain

So, Tom. I'm on my fifth Whiskey Code Red (which is just Bartrick's Bourbon mixed with Mountain Dew), and I'm really missing you. I miss when we used to write each other those long-ass letters at summer camp because I knew you were in the same bullshit position I was in. I know Camp Grittwood sucked ass. Camp Kleave was an absolute hellhole. I don't know why Mom and Dad kept insisting we "give it another shot, maybe you'll *like* it this year." The only thing that got me through four weeks of psycho Type A Counselor Kelly, those nightly rock-hard chicken nuggets, and those mosquitoes that straight up sucked out a kid's eye once—was knowing you were looking out at the same stupid lake I was. Camp Kleave on the west side, Grittwood on the east, Bartrick Lake in between. Sparkling in the sun like electrified glass.

I just wish you were here. That's all. I wish you were home. I know I ignored your texts for months. You *should* ignore me.

But you did *get* my text, right? I guess it was only half an hour ago, so maybe you're busy. Maybe I should just shut up and keep typing this all out. But . . . I can *feel* you out there. On your couch, watchin some dumb sci-fi show, per usual haha. So your phone *must* be right there, no? I'm not raggin on you, I just want to hear from you.

Just want to make sure you're still with me. That we're still . . . us. Maybe I'm just freaking myself out cuz I'm drunk.

But you know, Lawrence Renfield's family had been reporting changes in *his* behavior during the last few months before he killed them. He'd grown irritable. Mean. Distant. Spent hours standing at the edge of their property, staring up at the misty backbone of the Billowhills covered in pine. His wife, Adelaide, said to her sewing group more than once, "You know, ever since that mule kicked Lawrence in the head this summer, he just *hasn't* been the same."

Now, my research suggests that less than twenty-five percent of serial killers, including men who commit familicide, experience trauma to the frontal lobe as children, sometimes as adults. Men like John Wayne Gacy, Richard Ramirez, David Berkowitz, Albert Fish, Fred West. It isn't common, but it's also not *un*common. It is, therefore, not that unlikely that Lawrence's run-in with an ornery mule on August 28, 1927, provides an adequate explanation for his rampage through the Renfield home that December. So that's all well and good. Or . . . not *good*, but you know what I mean. It makes sense. And it's comforting because *I* haven't been kicked in the head, so . . . I'm still *me*. Even though I've been distant, I think I'm still *me*, Tom.

Except, of course, the Day of the Mule doesn't explain the weird-ass shit that happened once Lawrence reached the barn on December 20, 1927.

There's no evidence to suggest that Lawrence had any "demonic notions," which is the weird, archaic-sounding term investigators used at the time. He'd never mentioned anything to anyone about "strange ideas" (another quote from the investigators). Even Adelaide's claim that he'd had visions, nightmares, and dizzy spells since the mule kick lacked hard evidence. Lawrence couldn't even draw. He *didn't* draw. So nobody knew what the drawing on the barn wall meant, or why he did it. Which is, as most Renfield County residents will attest, what makes *this* the most frightening aspect of the entire case:

He dragged the headless Robert into the barn by the scruff of its shirt. He brought the body to the back wall, furthest from the door, where it was darkest, coldest. He drove his hands into the stump of Robert's neck, covered them in blood. And then he drew a man upon the wall. Six feet tall, five feet wide. Very minimalist—just a down-swoop for each arm, a bent vertical line marking each outline of a leg. Then a ragged mass of hair. Stabbing out in all directions, like dark red knives slicing outward across the wood. The rest of the figure is relatively calm. Orderly. Light, as if he only needed one layer. But the hair? The paint of the hair is thick. Rich. Feverish. Several layers deep. The hair is agitated. Angry. Maybe scared. Blood runs down off the hair in long lines, mixing with the rest of the painting. And below the hair, there is no face. Only two dark slanted lines for eyes. The edge of a fingernail pokes out of the left eye, where it broke off as Lawrence raked his hand hard across the wood.

Later, when the police asked Lawrence about this man, his eyes grew wide, and he said only, "Oh. You mean the *giant*."

You can see pictures of the giant online, of course, if you google "Lawrence Renfield Murders." Of the whole image, most people agree (and so do I) that the eyes are the worst part. Almost everyone who looks at them reports feeling cold and dark. They feel raw. Sliced open by those two straight, diagonal lines, hiding under that mass of hair, that swirling cloud of knives. Just two big slits. But they are the sharpest part of the entire picture. They cut right through you. All the way back from when he painted them there in the first place. They cut through time.

They cut through everything.

DETOUR

This is the only time you smoke. This five-minute window right after the meetings, every Thursday night. Clap the pack against your palm, slide out one long, slender stick. Light it with that shitty little book of matches from the gas station. Suck in. You used to smoke all the time, an entire pack a day, but now it's just the once a week. You don't even like the taste anymore. It's just to keep your hands from shaking.

Isn't it.

You linger in the doorway, half between the sick green light of the church vestibule and the parking lot. Everybody else filters out, gets in their cars. Waves at you as they drive away. You look at your phone as the summer night chirps and buzzes around you. It's so you look like you're *doing* something before you walk to your car (checking a text, maybe), but the screen is blank. The other group members—they all know it's a ruse.

Don't they.

When the cigarette dies, you grind the butt into the pavement with the toe of your boot and look up at the streetlight over the parking lot. The beam beneath is a swirling gray whirl of moths and flies, banging against the bright white of the lamp. You watch them for a while. You sigh, from deep in your chest. Yeahh, you get that feeling. Swirling around. Banging your head. Even after eleven years. Works if you work it, sure, but you feel like you're working in circles here.

Don't you.

The guy who usually runs the meetings, the one with the key to the church, comes outside. He turns off the light of the vestibule and ushers you, politely, all the way out. He closes the door, locks it. Always, he's the last one to say good night before he shuffles to his car. And always, something in your throat lurches as he goes. You move quickly to your own car, so you're not standing by yourself in the shadow of the church. You start up the engine and turn left out of the lot, onto County Road 7. Behind you, the guy turns right, leaving you—alone.

God, you hate being alone. You always tell yourself that one cigarette is just about the drive home, but deep down you know better. Your wife doesn't go to the meetings, so you don't have to hire a babysitter. She sits home with the kid, and you soak up the circle-the-drain Serenity Prayer bullshit for the both of you.

Every week.

Every week, she tells you, "You go for both of us." And you smile at her, tell a little joke. She's a very serious person. Tequila used to loosen her up, but that was a different time. Now? *You're* the jokes. *You're* the light. Every week, you have to swallow that scared little jerk in your throat when you leave her. You don't tell her you're not the light at all, you're the moth beating its head, beating its head. You don't tell her you're terrified. Instead, you smile at your kid, your little boy, doing his homework at the kitchen table. You say, "Alrighty then, party people, smell ya later," and off you go, whistling. Back down County Road 7 again. Scared as hell and by yourself.

You *have* to be strong. Even though sometimes you just want to gulp down an entire bottle of gin, smash the bottle into your own face, and laugh until you puke.

It's worth it, though. You've got a cute kid who adores you. An intelligent, attractive wife. What more could you ask for?

Well . . . you could ask to go *back*. Back before the kid. Before you moved upstate for "stability." Back when you and her were living simpler lives in the city. Back when you could (did) drink all night, every night, until it was a problem. But it was a problem you two shared, at least. Together, you were the life of the party. Even the parties you got kicked out of, or ruined, or burned (not that the fire at Abby's wedding was your fault *per se*). Booze was something you bonded over and then had to give up, because of the kid in her gut. But if you did go back, you wouldn't *have* that kid, who you love. Plus, at the rate you'd been drinking back then, you'd probably be dead now. So, thank God for that kid. He saved you.

And so, instead of being a dick about it, every week, for five minutes after the meeting, you stand around and have yourself one cigarette. Ground yourself a little before the scary drive home. What you feel here, when you leave here, let it stay here, right?

Hear, hear.

No harm, no foul.

But *that's* why you smoke.

We know it is.

We know you.

County Road 7. Stretches around the entire lake, from the middle-class iron and old paint of Bent, where *you* live, all the way north to the nice white-pillar, upriver town of Lillian, and beyond, winding deep into the hills. The church lies right outside the sleepy village of Edenville, and the redbrick spires of Edenville College. To head home tonight, toward Bent, you gotta head south from Edenville. You gotta head *further down*.

Seven is one of those wild roads that swoops and curves so hard, so fast, you can only see twenty feet ahead of you at any given time. No lights. Rarely other cars. Thick woods press against you from both sides. Branches droop over the road. Sometimes when it's rained, like tonight, the leaves are heavy. They scrape along the roof of your car. Like if you stopped driving, arthritic talons would stretch around you and squeeze. Begin to digest. Slowly. In fact, the entire road feels like the stomach of a Venus flytrap. The woods, its jaws.

Hills ripple along the landscape, billowing up and down and across. Bent, crooked trees spread between big swaths of brackish green, muddy fields. The abandoned debris of hotels and stores, rusted clumps of barbed wire and rotting wooden fenceposts. Miles and miles of deadland, shadow, and muck.

Mmm. We love that word *muck*. We love the way it hums and then cracks.

This road makes you nervous because it always feels much longer than it should be. You're sure the road is only supposed to be a few miles long. Shouldn't be more than about eight minutes until you're back in the safe fluorescents of town. But it isn't. Every time you take County Road 7 is a lifetime. A goddamn *journey* through leagues of mist and drear. Like the road swoops out and away from civilization in ways it shouldn't. Can't. It reminds you of that sadness swamp in *NeverEnding Story*, all murky and burbling. You showed that movie to your son the other night, his first time, and he loved it, but he sobbed when the horse died.

We know he did.

We watched him through the window.

And truth be told, your taste for movies like that—your proclivity for fantasy, that you're just beginning to share with your son—is giving you the gut sense that this road will kill you one day. Ever since you moved up here, you've heard the stories. You *believe* the stories. The land here is . . . different. The only cigarettes they sell are some brand you've never heard of. They're called Noxboros, and they taste like literal dirt, but beggars and choosers and all that. Even the drinks in this valley have alien names. They have things like Bartrick's Bourbon, Millet's Everclear, and stranger, unlabeled concoctions with live leeches swirling inside. So you know, you *believe*, that there are . . . *things* out here, in the Renfield woods.

There are houses along this road as well, of course, but they're all secluded. Spread far apart. They seem perfectly content here, nestled into the trees. All squat beams and gravel driveways. Slanted roofs and converted barns with ivy walls. They've dug themselves into the dirt. Jammed candles in their windows to wink away the evil spirits. Keep their warm interiors cozy and safe.

But that's no help to you. Because here *you* are. Outside.

We know what you're thinking. These houses all ooze suburban normality. Why can't *your* house be like this? All cozy and neat, without all the baggage. Why do *these* homes get to keep standing when you've known so many that have washed away? People keep breaking their lives with bottles, all around you, and you have to stay on the outside of not just *that*, but normality, too. On the outside of everything, even your own family, right now. All by yourself. Banging your head. Circling the drain. Every fucking week. Working hard to keep the fantasy alive.

You yearn for the city. For dim bars filled with bodies and warmth. This isolated dark makes you hunger for the close comfort of a gin-sticky, candlelit corner table. The kind of corner you and your wife used to *live* in. This road makes you *thirsty*. Makes your throat *work*. You wish you had gum in the car. You can feel your throat looking for something to swallow. Contracting, twitching. You can almost taste the cool juniper of gin. Can almost *feel* the sweet burn sliding down . . .

You swallow spit. You can't go back. You won't. You're not that guy. You can't do that to your little boy.

So you keep white-knuckling it through the sharp curves of a silent, lonely county road. The thousandth Thursday in a row. Alone in the dark. On and on through the muck. And every so often, out of the shadows, another house. More candles in windows.

Like they'd protect against anything.

Six minutes in (each half an hour long), you realize there must be a breeze. You can see the wet undersides of the leaves glistening in it overhead. Rippling like the scales of a massive, yellow-green fish. Inside the bubble of your car, you can neither hear nor feel it. You *sense* it, peripherally, at the nape of your neck. The part of you that still remembers, by instinct, why your ancestors left the woods. You keep swallowing spit. Your scalp itches. You're wringing the wheel a little. County Road 7 feels especially bad tonight, and you *really* want to get home. An addict alone is in bad company, after all, and everything here is trees and dark and candles and trees. Thin curls of hot summer mist spiral out of the grass and the asphalt. As you drive, your headlights suck them up, swallow them whole like they're ghosts, sliding their way into your engine, following you home.

The road sweeps past a dilapidated shed with a broken roof. A large bush sprouts through the split in the wooden boards, breaking the whole thing apart from the inside. The door is bent inward, like something shoved its way in. You glance at this shed for just a moment before the image makes your stomach clench and you force your eyes back to the road. A branch drags, squealing, against the roof of your car. You press your boot down on the accelerator. Another twinge at the nape of your neck.

You're not thirsty. You're not. Besides, nothing is so bad a drink won't make it worse, right?

You turn on your brights, and a pair of eyes flash on the side of the road, just at the edge of the light. A small, hunched thing. Fangs. It hisses and scurries away before you can see what it is.

A raccoon. Just a raccoon, you tell your body, which is cold now, covered in goosebumps.

Another branch grinds against the roof of the car. Something is reaching for you. You're sure now. It's that same fucking itch at the nape of your neck. That itch knows raccoons. It knows when there aren't any.

It *knows* us.

The trees go away for a while (*thank God*) and the road straightens. There's a wide, empty space you assume is a field. A large house sits far back from the road, surrounded by a tall, spiked fence. The house is just a black mass, but candles glitter in all the windows. You count at least eight before the house swoops away behind you. You probably think that's excessive.

It's not.

You keep your boot steady on the accelerator. Your throat is so freaking dry. Your jaw wants to open all the way like a snake's and swallow an entire fifth whole, glass bottle and all. But you'll be back in town soon, right? You can collapse through the front door, and your wife, your kid, will be waiting there to catch you. You'll throw on a classic, like the animated *Hobbit*, and you'll breathe, son curled tight against your side. Maybe maybe maybe you'll make it.

The road dips down a slight hill and—there's a red glow up ahead. Taillights? Another car? It's gotta be. You stop strangling the wheel. Loosen up a bit. Seeing people would be good. The company of another car.

When you come down the hill, though, you realize the red glow is actually three or four bright red road flares, laid across the middle of the pavement. A man in a reflective vest stands by the flares, hazy in the smoky light. You're probably relieved. Probably think something like, *Thank God. Company!* You hate being alone *so* much. It's almost sad.

The man watches you approach, hands on his hips. You flick off the brights. Strain forward, try to see what's going on. There are no police cars. No wreck. No sign of anything too bad. Just the flares. Sparkling against the wet road.

He steps into your lane and holds up his hands. You roll to a stop in front of him. Bring your window down. He walks over. Leans inside. His smile is too wide. Too friendly. Teeth too clean and big. But maybe he's just happy to have some company, too, you figure. Maybe he's just as spooked as you are, being out here all alone.

He's chewing gum.

"Hiya," he says.

"Hey, man. Road closed?"

Guy smacks his gum at you. "Ayeah. Whole tree fell we gotta clear. So you're gonna take *this* road down. Ten minutes, tops, spits you out on 11 South."

He's pointing off to your right. You follow his finger and your heart shrinks into a corner of your ribs. He's pointing down a narrow side road you've never noticed before. A claustrophobic one-laner. Trees knit tight together, branches spread over the pavement and all around. Thousands of pipe cleaners, warped and twisted together at odd angles.

Like a net.

Then you notice the street sign, and you can't help but laugh.

"You're kidding," you say. "Come on. Stump Rot Lane?"

Guy tilts his head. Lifts his eyebrows, conciliatory. "I know. But it's quick. Spits you out onto 11 South. Ten minutes, tops."

You shake your head. "Alright. Thanks."

"Thank *you*." He pops his gum, leans out of your window. Steps back from the car.

"Have a good one, brother," you say as you start to roll away.

"Hey, you too." The guy in the reflective vest raises a hand in farewell. He keeps it raised until he's far back in your rearview. You glance at him before he's all the way gone, and you notice something weird. He drops his wave, then immediately puts his hands back on his hips. Stands there. Still. Waiting for the next car to approach. It's like he's run through a dialogue and then reset himself, like a robot.

That's weird, isn't it? We think so, too. Quite frankly, he could show a little more tact.

Believe it or not, we actually don't know *what* he is. Just some other part of the ecosystem. But if you'd looked closely, you would have seen the long, slick appendage running down the back of his shirt and off into the bushes. We've never seen where it leads. But we figure there are other roads like Stump Rot Lane all over the county. Other men in vests. All connected. There have to be. Because as far as we can tell, the man in the reflective vest is just one finger of a giant, hungry fist. We don't know what the fingers get out of it. All *they* have to do is point down the right road at the right time. All *you* have to do is follow.

Which you always do.

Every time.

You drive for five minutes. Then six. Seven. Eight. Your eyes keep flicking to the small green digital numbers on your dash.

You're keeping track of time religiously. It's been nine minutes now, and Stump Rot Lane still isn't curving. It's just taking you farther *out*. No closer to the freeway or town. No closer to anything, just . . . deeper. A nearly straight line into the black. There are still houses here, but they're smaller, darker. The candles are gone. Some of the windows are broken. The living rooms inside are decaying. The only real light out here is your headlights, the moon flickering through branches.

Easy does it, though, right? This too'll pass. Serenity and all that. Eyes straight ahead. Just think how soft your son's hair is going to be. How sweet it'll smell, because he always takes showers at night. In twenty minutes tops, you can tuck him and his sweet, soft hair into bed. Drink in your wife's perfume. Maybe put your own candle in the window and sit in the corner on the floor with her. No gin. Just each other.

Soon . . .

It's been ten minutes now.

The wind must be getting stronger, because the branches are moving more quickly. Leaves fluttering in rapid ripples. You peer up at them every so often, watching them dance and waver in the breeze.

Finally, the road curves. *Finally.* You smile a little. You figure 11 South must be just around the corner. Maybe you'll wind around and—

A large blue shape looms out of the dark. Cocked at an angle against the shoulder of the road. You press the brake, slow down a little. You get closer and realize that this mass is actually a sedan. A blue Honda. Hazard lights flashing. Exhaust pouring out the back end. Relief washes over you so fast you don't even think about why the car's stopped here. You're just happy, again, for the company.

Since the road is so cramped, you have to slump down onto the other shoulder to pass the sedan. You roll by slow, and see a woman's face through the driver's side window. You try to catch her attention by lifting a hand in greeting. You've got a pale, scared smile on your face. Too wide. Too friendly. Overeager, like that guy in the vest. You know you look a little crazy. But she doesn't notice. She's staring straight down, illuminated by a pale blue light in her lap. It takes you a second to realize she's looking at her phone. Frowning, trying to figure something out. Her eyes move frantic in the light.

Goosebumps tighten the skin along your thighs, your arms, the nape of your neck. You drive away and sweep around another curve. This one is gentler, and in the opposite direction. So joke's on you because that means you're still heading in a generally straight line. You shake your head, mutter something under your breath. Glance at the clock.

Eleven minutes.

The branches above are dancing harder now. It seems like you're keeping pace with the breeze, doesn't it? But you're wrong. The breeze is keeping pace with *you*.

A little further down, you come up behind another car, hunched on the shoulder just like the last. It's a sleek red thing with two doors. A Porsche. Hazards going, engine running. When you pass, the driver doesn't look up from the phone in his lap. He's shaking his head wildly. Mouth moving in one continuous, angry babble.

Maps, you realize. These people are looking at maps. Their GPSs. Trying to figure out where the hell they are.

Maybe you should turn back. Maybe there's another way around the roadwork. Maybe you should give up on Stump Rot Lane. It's making your throat hurt.

But for whatever reason, you keep going.

How interesting. So many of you try turning back. *You're* stubborn, though. You *really* want to make it home.

Thirteen minutes now.

A branch swipes at the side of your car, clattering against the passenger's side window. You can't be sure, but you swear you saw a shadow—what could have been a bush—pick itself up and sprint away into the dark.

Now you start mapping things out. Where's the closest bar on the county road? How soon can you be there? Will there be people there? Because you never drank just to calm your nerves. It was never that. You drank for the company. You drank because other people did, and then you couldn't stop. Your wife was the same. That's how you enabled each other for so long. For *years*. You liked fitting in with each other. Being on the *inside* of something, rather than outside, looking in, like you are now. *That's* why you want a drink so goddamn bad. You can imagine the rough grain of the bar, rasping against your hands. You can taste the earthy froth of the beer. The salt of the nuts. The hollow clap of the empty shot glass *pow* against the—

Your knuckles are about to break out of your skin, you're gripping the wheel so tight, trying to make yourself stop picturing it.

See? We know you.

Sixteen minutes now.

The road curves twice more. Once right, then left. Evening itself out again. Still taking you deeper into the woods. Into the muck.

Then you come up behind the third car: a large beige minivan. It squats, hazards blinking, beneath a long, drooping branch. Leaves hang from the branch's underbelly in one wide, rippling swath. You haven't seen a tree grow like that before. Maybe it's moss. Some type of willow. Maybe it's like that tree in *Harry Potter*, it'll clobber you when you pass.

It doesn't. But you can tell it wants to.

You roll slow past the minivan. You can't bring yourself to look at the driver. Don't want to see the panic, the light of the phone. You just keep your eyes straight. Jaw tight. Swallowing swallowing swallowing spit.

Easy does it.

When the minivan vanishes behind you, you give in. You put on your own hazards and drift onto the shoulder, put the car in park. You arch your body up out of the seat, dig your phone out of your pocket, just like the others, and suddenly, you laugh because technically you're *not* alone now! You're in the company of the lost! And then, just as sudden, that isn't funny anymore.

You pull up the GPS, squint at the map. Okay, there's County Road 7, there's 11 South. But the little blue dot pulses, jumps, lands you about fifty yards west, then south, then east. You watch it hop around for a while until finally, you must realize that it doesn't know *where* the hell you are, because you mutter, "Screw it," and shove the phone back in your pocket. You put the car in drive. You almost feel safe, moving again. Moving forward.

You're not.

Stump Rot Lane swings in a long, leftward arc. You lean into it. Feel the car tilt along the road. You consider, for a moment, lighting another cigarette, which would be a first for you. Two in one night. But you feel *bad*. You're still shaking and thinking hard about stopping at the first gas station you see. Buying a six-pack. Just to steady your nerves. Just a little. A drop. Maybe, you tell yourself, you'll just have one (half of one) and throw the other five away. But that's a lie.

You look at the clock. You've been on this stupid road for over twenty minutes.

When that long arc finally ends, you see something strange. There's another car up ahead, but this one is facing you.

Odd. The road is so narrow you thought it was a one-way.

You slow down. Get closer.

And a small, high sound squeezes out of your throat. The nape of your neck starts to throb.

You are now facing the minivan. That same beige minivan you *just* passed.

You can't believe it. You can't fucking believe it. Stump Rot Lane is just a dead end. A big fucking circle.

We know what you're thinking. *Circling the drain. Banging your head . . . What a funny freaking joke. HA HA!*

You don't know what else to do, so you just shift into park and throw on the hazards because that feels natural and orderly. You need *some* kind of order out here. You need a moment to think. You stare through the windshield, feeling the engine rumble beneath you.

Then you notice something. Beyond its blinking headlights, something about the minivan feels different. Feels off. You sit there. Staring. Skin tightening and itching. Listening to the *click-clock* of the hazards. Trying to put your finger on it.

Then, finally, you do. The shadow of the car is wider than it was before. Part of it sticks out into the road. Because the driver's side door is open. The car is empty. The dome light isn't on. It's dark in there. A void. *Avoid.*

Your hand is shaking so bad now. You rest it on the gear shift and try to think (*easy does it*). Maybe you can make it back to the guy in the vest and ask if there's another way around. Maybe they finished moving the tree. Maybe he *knew* Stump Rot Lane was a dead end and he's laughing his ass off. Maybe when you drive back, he'll grin and you'll *both* laugh because it was all a practical fucking joke and you can go grab a beer together.

No.

You shake your head. Jesus, no. What are you thinking? A beer?

We'll just grab a beer? That kind of thought hasn't felt that natural in over a decade. You're regressing. You're losing it. You need to get home and hug your goddamn wife.

But you just sit there. Staring. The headlights of the minivan flashing at you. *Click-clock, click-clock.* Bright. Void. Bright. Void. You can't bring yourself to move. What if you start heading back and you pass the other cars and they're empty, too? The Honda, the Porsche. Nothing more than abandoned shadows. Then how would you feel? How badly would you panic *then*?

You can barely think straight. *Stuck in a circle. Banging your head* . . . You're getting sucked into the sadness swamp for sure. Gonna be deader than Atreyu's stupid horse. Gonna be . . .

Then something catches your eye. The leaves aren't moving. That sheet of moss hanging down from the branch above the minivan—is still.

The breeze must have stopped.

Everything is calm.

You relax. Take a breath.

"Okay," you tell yourself. "Alright, party people. Come on."

You put the car in drive.

And then that branch begins to turn. Slow. The leaves flutter and spread outward. The end of the branch unfurls into a long cluster of gnarled twigs. There's a flash farther up the tree. You look up. And something in the leaves looks back.

In an instant, it's all clear. That thing over the minivan isn't a branch at all. It's an arm. A long, thin arm. The branches are claws. And the sheet of leaves—is a wing.

This is when we pick ourselves up and move closer to the car.

You slam your boot down and *go*. Push fifty miles an hour past the minivan, engine roaring. A large shadow breaks from the tree, wings bursting out as something launches itself into the air. You don't even look. You're just *moving*. Speeding away for your life. You can make it back to the church. Take a different road home, the long way. You know you can. You press your boot down harder, tires screaming around a curve.

The red Porsche looms into view. Sure enough, the driver's side door is open here, too. The man is gone. His phone still glows, abandoned on the driver's seat. It whizzes past as you drive. You don't slow down. And a minute later, you pass the other car, the Honda. That one's empty, too.

Your blood is rushing fast now. Loud in the night air. A pounding, wet roar. Beating through your heart like water from a broken dam.

They can almost taste it.

The road veers to the right. You crank the wheel, grinding against the shoulder, almost barreling into the trees. You're cursing, sweating. You turn and turn and turn. The road straightens—

And spits you out behind the Honda. Again.

You slam on the brake. Grind to a stop mere inches away from the other car's bumper. You smell the burning rubber. See the smoke drifting into the air. You sit there, panting.

You're probably telling yourself it's impossible. It's fucking *impossible* that you're now trapped in a big circle. Where did the county road go? Where's the guy in the vest? What is *happening*?

We know that's what you're thinking. It's what you all think.

Something big drops onto the roof of the Honda. You can hear it *thunk*, see it dent the metal. You watch as it bends, unfolds. Limbs crack and twitch. In your headlights, you can see the thin flesh. The lines of bones beneath. The spiderweb of green veins pulsing over the skin. The wings, the light green feathers. The sharp yellow beak, spit trembling down in long, hungry drools. The eyes like thick red spirals. The rows and rows of teeth, the ragged shreds of meat stuck between. Torn strips of whoever used to be in those cars.

You'd heard the stories about Renfield. You knew. But you never ever expected . . . *this*.

This hisses at you. This glares at you through the windshield. This stretches its wings, leaves fanning out, stretch and stretch and stretch, and there's noise overhead. You look up. The leaves all around you are dancing. Unfurling themselves from the trunks of the trees. The woods themselves are molting. Coming apart and casting red eyes down upon you. Ruffling their feathers.

It occurs to you then. Really strikes you: All these trees are bare. All these leaves, rippling in the breeze, were never leaves at all.

The trees are all alive, leaves and branches becoming limbs and claws, crawling down the trunks—toward you.

You jam your foot on the gas. The car jolts forward, screams. There's a crunch of metal, a whine. Sparks. The car won't budge. While you were distracted, we ran up and fucked with your engine.

You're going to have to get out of the car.

There's another hiss. A crazy, wet rasp. You look in the rearview. The spiraling eyes are behind you now, too. Another crimson-stained beak. Coming at the back of the car fast on long, pumping legs. Screaming at you. You can feel your bones freeze at the sound, like this thing is already eating you, crunching you down between those teeth. Like those long, black claws reaching for your car, glowing red and dripping, are already sunk deep in your skin.

You're going to have to get out of the car *now*.

You fumble with the seat belt. You're shaking so bad you can hardly get it off. But just as something slams onto the hood of your car, cracking your windshield, you're free. You tear open the car door and book it. Something behind you hisses, reaches for you. Nails swipe at the back of your neck, drawing blood. Right at the nape.

See? You knew. It's that nape. We see it all the time. Part of you always knows. And always, always, you ignore it. Always, *always*, you turn down Stump Rot Lane.

You run from the car into the woods. It's started to rain again. Hot, fat drops of summer storm. You can barely see through it. Barely see your hands in front of you. You're sprinting through the undergrowth. Branches hiss, tear at your face and your palms, but you don't stop.

One of us trips you. Giggles, runs away. You tumble down onto a boulder, slamming your knees and hands. Something in your elbow pops. You stop, feeling your wounds throb. Feeling blood roll down the side of a leg. Panting. Heart racing. You look up at the sky. You wipe the rain out of your eyes. The air stinks.

Then a shape in one of the trees gives you pause. You gaze up at it, squinting. In the pallid haze of the mist and the moon and the rain, you can't tell what it is at first. Something lurching back and forth, kicking at the branches. You stand, step toward it. Take out your phone, turn on the flashlight, shine it up. All you see is the lower half of a woman's body. Suspended in midair, limbs jerking. Reaching down are three different pairs of hands. Reeling her in. Dragging her upward in slow, violent jerks. You step back. Bile burns the back of your throat. You turn, see another pair of shoes dangling from the tree behind you. Another, off to the side. You stumble around in circles, craning your neck up to see. There's another. And another. Dozens of bodies. And all over them, dozens upon dozens of black-nailed hands, yanking them up into the shadows. You can hear it now. The teeth gnashing. The feathers whispering, rustling. Small barks of pleasure. Happy murmurs as the trees begin to feed.

"Christ," you say, like He can hear you.

Something slaps onto the dirt at your feet. You shine the light on it. Guts steam upon the ground.

See, it's not raining at all. It's *bits*.

And this is our favorite part. Because without fail, every time, this is when you lose it. Snap. Done. Gone. You see all the blood. You open your mouth to say something. Nothing comes. And you stand there, open-mouthed. What seems like hundreds of bodies twitch and jerk amongst the trees. Something in you cracks—and you give in.

You grin. Tilt your head back. And you stand there, blood raining into your mouth. Pooling under your tongue. You close your lips, and swallow. Stick your tongue out, swallow again. You laugh. It feels so good to swallow. To finally . . . let go.

It's sweet watching you accept that you're lost.

You were so thirsty. All night, you just wanted that drink. Your body *craved* it. Kept gulping spit like it could pretend that was booze, but now booze is pouring from the sky! A dream come true! It's a fountain of champagne, gushing right down into your mouth! It's your wife getting that same old trusty corner seat. She hands you the glass and the can, and you swallow another shot, crack open another beer, swallow that, too. Swallow swallow swallow. Good music pouring out of the speakers. You dance. You laugh. The room spins. Your shoes are sticking to the floor. You can hear them, even over all the people singing and laughing and dancing, *slick slock slap*, and there's your kid in the corner, too, doing his homework, all sweet-smelling, and nobody is scared, nobody's scared at all, because there are no roads at night here, no stories, no County Road 7, no candles in windows, no circles, just everybody together inside in the warm and the fountain of champagne and the good times roll and you keep swallowing swallowing swallowing it all down like you always have and one of the things in the trees dives at you and buries its claws in your ribs and yanks you up like a fish on a fuckin line.

Now. *We* are not like the things in the trees. We don't eat people. *We* live in the undergrowth, and we just like to watch. Just for fun. We think it's funny when you try to run, and it makes us horny when we hear the sounds you make as the stuff inside you pours down from the branches in chunky red rivers. When the things in the trees are done with you, we take your car and scrap it for parts. We're building our own machines in the bushes. You don't have words to describe them. Or us for that matter. So don't worry about it. When we turn our engines on and sic them on your towns, you won't *need* words anymore.

None of you will.

But for now, you scream. You shove against the hands as they tear at your clothes, your skin, your muscle. People always think that might save them. The screaming. Even when the claws pop up their tendons and chew them apart, they scream. Like it will do any good. But that's alright. And it's alright that you puked. That you tried to get everything you swallowed out just before you died. To repent at the last second. That's okay. Almost all of you do. You ran through some puke yourself when you ran beneath the others. The trees don't care. They eat you anyway. And when your bones crack between their teeth, they will neither remember nor care that those bones ever had a name in the first place. A wife, a son, anything at all. They don't care. And we don't care that they don't care. They're good company.

They've never been sober at all.

From: Rachel Durwood <radurwood@bhs.org>
To: tom.durwood@gmail.com
Re: The Stain

It was below freezing when Lawrence killed everyone in his home, and all the blood froze into a red-brown bark. It pooled across the kitchen in a glossy frozen lake. The stairs were hard to climb, all covered in human frost. The neighbors, feeling for some reason responsible for the house, had to crack apart the blood with hammers. Pry it off the floor with screwdrivers. They broke the blood into square-foot sheets, carried these dripping sheets to the back, and buried them.

They buried almost fifty sheets.

In the spring, when the ground thawed, the neighbors discovered a narrow red river trickling down into their property from the shared boundary of the Renfield plot. It didn't take them long to realize what that stream was, and worse—what it was capable of.

But more on those neighbors later.

Meanwhile, the Renfield blood spread, pouring into a brook behind the Renfield barn. The brook fed a river, and the river fed a lake, and the wide, scenic bowl of Bartrick Lake in turn (that big slice of electrified glass) fed several wells for the people of the surrounding towns. Tinker's Falls, for one: a small mining town named for the miniature rapids feeding the Bent River on Bartrick Lake's eastern end. Not to be confused with the larger and more scenic *Bartrick* Falls on the Lake's southwestern side (where Dad proposed to Mom). *Those* falls gave rise, of course, to the town of Bartrick Mill, just south of Bartrick Falls. You can always spot a county outsider because you say "the Falls" and they think you might mean Bartrick Falls. But true Renfield folk know the Falls is always *Tinker's* Falls, and the Mill is always Bartrick Mill.

Ha. Sorry. I feel like I'm talking down to you, Tom. I mean, you *know* all this shit. But it's part of the report. Part of the *history*. And here's some interesting shit you maybe didn't know:

In 1927, the Falls got most of its well water from the Lake. But by the fall of 1928, more than a few of those wells were abandoned. People claimed the taste of the water had changed since the Renfield murders.

Did you know that? There are even reports of people attempting to *explain* that taste. In each one, the subject's eyes become "sharp but distant," and they say simply, "It tastes like madness."

If they could, people living in the Falls started to move away from the Lake, to the town of Edenville, which gets its water from Billowhill springs to the east. Some people fled upriver, too, into the upper-class haven of Lillian. Lillian has always been a prosperous town, home to a number of old-money families like the Mithers, who grew rich off the lumber they reaped from the surrounding Shembelwoods around the turn of the nineteenth century. The Shembels is, of course, the endless dark forest blanketing Renfield County, all the way from the eastern wall of the Billowhills to the unnamed western reaches of the valley. They're named after one Arthur K. Shembel, Dutch trader and fellow founding member of the Lillian elite, along with the Mithers and Haywood-Fryes.

See? Told you I kicked ass in history.

Anyway, *some* people claim that Lillian is the county's most affluent community because it is slightly north of the Renfield farm. It is, therefore, less "poisoned" by the spread of the Renfield blood. Whether or not this is true is, quite honestly, difficult to say (causation vs. correlation and all that). But the "downstream towns"—the Falls, the Mill, and Bent—*did* all sink into a sleepy stagnancy by the 1970s. After The Big Accident, that infamous mine collapse in 1968, the Falls became more or less a dusty trailer park sprawl, locked in a permanent recession. In 1846, the rise of kerosene tanked the whaling industry in Bent, and the excess whales they used to haul up from Hudson stopped coming. The men in Bent who'd hack them apart for their blubber, oil, and bone began fishing the river instead, which worked well for the town for about a century. But by the mid-1950s, they stopped doing that, too. Because ever since the summer of 1928, men had been hauling things out of the depths that they couldn't name. Small wriggling things that'd leap into their ears and *push* into their skulls. Things that'd whisper through the net at them in a river-bottom language no one could identify. This apparently drove one Bent fisherman so insane that he blew up his trawler, burning half the town in the process. And since that great trawler-fire of '53, the town has crusted over into a middle-class swamp. I mean, I've lived here a few years now and I don't think it's that bad. I like my view of the river. But the town's brilliant brick buildings, wide streets, and riverfront park have all faded into a cracked and dismal gray, and the fishing industry has died completely. As the twentieth century wore on, people in Renfield County tended to care less and less for food that comes from the water.

See, over the years, the Renfield blood pulsed deeper into the valley's veins. And in its wake, the stories followed. People moved away from Bartrick Lake because they claimed the things living near the Lake grew strange, as that Renfield blood soaked into the land. Bartrick was a nondescript, nearly cliché, pine-surrounded lake before 1927. Wooden docks and cabins up the hill. But people began to spot new creatures lurking near the lakeside, in the alleys of the Falls, sniffing around trash cans in Bent. Mutations wandering free. Like coyotes with antlers and red teeth, moaning as they sulk through backyards. Slumped and faceless quivering masses of fur, running along rusted sunken train tracks on five legs. Half-squid insectoids crawling up out of the lake. All this, and worse.

Nobody really touched the Lake after the stories started. Except the occasional high schoolers, daring each other to dive under the surface for five seconds a pop. They do that to this day. Some of them even resurface.

As you know, Tom, there is such a *variety* to these myths in Renfield County. Such a wide, chaotic sprawl. But the first verified report of anything supernatural comes from March 9, 1928:

A young couple from the Mill report entering a circular grove of trees in the woods by Bartrick Lake and immediately feeling watched. They look around and discover "four or five pairs of big eyes" surrounding the grove, in the undergrowth. Before they can react, they feel the trees begin to move, bend, and close around them. The couple both refer to these trees as "fingers from a giant fist—like a hand moving underground." When asked where the hand might have come from, like what it would've been *attached* to (and I love that some cop asked this), they both asserted that they had the impression the hand grew from an arm coming from the direction of the lake. When the police went to the grove to investigate, there was just some lumberjack guy standing there, smiling at them, hands on his hips, all "nothin to see here." One officer swore in his report that the guy had some kind of appendage unspooling out of his shirt, slithering out into the lake.

I actually found the exact location of that grove in an old report and went there last night to check it out. I know, that's stupid of me, going out alone at night, but please don't give me shit about it. I mean, nothing *happened*. I didn't see anything. The dumb trees didn't even *move*. But not gonna lie, it was fun. Like, spooky fun. I wasn't even scared driving alone through tree-demon country. I was . . . sort of excited. I was *daring* the dark to come get me. So far it hasn't, but . . . fingers crossed?

No. I shouldn't say that.

Anyway, the point is, this *history* of Renfield County—the way its towns were established and grew away from Bartrick Lake—is an intriguing one. None of it can, of course, be mapped directly to the spread of the Renfield blood, nor can the county's many stories of unexplained phenomena. Even if they *could* be mapped effectively, it's nigh impossible to connect these occurrences to any mutating effects *of* that "cursed" Renfield blood. Paranormal phenomena are, to say the least, characteristically impossible to explain.

That said, there *can* be noted a direct correlation in timelines. There are no such stories *before* 1927. And beginning in 1928, many of the people in the Falls who did *not* abandon their wells feeding from Bartrick Lake are said to have grown strange. To have acquired peculiar habits and appetites. There were disappearances. *Lots* of disappearances. Parents began to urge their children to be careful around "that area." To avoid Tinker's Falls at night altogether.

But regardless of what we may believe (or really *want* to believe) about stories, waterways—lakes, brooks, rivers, ponds—are *all* connected, no matter what. And soon enough, "that area" became not just the Falls, but the entirety of Renfield County. The blood had completely saturated the landscape, spreading out in a massive radius around Renfield's giant. Twisting everything in its path into strange, complex, and unpredictable new shapes. The trees, the birds, the foxes, the deer.

Even you and me.

WAG

Old Wag lived in a bathtub by the side of the road. Technically, he lived in the decaying shotgun house a few yards behind it, but he spent his time in the tub, watching cars. The tub was a rusted red and white porcelain beast of questionable origin. When he sat in it, Wag's head tilted back over the lip on one end, his bare feet over the other. The house was a faded, peeling green. The windows were cracked and part of the front porch sagged.

Old Wag had three chickens and a border collie with misty eyes. At dusk, just before the Shembelwoods swallowed the sun, you could catch him clearing his throat and clambering out of the tub. He would pass his decrepit toolshed and amble back to his house, collie at his heels. Sometimes at night if you listened close, you could hear the whir coming from his kitchen. Mrs. Wilson, Wag's neighbor down the road, thought it was his blender. Maybe he liked margaritas. At dawn, he slunk out his front door. He scattered chicken feed across the dirt. And, clearing his throat once more, he got into the tub.

Everybody had questions about Old Wag. Parents told their kids to stay away from him. No one had any real inkling about where he came from, no one ever saw him in town, and no one knew what his real name was. No facts; only questions. Mrs. Wilson wanted to know: "What's he always got stuck in his gullet like that?"

* * *

"My mom said it should snow tonight." Harmony looked up at the sky. Bleak gruel-colored clouds gaped back at her. "Doesn't seem cold enough."

"Be colder when the sun goes down." John followed her gaze. Looking at the clouds scared him in a way it never scared her, and he dropped his head back down.

Harmony and John sat on the edge of a granite outcropping by the side of the highway. They were a mile or so south of Babylon, the trailer park where John lived. And *that* was a mile south of Falls proper, where Harmony lived in an apartment that stank like glue. *Removed*, was how they felt right now. It was a good feeling. They were fourteen. They kept pushing their limits, stretching the bubble of their small-town life wider and wider until one day, hopefully, it might pop and let them run free. This outcropping was about as far as they had ventured. For now, they were content to sit on the granite hillside, watching cars.

Harmony had his dick in her hand.

She jerked mechanically up and down. "It can't snow before Halloween. I'm not going trick-or-treating in snow."

John was leaning back on his hands, head scrunched back onto his shoulders, dick way out in the open. His jeans pooled about his ankles. "You're going out this year?" he asked. His voice came out more surprised and indignant than he meant it to.

"This is my last year," Harmony said carefully. She didn't want him to chastise her, but she *did* want to defend herself. "I'm going as Buffy Summers."

"Who?"

"Forget it."

They were quiet.

A small green Volkswagen came rushing round the curve in the road. A pale girl had her face pressed up against the glass. John made eye contact with her hard, pressing the scene down upon her. He hoped it stamped itself on her mind and stayed there forever— two enigmatic, skinny ghosts on the hill amongst the fire-trees. Bored, half-naked, and watching.

The car vanished around the bend.

Harmony gazed out across the tops of the trees in the field below. Smoldering embers of October leaves in dull sunlight. Yellow and orange and dying. She sighed. "What should we do this afternoon?"

John shrugged. He prodded idly at a neck zit. "Don't care."

Harmony felt a twinge down her spine. Suddenly, the stillness felt oppressive instead of serene. "Let's do some kind of adventure."

"What kind?"

"Any kind."

John screwed up his face in thought. "We could see what Jackson and Gwen are up to."

Harmony knew that if they saw what their two friends were "up to," the day would be spent drinking stolen beer and throwing rocks into the river. *Kaplunk swig kaplunk.* The thought made her spine twitch again. She shook her head. "Nah. Something bigger."

"Harmony, what could be *bigger*?"

She considered for a long moment. Finally, it came to her. An arcane whisper she somehow knew she'd always voice: "We could visit Old Wag."

She felt John start in her hand. A quick jolt of surprise. He looked at her. "Old . . . Wag?"

"Yeah."

John gulped. A genuine but cartoonish *ulp*. He sounded younger when he asked, "W . . . why?"

"He always sits there. Don't you wanna know—"

"But our parents told us to leave him alone."

"I know, but—"

"Ever since I was *born*, they've been saying."

"Right, but he's *always* there," she insisted. "Don't you wanna know what he's like? I drive past him, like, four times a week. What is he thinking? What does he *do*? Is he watching for something specific? What does his *voice* sound like? Why the tub? We can go find out, John. Please? It'll be fun."

Her hand paused. She felt him pulsing a little, slackening.

He frowned. "Fine. We can check it out. If you . . ." He nodded at his lap.

"Oh, great! *Thank* you. It'll be *so* fun. Here."

She went back to jerking him up and down, up and down. As she did, she looked out over the valley. It stretched wide in front of them, rolling away in an endless grim expanse. Dark gray Billowhills loomed to their right. Tired, ancient, sacred. Harmony watched them. She felt very, very small.

"I'm coming," said John.

Old Wag wasn't far away. Took them maybe four minutes to walk there. As they approached, they could see the house, the little wooden shed, a beaten-down Oldsmobile that looked like it was sinking into the mud driveway, and the tub. Just over the edge of the tub, they caught a glimpse of Wag's bald head. His toes.

Chickens were circling the foot end of the tub as they walked up. The collie lay on the dead grass a few yards back. Wag blinked at them as they came, hazel eyes squinting hard. He wore a dirty white-and-brown plaid buttoned shirt, half its buttons missing. His jeans were riddled with holes. They hung in snaky white spaghetti strands across his legs. A few sprigs of bristly chalk-colored hair stood out all around his head, across his cheeks and over his scalp, running down over his shoulders in long greasy tendrils. His skin was old and dry, covered in deep wrinkles and broken veins. He cradled against his chest what Harmony assumed was a bottle of beer.

Harmony and John stood silent for a moment before Wag coughed and said, "Hello."

Harmony's voice cracked dangerously: "H . . . hello."

"What can I do for you?" Wag's voice was higher-pitched than she expected. A little whiny and thin. Raspy, even. Warm sand rubbing against metal.

"Um," John began. "We just wanted to say hello. We always pass you. And. See you sitting here."

Wag nodded. "Indeed."

"We wanted to ask you some questions," said Harmony. John shot her a look. She bent her head to the ground. Watched a chicken peck at the old man's bare toes. Peck, peck, pecking.

"Is this for some sort of school report?" Wag asked.

"No," said John.

"School newspaper?"

"No."

"You just had some questions."

"Yes."

"You were just *curious*."

"Yes."

"Uh-huh." Wag shifted his weight. There was a loud clatter of glass bottles moving in the tub beneath him. *How much beer does he drink*, John wondered.

Almost on cue, Wag lifted the bottle he'd been nursing to his lips and took a long swig. He swallowed, grimaced, gave another small cough. "So. You want to know more about me."

"Yes," said John.

"You know my name?"

"Wag," answered Harmony. "They call you Old Wag."

"Hm." He seemed amused. "That's a new one. Who's *they*?"

"Our parents."

"They tell you about me?"

"No."

"Otherwise we wouldn't have come," said John.

"Otherwise," Wag widened his eyes sagely, "you wouldn't have been *curious*."

"Right," they said together.

"I see." Wag shifted upward a bit in the tub. The bottles under him gave out another clattering cacophony. The collie came trotting over, tongue lolling. Wag lifted a long, arthritis-warped finger and pointed to the shed. "I've had many people come asking about me. Over the years. So I made a little museum about myself for curious people like you. It's in *there*."

They followed his finger to the shed. Through the little window in its side, they could see a bare bulb hanging in the center of the space. They glanced at each other.

"You can go in and have a look around," Wag continued. "It's free. Go on." He gave a light wave of his hand. John took Harmony's wrist, smiled at the old man, and pulled her along with him toward the shed. She looked over her shoulder. Wag rubbed the collie's head with one hand, cradling the bottle with the other. The chicken was still pecking at him.

"Doesn't that hurt?" she called.

Wag beamed. His teeth were gray. His toes wriggled. "No. No, it does not."

John pulled the cord for the light in the shed. They stood in its center, holding hands. They looked up at the walls, the shelves, the tool bench, the dirt floor.

Nothing.

The entire shed was empty.

The light waved overhead.

"The fuck," said Harmony. She swore when she was nervous. "There's nothing fucking here."

"Maybe it's a joke. Like, there's nothing *to* know about him?" John looked under the tool bench. Not a single nail or screw or anything. Just empty space.

"Fuck that. What the *fuck* ever." Harmony bit her lip. She kicked a clod of dirt across the cramped shed. There was a rusty hook sticking out from the wood in the corner. She went up to it and flicked at it.

"Hey," she said.

John didn't answer.

"Hey." She smiled. The darkness of the space, the closeness of it, made something inside of her turn over. Like an engine. "Johnny, I dare you to go down on me in here. It *is* my turn."

He didn't answer. She spun around to face him.

And there in the doorway was Old Wag, fingers gripped tight about the sides of John's head. His eyes glowed. The glinting green of hungry animals in the dark. As Harmony turned, Wag dug his teeth into John's throat. He jerked his head back, ripping out a series of cords and tubes. John spat out blood between his teeth, spraying it onto the wall. His fingers twitched, his eyes rolled. Wag gnashed meat between his molars, sucking up tendons like pasta. Harmony screamed. Wag dropped John in a bloody, epileptic mess and rushed at her. He took her head in one hand, slammed it against the wall. The hook caught in her eye and half her vision went black. Wag brought her head back and she felt the eye yank out of its socket. A hot wet stream rushed down her cheek. Wag slammed her head into the wall again and, instantly, her mind broke open. Everything she had ever learned evaporated. Speak, read, ride a bike, anything—gone. Her skull cracked. Her brain seeped out. She was still conscious, could still see the shed and the light bulb swinging, could hear the collie yapping happily, and could feel the fingers rooting around inside of her, splitting her like a nut. She felt his chin dig into her as Wag stuck his mouth down into the concave mess of her head, guzzling gray matter. And as he ate, she let out a small squeak, and her body finally shut off.

They lit the dining room with the long white candles Gwen's mother left behind when she passed. Jackson had never really liked those candles. Too exquisite. Too polished and rich. They stuck out sorely from the cozy mundanity of his everyday. They stretched his circle of familiarity too far, and they made him frown.

He glowered at them as he chewed his dinner. The room pinged and clanged with the sounds of his family's cutlery against the plates as they ate.

Jackson caught his wife's eye, smiled to her. Gwen smiled back, not showing any teeth. Her head dipped down again, and she shoved another forkful of meatloaf in her mouth.

He found the silence comforting. To his right, his sixteen-year-old daughter was drowning in it.

"Dad," she said suddenly. She scrutinized him from between the candles.

He looked up from his plate. "Yes?" he asked.

"Who's that old guy in the tub?"

Jackson felt his blood freeze. He glanced up at Gwen. She looked pale, eyes wide.

"What makes you ask that, hon?" Gwen said.

The girl shifted, uncomfortable in the growing tension. She glanced between her parents. Feeling cornered, her voice grew small and faraway. "I . . . just wanted to know. He's always sitting there. Who is he?"

Jackson and Gwen hadn't spoken about him for a long, long time. Not since high school. Since the Monday their two friends stopped coming to school, and nobody would tell them exactly why or what had happened, even when they stood above the hollow caskets at the funeral. He vaguely remembered there being a police raid, but nothing came of it. The house had been empty except a battered futon, a ham radio, and some kitchen appliances. They had to let Wag go.

Another, even blurrier memory bubbled up: a town mob of angry fathers who made it all the way to the shed, then marched back, shaking their heads. Some of them laughed madly. Others cried. And afterward all of them drank.

Jackson's father had seized the back of his neck one night, brought his face close to him, so close Jackson almost choked on the stench of whiskey boiling out of his father's mouth. "Stay the fuck away from that man," his father hissed. "He was old when I was young, and now he's still old. It isn't right."

After that, Jackson had never so much as asked. He steered clear of that road as best he could. Even if his detours took him a good hour out of the way, he never went near the tub.

He leaned across the table. He enunciated every word carefully: "Do not. Go near. That man. *Ever.*" He looked back up at Gwen. She gave him a light nod.

"But . . ." The girl started to say something else. She'd heard rumors at school. They called the old man King Tub. If Wag had heard that, he would have chuckled and said, "That's new." But then again, his name changed all the time.

"Listen to your father," Gwen chimed in. "That man is dangerous. *Very* dangerous."

Their daughter looked back at her food. Her cheeks burned. On either side of her, the candles flickered. Each time the little flames rippled, they seemed to move closer and closer to her, until she practically felt them licking her chin.

They finished their dinner in silence. The fact that nobody had answered her question was, of course, what made her go visit him.

The next night, Old Wag burned her clothes behind his shed.

Wag's tub was a vintage Renfield. When Lawrence shot his daughter May through the bathroom door, she slumped toward the tub at her side, and bled heavily into its wide porcelain maw. Wag—back when he was human, and had a job, and a different name—purchased the item from a collector in the Falls. That woman had *shelves* full of Renfield memorabilia. Lawrence's razor, Adelaide's housedress, some of Robert's old toys . . . Wag wasn't interested in any of that spook-show crap. But the tub was rumored to have healing properties. He'd heard that in the mine, from the other men who dug with him, deep in the bowels of the Billowhills, clawing further and further into the rock, inhaling greater and greater gouts of sulfurous grime. They all had mortal ailments, and cures they wanted to believe in.

Wag saved up for that damn tub. Took him twenty-three paychecks. But when he finally climbed inside, his throat didn't feel any better. He lay there, nude, submerged in lukewarm water, feeling silly. His breath rasping around the cancerous lump of mine dirt lodged within his gullet. He lay there all night, until the water was freezing. Gazing up at the stars, for he could not drag the tub into the house by himself.

Just before dawn, the tub began to whimper. A vibrating cry, bubbling up from the drain: *Meat . . . meat . . .* The word made Wag's eardrums ring, dangerously close to bursting.

He knew exactly what it meant.

So Wag stole and blended his first child, and sat in the tub as he drank him whole. He poured half down the drain, and the tub moaned happily. But Wag's throat did not heal. He took another child, and another. His throat continued to ache. The tub lengthened Wag's life, made it endless, but it did not cure him. Not once did he suspect that it was only using him.

Yet still, he hoped. For years, he hoped.

And he never ran out of food.

When the fire behind his shed died down, the girl's clothes all crisped to ash, he went back inside, tossed her hand into the blender, and flipped it on. It whirred terribly. The bone crunched and groaned. He turned the blender off. He opened the lid. Sniffed at it. It smelled good. He went to the kitchen table and sawed off the other hand. The girl gaped up at him. Her mouth opened and closed soundlessly. In the corner of the room, the collie chewed complacently on her tongue.

This was a good get, Wag thought as he tossed her meat into the blender.

Many days passed without a catch. Sometimes months. Sometimes, though, Wag got lucky.

He popped the lid off the blender. He poured the juice into a bottle and shook it, turning its contents frothy. He peered inside the dark brown glass, trying to find bits of bone. It didn't seem like there were any.

Wag went to the futon in the living room, leaving the still-breathing leftovers of the child on the table. He sat with a sigh. He used a plastic milk crate as a kind of makeshift coffee table. On it was a ham radio. He turned it on. Through the static, a voice crackled into focus: "Hello?"

Wag picked up the microphone. "I'm here."

"You get anything today?"

"One. First in almost eight months."

"Luckier than me."

Another voice chimed in: "Anyone else score?"

"No. You?"

"Nah."

A third voice came on the air, asked the same question. A fourth, a fifth. On and on, until out of the radio flowed a fracas of over a dozen voices. The living room swelled with the sounds of what might have been an invisible party.

For a while, Wag listened. He caught a voice out of the crowd, a young woman's: "Someone called me Old Wag today."

Wag spoke into the mic, "I had that a few years ago."

"Same," another one put in. "They call me the Bottle King now."

"King Tub," said Wag.

"Treemonger."

"Childeater."

"Potbelly."

"Yaga."

"Yeah, I had Yaga once," said an old voice Wag had never heard before. "I *liked* Yaga. They call me Bone-Guzzler now. Not nearly the same ring . . ."

Some of these were fellow collectors. Fellow believers in Renfield remnants. Some of them Wag even remembered from the mine. Some were strangers. He appreciated their company regardless.

He leaned back, sighed again. He raised the bottle and took a long drink, draining half of it. It tasted good. He licked his lips.

The girl would be gone soon. He'd be dry again before he knew it. As always, he'd worry about his next catch. He'd worry about running out of meat before the cure had a chance to really work. But no matter. They *would* come again. Always had. Always will.

As long as someone held tight to that dark fascination. As long as no one had anything more than questions and curiosity. As long as there were kids to ask and parents to answer with nothing more than a hollow, despondent shrug—they would come.

All he had to do was wait.

He coughed. Swallowed hard, cleared his throat. Plucked a splinter of knucklebone from his tongue. He took another sip of the girl's blended hand.

And still, he hoped.

From: Rachel Durwood <radurwood@bhs.org>
To: tom.durwood@gmail.com
Re: The Stain

When it first began to thaw, the Renfield blood melted down into a line of peas on the neighboring property. In June of 1928, those peas were full-grown and ready to sell. The neighbors I mentioned before, Edna and Otto Mason, were superstitious but relatively poor. So they ignored their intuition and sold the peas at a farmers market. Since Otto had been a member of the party who disposed of all that blood and discovered the giant in the Renfield barn, you'd think he would have been a *little* more cautious, but alas.

Edna and Otto's son, also Otto, was seventeen. He said, joking, that they should up the price of the peas and make a sign: WATERED BY THE RENFIELDS. He wasn't invited to come to the market that day. He sat at home, irritated and bored. When his parents came home, they found him hanging in the attic, clutching a half-eaten pea shell in his hand.

This is, arguably, the first death caused directly by Renfield blood.

Luckily, not many people came to the market that day, but Edna and Otto *did* sell some peas to a schoolteacher named Elaine Westfield and an old farmer named Porter Brim. After Otto discovered his son, he and Edna tracked Brim down to warn him something might be wrong with the peas. They found him feeding his hands to his pigs, knuckle by knuckle. As they pulled him away and tied him up to make him stop, he told the Masons he could feel things. Maddening things. Echoing around in the air, in objects. He claimed he knew how to contain them, to help them stay still. Legend has it he figured out a way to do exactly that, sans fingers. Old Porter Brim even passed the trick down to his son Hector, who passed it down to *his* son Hector, but no verified record of that exists. It's just a story.

The Masons tried to find Elaine, too, but she was gone. Her house in the Mill stood empty. No note, no sign of struggle, nothing missing that would have indicated Elaine's flight from town. Nothing at all but an overwhelming stench of lavender. People who live near the old Westfield place claim to have seen strange lights hovering over that area at night, but I camped out there last weekend (I know, I know, it was stupid of me, etc., etc.) and I didn't see anything. I just lay there in what used to be Elaine's pumpkin patch, shivering in my sleeping bag, counting shootin stars. How many wishes does it *take* to get answers around here? Why does every urban legend in Renfield seem like such a grab-bag of random, weird-ass shit? And why does the Westfield property *still stink* of lavender? I could barely fuckin breathe.

Anyway. At the end of the day, Edna and Otto Mason burned the rest of their peas and salted that part of their land. That night, they sat at their kitchen table. Otto Jr. lay under a sheet on the table between them. According to Edna's diary, they talked about it for a long, long time. Then they burned their son, buried the ashes, and salted that land, too.

We probably should've done the same thing with Mom.

Ya know. Just in case.

RED X

—pped her out of bed, carried her spiraling up. She awoke in the middle of it, trying to scream. All that came was a tiny whimper, "Dad?" Which she held as she flew at the ceiling, hands clawing in mad arcs, the room reeling around her, "Daaad!" As light shattered the air and her ears filled with a high-pitched vibrating whine— the *twang-whizz* of whipping metal wires, constant, deafening. She closed her eyes. Colors burst behind her lids. She was still asleep, she had to be. It was a dream, a dream, a dream. Not real. Not happening, not—her mind emptied. Nothing. Limp, scared nothing. Insane, blank, blind. A fish reeled in to the surface. Gasping. Spinning. Falling endlessly up out of bed, into what felt like the metallic roar of the sun itself.

Kelly's feet landed gentle against something cold and hard. She tried to move. To scramble away. Maybe go for her phone, charging on the nightstand. Call the police. The neighbors. Something. Anything.

But her arms wouldn't move. Nor her legs. Something held her tight in place.

The air was freezing.

She realized she still had her mouth open. Was still frozen in that half whimper of a mid-dream scream, sound leaking out of her as she cried for her dad down the hall like she was six years old.

She wasn't six. Dad wasn't down the hall. She made herself stop. Tried to close her mouth, but couldn't. Something was cinched tight between her teeth, stretching her lips to the point of splitting them open, almost, and when she prodded it with her tongue, the flavor of old sweaty leather hit her taste buds. Something was lodged in her nose, too. Sharp edges that stank of copper dug into the tender flesh ringing each nostril, so that when she tried to move her head, she felt like someone was shoving twin metal tubes up her snout. It kept her pinned in place.

So . . . wherever this was, it clearly wasn't an *awesome* place to be.

Kelly kept her eyes closed. Her whole body trembled in the cold air. She began to talk to herself. *Okay. Calm the hell down, Kel. Assess the situation.* That's what her dad always said, back when he was still alive. In *any* situation, no matter what. Think in straight lines, not branches. Branches lead nowhere, turn in on themselves, make you panic. So follow the trunk. Get to the root. *Focus. Assess. Don't panic.* That'd been the mantra she'd *always* been able to use, her entire life. One she was grateful for, because it always calmed her down. Always seemed to work. And if she was ever really going to need it, *now* seemed like the right fucking time.

So she took a moment, and breathed. Sucking in frigid, coppery air through the thing in her nose. *Focus. Assess. Don't panic.* She took slow, whistling breaths until her heart went relatively calm. Then she focused, eyes still shut, on her legs.

From what she could tell, they were spread about shoulder-width apart. She could feel straps constricting her ankles, her calves, her thighs. Holding her fast to the wall. She moved her attention up, and felt more restraints around her waist, her neck. She felt her arms stretched out to her sides, crucifix-like. Three more restraints on each of those as well. One at the wrist, another at the elbow, and a third right up against her armpits.

She couldn't move a single part of her entire body. Except her head—she could turn her head a little side to side, but not more than half an inch each way before the rigid metal thing in her nose bit into her.

Scared anger began to boil along her skin. *If this is some kind of alien sex thing, I swear I'm gonna be so fucking pissed. I'm not getting sucked up into the sky just for some fucking . . . I'm gonna crash this UFO and I'm gonna . . . I'm gonna . . .*

Hey, hey. Come on. Focus.

She breathed. It took her a while, but she calmed her heart again. She felt like she was ready to open her eyes.

She eased them open slow. Had to blink several times to adjust to the light. She squinted upward. A rectangular fixture glared down at her from the ceiling. Yellow and buzzing.

She looked down from the light, and jerked back, surprised. She was facing another woman. A few years younger than her, maybe just shy of thirty, and equally stuck to the wall with her own web of black nylon straps, wrapped tight around every single joint in her body. She had a strap between her teeth as well, so she could do nothing more than gargle muffled syllables. And she, too, had something in her nose. A long metal pipe with a funnel welded to its end, pointing up at an angle so the woman's head was tilted slightly back, as if she were being led somewhere by the nose. The woman's eyes were wide, and she kept making sounds Kelly couldn't interpret.

But at least, Kelly observed, *she isn't naked*. If this were indeed some weird sex thing, she assumed they'd be nude. But no, this woman wore some kind of yellow jumpsuit, covering her from ankles to neck. It zipped open down the front, revealing the woman's skin from her cleavage down past her belly button. As if her pale skin was exposed only out of necessity for ... whatever operation this was.

Kelly shifted her body and could feel fabric rustling against her skin. She, too, must be in a yellow jumpsuit, zipped open down the front. Cold air slipped in around her hips, up her back.

She attempted to speak, because that seemed like the thing to do. The woman across from her returned the favor, and they gargled at each other against their gags for most of a minute.

Then Kelly heard the other voices. From both sides. Surrounding her.

She turned her head, wary of the thing in her nose, just enough to see that she was actually in the middle of a very long hallway. Three more yellow lights ran down the ceiling on either side of her. The floor was a thick, dark black. The walls were deep brown. And lining these walls, each clamped in place as tight as her, were over thirty people. All different ages, races, shapes, genders. Over thirty pairs of wide, terrified eyes. Thirty yellow jumpsuits, zipped open down the belly. And thirty long metal nose-tubes with funnels at the end. Like they were all part of a long, multi-human brass instrument. Some of them were trying to scream, to wrestle free of their restraints. Others sobbed and trembled. Some were silent. Some moaned. None of them could move an inch.

So this was, like ... *really* not a cool place to be.

A sound. To her left.

All eyes whipped toward it. Kelly could see, far away, in the very corner of her eye, what looked like a door. She watched it slide open. More cold yellow light poured forth from beyond, and a young man moved into the hall. The door rolled automatically shut behind him.

Kelly's mind began to reel. Panic coiled about her stomach.

She realized in that moment, a *man* was the last thing she'd expected. In fact, a human was actually more frightening than . . . the alternative. Because that meant something more complicated was happening here than she'd assumed. Something . . . maybe even worse? Something . . . It meant . . . It . . .

She closed her eyes. Breathed. *Just observe. That's what Dad would say.*

She took a moment, reopened her eyes, and became instantly aware of several noises at once. The wet gnashing of gum, the far-off crackle of music through earbuds, the clatter of someone shaking a can of spray paint. All distinctly human, and unsettling. And over it all, the cacophony of everyone in the hall howling around their gags. Begging, pleading. Their words no more than a drooling muffled roar.

The young man took a few steps deeper into the hall. Kelly couldn't see him well enough to see what he was doing. But she heard him shake the spray paint can. Heard the long hiss of spray. Someone wailed, went silent. More footsteps. The sound of the gum and the music came closer. There was a rustle of fabric. The clatter of the can. A long hiss. Another wail. More footsteps. Coming closer.

Finally, he entered her field of vision enough so that she could see him clearly. He was just some kid, a goddamn *kid*. Barely eighteen. Peach fuzz lining his cheeks. A mess of dirty blond hair. He wore a baggy hoodie, skinny black jeans. The thin white noodles of earbuds snaked down from his ears to the back pocket of his pants. In the other pocket, a can of green spray paint. He held a can of red at his side.

The kid stood before a man way down the hall from Kelly. He glanced at the man. No more than half a second. Then he shook the can of red paint and scrawled a long, wavering X across the man's exposed belly. The man shook against the spray. He howled, tried to shrink back against the wall. But it was already done.

He was already marked.

The kid nodded. Once, perfunctory. Smacked his gum. And moved on.

He turned to the elderly woman bound directly across from the man he'd just tagged. He glanced at her. No more than a second. He exchanged the red spray can for the green. Shook it. And sprayed. The woman railed against the wall. Tried hard to wrench herself free. A spidery, bile-colored X bled across her belly.

The kid nodded, satisfied with his work. And moved on.

The woman across from Kelly sounded like she was saying, "Hey. Hey."

Kelly looked at her. She made several rapid grunting noises. Speaking earnestly and pointedly against her gag. It sounded like she was trying to form an escape plan, to loop Kelly in on it.

Kelly blinked at her.

"O-ay?" the woman asked, clenching her teeth.

Kelly splayed her hands in a gesture she hoped said, *What the hell do you want me to do?*

The woman gaped at her for a moment. Then deflated against the wall.

The next stomach got a red X. The three after that, green. Another two red. And each time, the kid barely glanced at his mark. He seemed like any other teen working a minimum-wage job. Kind of bored. Listening to music. He might as well have been flipping burgers. He nodded consistently after each spray, taking inventory. Whatever the kid saw when he glanced at them—however he decided who got what color—it wasn't based on anything immediately apparent. Not to Kelly, anyway. Maybe it was random. Maybe it didn't matter. But no, no, he *did* seem to have a system. Some method for judging red from green. She could tell. She just wasn't sure what it was or which color she should hope for when, inevitably, he came for her.

Slowly, he made his way down the hall. Marking everyone in his wake with the same spidery X. As he came closer, closer, Kelly couldn't stop the panic from chewing at her bones. Needling against her skin. She had to close her eyes again and conjure up a physical image of her dad. His salt-and-pepper beard, his big glasses. She had to zero in on his voice telling her to focus. *Think in lines, Kel. The crazy branches, all those uncertainties and hypotheticals, are where you panic. Think of the trunk . . .*

But when she thought of straight lines, she thought only of the kid. Moving carefully, methodically. Down the line. Toward her.

At last, the kid stopped diagonally from her, in front of a man in his mid-forties. The man's eyes were bloodshot, furious. He formed rapid, wordless pleas against his gag. Pumped his fingers into and out of fists, lurching against his bonds. The kid's face was impassive. He just kept chewin. The buds in his ears kept cracklin music. He bobbed his head a little with the beat. Did his usual glance, flicking his eyes up into the man's face. He took out the green can. Pocketed the red. Shook the can. Aimed the nozzle at the man's belly button. Held down the valve. The man yelped. Clenched the muscles in his stomach.

But nothing came.

A thin green drizzle trickled onto his flesh, onto the floor. Kelly could almost taste it, coating her tongue. She gagged. The kid frowned. Shook the can again. Again, no more than a fine green mist sputtered forth.

"Goddammit," he muttered. He trudged back down the hall. The door slid open as he approached, and shut as he went.

The tension in the hall lifted. The faint sound of crying echoed down its length. Those already marked with Xs breathed in ragged, frightened gusts. They seemed, for the most part, beyond sense. Minds numb. Unsure of what was coming. Just expectant. Afraid.

Kelly looked around as best she could. Her eyes locked again on the woman across from her. She breathed evenly, salt lines drying across her cheeks. They stared at each other for a long time. Kelly wanted to say something. But even if she could, she didn't know what it would be. *Look, I'd love to formulate an escape plan with you, but—*

The door at the other end of the hall slid open.

Kelly could just barely make out a tall figure stepping through the doorway. No more than a vague gray shape. A shadow in the corner of her eye.

But she knew immediately it wasn't human.

A swollen humpback bobbed against the ceiling. A slow, fleshy dragging crept down the hall. A limping, slapping *plod-plod* as the figure moved toward her. The people lining the walls howled as it passed them, as they saw it. And when it passed her and she, too, saw it, something in her stomach gave. The image of her father left her entirely.

The thing was double Kelly's height. Rail-thin. Skin gray and sagging. Ribbons of flesh hung off its bones, sliding along the floor in a long train. Its knees buckled backward, so that it walked chicken-like on large, gray pads. There was nothing along the length of its body except the ripples of gray skin and the deep grooves of its skeleton. Its face was no more than a crease of puckered muscle, running vertically from its chin back up over its forehead.

It swung its head slow from side to side. It looked—if it could do so without eyes—at the bodies lining the walls. The offerings. Kelly caught a strong scent of lavender wafting off its hide as it passed. The smell wormed its way into her open mouth. Made her gag again. Like someone was shoving a flowery fist down her throat.

She'd always loved the smell of lavender. And for months after this night, she couldn't help but wonder if maybe, for some insane reason, that was why she was chosen. If maybe *everyone* in that hall loved the smell of lavender. Maybe it was some kind of psychological trick. If it was, it worked. Because she never let that smell into her home again.

The creature dragged its way to the first X in the line: a young woman, painted green. It stopped before her. Lifted its gray, sagging face to hers. Her body trembled. The nose-tube whistled as she shivered. The creature bobbed its head. Seemed to sniff at her for a long time. Then moved on.

The woman's body sagged with relief.

Next down the line was a red X-ed man, about forty years old. He kept still as the thing came to him, sniffed at him. He watched it, as if daring it to do something. Challenging it to make a move.

Which it did.

Positioning itself directly in front of him, head mere inches from the funnel-end of the tube lodged in the man's nostrils, it reared back, arms slapping onto the floor. It shuddered, sending waves down the loose folds of skin. Its entire body shook, letting off a rattlesnake clatter. Fingers twitching, dancing against the floor, hands flopping. Then the slit in its face opened. Kelly could hear it. A sickening wet *slllick*, revealing layers of white flesh surrounding a bright red hole. A toothless mouth that puckered in, out. In, out. As if it were tasting the air through deep, wheezing breaths. As if it could only breathe when it blossomed like this.

Its head wavered side to side for a moment, then it threw itself forward. The head splatted onto the funnel at the end of the man's tube. The folds of flesh wrapped around it, and the creature— began to vomit. A loud, violent rush of fluid that Kelly couldn't see, but only hear. She heard it splash into the funnel and echo fast down the tube, like the breaking of a dam. The man's eyes widened, and he screamed as the surge hit his nose and punched its way up his nostrils, down his throat. She saw his throat bulge hideously. His eyes rolled back into his head. Black ooze dripped from his nostrils. He snorted, coughed, and oily fluid flew out between his teeth. The creature rocked back and forth as it retched, pumping a high-powered jet of more and more goo into the tube. More than the man's body could possibly contain.

It went on for a dizzying length of time.

At last, the creature lifted its head from the funnel. Another moist *shlllick* as it peeled its flesh from the metal. Its face resealed itself, and without another glance at the man it'd just vomited into, it turned and moved on.

The man was still. His eyes glossy and blank. He still breathed (or at least it looked like he did), but for the rest of the time Kelly was there, he never moved again. A slow stream of blood trickled out of his nose. It dripped like a metronome onto the floor.

Kelly had no idea how to assess . . . this.

The creature passed over the next green X, and came to another red, painted across the belly of a woman about thirty-five, just a year or two older than Kelly. Again, the thing reared back. Shuddered. Its face split open. And it latched itself onto the funnel. She screamed as the flood of goo hit her, and she gargled wet, horrible sounds for a long, long time. The woman seized, bled, and was still. Eyes cloudy. Nose dripping. She, too, never moved again.

So that settled it. To receive a red X was, apparently, to be damned.

The creature resealed itself and moved on.

It came to the next red X, lying crimson over the beer gut of a middle-aged man. Kelly watched the creature quiver. Watched the man shake his head. She shut her eyes. Heard the rushing stream down the tube, the sudden retching as the bile hit home. She imagined the feeling of a neti pot. The warm saltwater rushing into your throat . . .

When it was nearly over, she could hear the door at the end of the hall open. Heard the familiar sounds of the kid. She opened her eyes just in time to see the older man's body shake, and go still. He slumped forward. His nose wept onto his chest.

The creature's face closed and turned toward the kid.

"Sorry," said the kid. "Had to get another can."

Kelly blinked. *He's speaking to it.* She tried to move her head. She had to see them interact. *Had* to see if the creature said anything back. But the tubes in her nose threatened to break into her skull if she turned her head any farther. She could only barely make out the kid's face.

"Ran out of green," he said, gnashing his gum. He held up a new can so the thing could see.

It didn't react.

"I'll finish the rows here first," said the kid. He jerked his chin at the seeming-dead. "Guess you already started treating that end, so just gimme a minute to finish this one. I know we're kind of behind, but . . ." He shrugged. "What can you do."

He went up to the man he'd stopped at before. Glanced at him. Exchanged the can of green for the red. And began to spray. The man railed against the wall. Kelly could almost make out the words around the gag: *"This is a mistake! I was green before! I was! Goddammit, I was green . . ."*

The kid ignored him. Continued talking as he sprayed. "I did the east halls first, so. Only about ten more on this wing. Not bad, but I know we're still behind your estimates."

He glanced at the woman across from Kelly. Painted her green. She managed a wet, weeping *thank you*.

The creature stood still, almost statuesque, watching the kid work.

"We'll still be *done* before dawn," said the kid, as if scolded. "Look, I'm *going* as fast as I can. You picked a good crop. They'll all take. See?"

He pointed at the slumped, bleeding figures down the hall. The thing turned its head toward them, and back to the kid. It gave no sign it understood.

The kid shrugged again. "We can always repropagate if we have to."

Repropagate? Kelly's mind seized at the word. It sent waves of ice down her skin. *Repropagate . . . us?*

She watched the kid approach. She could hear the creature move down the hall. Shaking, opening. Preparing itself for someone new.

Her mind continued to spiral. *Propagate? Like, crops? Like a fucking garden? Of what?*

She told herself to stop. Think in lines. *What lines? What the fuck am I doing here? This is . . . I don't . . . I can't . . .*

The kid glanced at her. Looked down. Picked a can.

But Kelly couldn't see which one it was. The way he moved his hands, the way he was standing . . . She couldn't see.

She jerked forward, pressing away from the wall. The edges of her nose-tubes bit into her flesh. She felt blood fall onto her upper lip, dripping into her teeth as she snarled at this stupid kid, this fucking *punk*. Her nose burned with pain, but she pressed farther, farther. She *had* to know. She peered down as far as she could, but his hands remained out of sight. She couldn't see which can he held.

She slammed her back against the wall. Arched her spine. Screamed in a jagged, breathy rush. The sound of the shaking can was a roar. Down the hall, she could hear the sick, wet slide of fluid against metal. Heard someone retch.

Kelly gave the kid a fierce look, and he grinned, he fucking *grinned* at her. His first and only show of emotion.

She wondered, for a long time after, why *she* was the only one he grinned at. This detail stuck with her more than anything else.

"See?" he called down the hall. "It'll be done tonight. No sweat. Still on schedule for settlement."

And with that, he sprayed her. The cold slash of air stung her skin. She tried to get away from it, like the others. And, like the others, it didn't matter. She tried to move her head, her stomach, *anything*, to see what color she'd gotten.

But she couldn't.

Her mind exploded into branches. Her father evaporated, his advice dust. Down the hall, the creature readied itself for another red X. Moving faster now.

The kid went past her. She yelled at him as she watched him go all the way down the hall, spraying every body in turn. Then he vanished through the door, and she never saw him again.

Far off to her left, she heard the creature turn and begin working its way back toward her. Slow, red rivers ran from the chins of the glassy-eyed red X-ed, keeping time as they tapped against the floor.

The creature lumbered closer. She could smell it fully now. The lavender stench punched through her, singeing her nostrils. Strong and sickly sweet. Coating the back of her throat.

It stopped in front of her, mere inches from her face. Its arms dangling, the slit in its face coated in a thin layer of black slime. It sniffed at her. The lavender drowned her until she thought she might vomit or pass out or both. She made promises to God she knew she'd never keep, but meant anyway. If she woke up *right* now, she'd do anything. *Anything*. Swear to God. *Please*.

The thing bobbed its head, scanning her body for the X. It looked up at her. The muscles in its face bunched. Dark ooze dribbled down in slobbery lines across its chin.

She felt faint. Woozy from the stench. It made her dizzy. Made the hallway spin. She looked up at the ceiling light, too afraid to see what would happen to her. She heard the creature make some kind of noise. And—

And she's falling. Spiraling upward into the light. Twisting into its bright, hot embrace. The light flashes, turns, whines, breaks—

And became the morning sun. Flickering golden-green upon her ceiling. Bouncing off the leaves outside.

The window was open. Through it, she could hear the songs of robins and the rush of the wind through the leaves. A power drill somewhere, a lawn mower. Kids screaming on scooters down the street.

She was back in her room. In her house in her neighborhood in the Mill. On Earth. She could look outside right now and see the edge of Bartrick Lake, shimmering through the trees. On *Earth*.

Kelly sprang out of bed, ran down the hall into her bathroom, and threw herself in front of the toilet. She vomited for an eternity. When she was done, she stared down into the bowl. Nothing black or slimy had come out of her. No alien bile. She stuck a hand in, rooted around. Nothing.

"Fucking hell," she breathed.

She flicked the sick off her hand, wiped her mouth on her shirt. Flushed. Went to the window next to the sink. Looked outside. The lawn smiled back at her, simple and warm in the summer morning sun.

She lifted her shirt and studied herself in the mirror. Turned left, then right. Her stomach looked normal. No paint. She ran her hand over the skin. Tried to feel something there, anything. Looked at her hand. Rubbed her fingers together. Again, looked at her reflection. Tilted her head back, examined her nose for dried blood. Nothing.

She shivered. Stared at herself for a long time. Then got in the shower. Worked her jaw in circles. The restraints had left no ache. No stiffness. No mark. The taste of blood was totally gone. She moved her arms around. Her head. Pumped her legs up and down. Nothing. No sign of any trauma or strain. She watched the water running into the drain for any sign of green or . . . or red. Maybe she couldn't see it. Maybe it was a special *kind* of paint. Maybe it . . . Maybe . . .

"Fucking hell."

She reached for the bar of soap on her shelf. Stopped. Gagged. Almost vomited again. She held the soap at arm's length, staring at it like it was alive.

Lavender.

She reached around the shower curtain and chucked the soap into the trash. She realized her entire body was shaking. She could still feel that cold air against her skin. She turned up the hot water. Breathed in the steam. Let it scald her for several minutes before she got out. She wrapped herself in a towel and padded, dripping, trembling, back to her room. She slipped on her bathrobe and went outside, leaving her towel in a wet heap on the floor.

Kelly was an estate planner at a small law firm in the Mill. She was a very neat, orderly person. Her dad's advice affected nearly every aspect of her life. Each morning, she awoke at six a.m., showered for exactly seven minutes, and never once needed to pause to vomit because she had never once, in all her adult life, been hungover or had food poisoning (she was not an adventurous eater). So already she could tell, as she stepped outside in her bathrobe, that this event would throw off her entire fucking year.

She stood on the lawn. Looked up at her bedroom window, at the trees, for any sign of . . . of anything, really. She didn't know.

Nothing.

She went quickly back into the house, to the bathroom. She opened her robe and, once more, examined her skin in the mirror. Nothing.

She stared at herself for a long time. A faint nausea churned inside her stomach. She put a hand to it. Began breathing hard. Heart slamming. Suddenly, she felt like she knew. She *felt* it. That cascade of black bile. Swirling inside of her. She could feel it moving. Pumping through her entire being, replacing all her blood and normal human juices with . . . something else.

She sprinted into the kitchen. Grabbed a knife from the rack on the counter. Held it over herself for almost a full minute before she dropped it and sank to the floor, sobbing.

For the first time ever, Kelly called in sick.

She'd always had trouble making friends. She just didn't *like* other people. Didn't find them interesting or safe. In elementary school, she spent recess playing by herself in the corner of the Haywood Elementary playground, close to the woods where the other kids wouldn't go. She'd tromp around in circles, concocting complex stories in her head about criminals on the run. Criminals *she* had to catch.

Her father, who always let her stay up late to watch *JAG*, visited her one day at school (some PTA thing they needed volunteers for).

He was the only one who understood the convoluted stories in Kelly's head. *He* was safe. And for the whole recess that day, he chased her around the entire playground in a pretend shootout.

It was the happiest moment of her life.

When the heart attack took him on Kelly's thirtieth birthday, she decided she was fine being alone. Other men had never interested her, and neither had women, for that matter. She didn't *need* anybody else. She could even plan her own estate, donate all her leftover money to the Haywood Educational Fund.

But that was before . . . this. Before she needed, really fucking *needed*, to know if she was, or was not, full of alien bile. *Then* the loneliness hit her in a way she'd never understood before. She needed someone to validate this.

Two days after her abduction, she managed to drag herself to work, bleary-eyed, still shivering. All day, she eyed her coworkers, flicking her eyes around the office and analyzing their faces. Trying hard to see if she recognized them from the hallway. Or if they recognized her. But no. Those people in the hall remained strangers.

She spent the workday hunched over her desk, scouring Facebook groups and neighborhood watch forums (of which Renfield has many). Not anywhere did she find mention of the hallway, the yellow jumpsuits. The bile.

She began to wonder if she was alone in this experience. If perhaps this, too, had been in her head. A complex nightmare that eight-year-old Kelly would have been proud to have invented, it was so clever and . . . effective.

If her dad were here, he would have believed. *He* would have validated her. He always did, back when she had nightmares and he was just down the hall . . .

She spent weeks surveilling all the high schools in the area, alternating which school she watched each day, keeping a color-coded record on Excel. She'd leave work early and park by the school's front entrance, by the buses. She'd wait for the final bell to ring, then scan the crowds of teens pouring outside into the parking lot. Hawk-eyed. Waiting for *him* to appear. That little asshole.

Nothing.

She tried Bartrick High School, Tinker's Falls High, Bent High, Grittwood High, Lillian Academy . . . She returned to Lillian Academy several times, actually, thinking maybe the kid was one of the many blond douchebags who haunted its halls, in their stupid uniforms. Their silver and blue ties, their khakis, their smug Richie Rich grins. She glared at them all through her windshield, wringing the wheel with one hand, scratching idly at her stomach with the other.

But no dice. She never saw the kid again. He must have been from some other county. Or . . . from somewhere else entirely.

Every morning, she awoke on the couch in the living room, the tv still droning on from the night before, keeping her company. She took a shower first thing, emerging half an hour later bright red and burnt. Every morning, the distant rumblings of nausea crept once more into her gut. She'd go into the kitchen, drum her fingers on the counter. Staring at the knife block next to the stove. She'd grab a paring knife. Press it to her skin until she bled. She'd examine the blood for streaks of black. She considered, seriously, every single morning, burying the knife to the hilt in her stomach and moving it in circles. Letting the slosh of bile spill out of her in great, dark waterfalls.

But she never did. Because she couldn't be entirely sure. Because maybe she'd cut into herself and find nothing. Then her innards would slosh out onto the floor and she'd die feeling ridiculous.

Or maybe there *was* something. Maybe she'd been fertilized with the beginning seed of a vast and terrible settlement. Or maybe she was just an insane person, and a person who now cut themselves.

She started eating like a hummingbird. Meals became strangers, traded in for small bites of things here and there. Things she often threw up, in long, silky ropes. Often, she *made* herself throw up, just to see what was inside of her. Her skin sagged, and then tightened around her bones until she was totally flat, nearly translucent. Eventually, nothing ran along her body but the deep grooves of her skeleton.

The nausea came several times a day. She'd find herself back in the kitchen, blood leaking down her waist. Knife in hand. Staring at the spiderweb of thin cuts along her skin. She started bringing the knife to work, until they asked her to stop coming to work. Then she spent her days on the couch, staring into the tv without seeing it. Thinking in spiraling, labyrinthine branches. *What if They're way more advanced than us? What if They have some kind of masking technology? What if, no matter what our charts show or doctors say, there is still something in me? What if I'll never ever know? What if that was the point? What if that's the experiment? To see how I react . . .*

Time rolled past. She didn't find a new job. Ate away at her savings. She was surprised she wasn't dead. Maybe the bile was keeping her alive.

She thought often of those glassy-eyed people in the hallway. Waiting for their turn to be freed or doomed. Not knowing what was happening. Just expectant. And afraid.

She swore she'd figure this out. She wouldn't be like them. She wouldn't be trapped in her fear. She could find that root, dammit. She always had. She just needed to *focus*.

She watched a lot of tv. Letting the shapes and colors wash over her without really seeing them. Going over it all in her head. Over and over again. Clawing deeper and deeper into her stomach scabs. She kept peeling them off, flicking them into the corner. The skin underneath was a raw, bright white. She kept her nails short and stubby so she wouldn't open herself in the night as she dreamt.

But one day, she knows, she probably will. Just to have something tangible she can point to and say, *See?? I'm not fucking crazy!* That'd show those goddamn kids at Haywood Elementary. Those assholes who called her *weird*, called her *alien*, told her she *smelled*. She'll probably cut all the way down into her stomach, reach into herself, root around for something, anything. Feel her organs squish and pop around her fingers as she digs. She'll feel the stomach acid ooze out, burning its way through her. And she'll let it happen. She'll let herself go. Just to be done with everything. To have some modicum of peace. Be free of herself. She'll just . . . let it happen. Just let it happen . . . let it happen . . . let it happen . . . let it go . . .

On the one-year anniversary of her abduction, an officer from the Bartrick Mill Police Department breaks down Kelly's door. He's responding to an anonymous tip from a neighbor who heard screams, howls, laughter, coming from within. The officer arrives quickly, but he doesn't expect much when he enters the house. Everyone in the BMPD has seen plenty of nightmares.

So it isn't with horror that the officer looks upon the situation in Kelly's kitchen. The smears of brilliant red across the counters, the spray of it across the ceiling. He doesn't retch or gag. He simply holsters his weapon and sighs. He's not even saddened by scenes like this anymore; he's just . . . numb, when he discovers Kelly sitting on the floor, slumped against the back of the kitchen island so he can only see her legs sprawled out in front of her, and the mess.

Her intestines blossomed around her in an impossibly wide net. Other throbbing chunks and sacks stretch out across the floor. She has unpacked herself completely, digging as deep as she can for any sign that this was all real.

The officer turns his chin to his radio, is about to call in a probable homicide, when Kelly's foot—twitches. He takes a step closer, says, "Miss? Can you hear me?" Peering over the marble island, feeling silly because of course there's no way she's still alive. That's the only small mercy here. She *must* be dead. But he can't quite see her face, just the spread of her.

He says it again to be sure. "Miss. Can you hear me."

Kelly is still scraping the knife around her eye socket when she looks up and says softly, "Dad?"

From: Rachel Durwood <radurwood@bhs.org>
To: tom.durwood@gmail.com
Re: The Stain

Okay, little bro. So . . . you don't want to write back. That's cool. I know I said I'd try to give you a little space, but I'm worried now. Sorry.

You *are* reading these, right? I know it's a lot, but . . . I'm trying to reach out. Fuck. I'm sorry.

Look, I'm gonna call you as soon as I hit Send on this one. You can ignore my texts, fine, but please don't be a total asshole and send me straight to voicemail? I'm all outta Mountain Dew, so I'm just drinking straight from this huge thing of Bartrick's Bourbon (I love that bottom-shelf shit), and every time you ignore me, I'm taking another shot, so. Pick. Up.

Cheers.

Now listen:

After the murders, inside the Renfield home, the stain stretched all over, across the entire house. The upstairs toilet was stained a faded brownish pink. The stairs, a dark crimson oak. Bootsteps of stain went down the halls. Little bare feet of stain led through the foyer toward the back door.

The police took pictures of the cave-drawn giant in the barn, of course. There are at least five different written descriptions of it as well, archived in the Renfield County Sheriff's Office (although the Edenville Library was gracious enough to let me peruse their copies).

The detective assigned to the Renfield massacre, one Walter George Harren, returned to the barn several times during the winter of 1927–28. He sketched the giant repeatedly. Kept drawing it, drawing it, drawing it. Every day for months, according to his colleagues. He filled an entire notebook with the jagged lines of hair. The sloped shoulders. The eyes. Some of the sketches were highly detailed, in color, depicting the very grain of the wood in the barn wall. Some were hurried and simple. Others were angry, his pencil cutting through several layers of paper. When the notebook was full, in July 1928, he simply vanished from the county, and never returned. As if filling that notebook was his only task in life. The only thing keeping him sane. He left the book with Mrs. Harren, who immediately handed it back to the Lillian PD, claiming it wasn't written by "any Walt *I* know."

You can see pictures of Harren's notebook online. The *Bent News* (Renfield's own *National Enquirer*) published them in 1933. The *Lillian Journal* (Renfield's classier local news source by far) did not.

Throughout the notebook, alongside Walter's sketches of the giant, are thousands upon thousands of notes. They begin neat and orderly, but quickly turn chaotic as the book goes on. As if just being *near* the giant was enough to warp Harren's mind. Like the entire barn was radioactive. He drew the giant nearly eight hundred times over the span of his little notebook. Cramped and near-illegible marginalia encircle its hair, its shoulders. The eyes. These notes refer to local folklore, mythology, even fairy tales containing references to giants. But almost all of it is nonsense. None of the stories Harren references seem to exist. Unless *you've* heard of "The Swallow and the Bone" or "Mrs. McCready's Little Friend." No?

Cool, me neither. Nobody has. So you can believe that Renfield's giant was telling Harren stories whenever he stood near it. Stories from another world. Which is what *he* claims, in the notebook. Or you can believe the doubters over at *Lillian Journal*, who refer to Harren's disappearance as "the inevitable result of a very troubled mind. For who could gaze upon that grisly murder scene, that poor hanged Mason boy, *all* of it—and not go at least a little insane?"

So. Tom. Here's the one. The one you're *really* going to give me shit for. But please just hear me out: I *found* the goddamn notebook.

At the same Edenville Historical Society Halloween Auction where somebody bought Adelaide Renfield's half-an-eye in a jar, there was also the original Walter Harren notebook. It sold for about five grand to a guy up in the Falls named Andrew. I reached out through FB (his profile seemed normal enough—just some construction contractor dude), and he agreed to meet me. I know, I know, the Falls is all cannibals and freaks. Yes, I shouldn't have gone. This is an obsession. *This* is what I was doing instead of reaching out to you. Yes, Tom. I know. I'm sorry.

But the guy didn't even *have* the Walter Harren anymore. Said he'd burned it. And I wasn't the first person who'd come looking for it.

"Oh, there are many other . . . collectors around here," Andrew told me in his kitchen. We were sitting at this wooden table. I kept my hands in my lap. I was perched on the very edge of his chair, trying to touch as little wood as possible. After my run-in with that creepy guy who'd had a big slab of Renfield oak in his fuckin living room, I wasn't taking any chances. Even *being* there felt like playing Russian roulette.

"I thought it would be cool, ya know," Andrew explained. "I love a good urban legend. But I think people like us," meaning me and him, "know when to quit. Right? You're all down for exploring a cave, for example, but you get a gut feeling that tells you when to stop. When to turn back."

I told him I didn't have that.

He laughed, then cocked his head and sucked in air between his teeth. "Then good luck to ya. Point is, I burned the thing so it wouldn't bother anybody else anymore."

I swallowed a sting of baffled anger. I can't imagine *burning* something like that. I asked him if there was anything he could glean from the notebook. About Renfield's motivations, the giant. Anything.

"Three things, actually." And he counted them off on his fingers. "One: Lawrence was out cold for three minutes when that mule kicked him. It was Harren's strong belief that something *spoke* to Lawrence in those three minutes. Giants? He doesn't say. And he has no way of knowing. Harren didn't *talk* to the guy, this is all just his speculation. But two: When Lawrence woke up, he'd been given orders. He killed his family *on* orders. And Harren thinks this because? *He'd* been hearing orders inside the barn, too. Every time he visited the giant, something whispered to him from behind the blood-painting. Telling him . . . to *eat*. Harren left the entire damn county behind because he didn't want to kill his wife and kid, didn't think he could last much longer before he gave in. He details all this pretty explicitly in the book's last few pages. 'Eat them whole,' said the voice. 'Come. Birth yourself into something . . . *better*. For me . . .'"

Hearing Andrew say that made me feel cold and prickly. Scared, yes. But excited, too. I can't explain it. I felt . . . *close* to something, Tom. For the first time since Mom. I don't mean that to be frightening, but . . . I felt it.

"Harren wrote that over and over," said Andrew. "'Something *better*.' Like he wasn't *made* well. And the giant was trying to . . .

remold him. Something like that. Who knows. If you've ever seen that play, *No Longer Lawrence*, Harren is a character in that. I actually . . ." He smiled a little. "*I* played Harren. In high school. We did *Lawrence* when I was a senior at Falls High, and, uh . . . I had such a crush on Mrs. Harren. Anyway. Not the point. Point number *three* is . . ."

And here, he paused. He picked at something on the table between us. He worked his jaw for a long time before saying, "Three, Ms. Durwood, is that several pages of Harren's notebook describe the benefits of consuming human flesh, and fresh, pumping blood. Harren suggests that Renfield knew this as well. That given enough time, Lawrence may have begun to *eat* his family. Or the parts the giant didn't want, anyway. The barn voice spoke of this. Encouraged it, even. 'The consumption of man,' Harren writes, 'allows one to see beyond time, beyond death. Beyond the *walls*.'"

I asked what that meant. Leaning forward.

"Well, we *all* live in walls, Ms. Durwood. Surely you know that."

I said that sounded like bullshit. Andrew laughed and said, "Well . . . sure. But hell, transumption rituals were and *are* a fairly big deal in some cultures, for a number of reasons. And Harren never *denounces* cannibalism outright. He just didn't want to eat his *own* kin. He figured he'd maybe make a new life in the city, so his kid would be safe. Or *safer* at least. Down there, Walter figured he could either resist the giant's call or, if not? There'd be plenty to eat."

I said it still seemed like bullshit. I don't think I sounded convinced of that, though (and I wasn't, I'm not).

"Well, Ms. Durwood." Andrew smiled. "That may be. But who am I to say you couldn't prepare yourself a nice, rare man-steak and 'live beyond death' or some such profane bullshit? Even in the Bible, they talk about it, in Deuteronomy. 'The blood is the life,' and all that? Taking Communion? Just sayin. Who knows. Besides . . ." His smile grew. "Blood tastes fuckin *great*."

At that, I was back in my car faster than you can say *boo*. Shaking head to toe. Too close, Tom. Way too close. Stupid of me. Selfish, even. You don't deserve to lose two people this year.

As I backed out of his driveway, Andrew stood on his porch and waved to me. He called something out. Ever the idiot, I stopped and rolled down my window. "What?"

"I said, be *seein* ya," he called again. And waved.

I couldn't even respond, I was shaking so bad. I was so spooked.

I mean . . . I was scared, yes. Sure. But if I'm being honest, I was also shaking because I felt fucking *alive*. I almost *wanted* him to try something. To take a bite out of me so I had a reason to hit him.

I don't know. Sometimes I feel like I'm looking for someone to bite me, so that *I* have an excuse to go apeshit.

10 PM ON THE SOUTHBOUND G

It's night, and Nick's watching this man nibble on the nubs of a baby's hands on the subway. The man is hunched deep over his lap, the child sprawled across the top of a duffel bag strewn over his knees. The arms and legs writhe, as baby limbs do. And the guy nibbles so intently on those tiny little digits. Gumming them with a goofy kind of baby-love. Then he pulls his head back. Mutters. Grins. Shakes his head slow. Mutters something else. Nonsense. Googly noises.

He is loving that baby up.

Nick's watching this from a ways down the car, standing against the wall. He has a grocery bag in one hand. The other holds the railing. He bobs along gentle with the movements of the train, watching this guy and his baby. He keeps watching for maybe five stops. The guy just keeps on going.

Lovin his baby up.

Nick is laser-focused on this guy because he's soothing some deep worry inside of Nick. He can't look away because his wife, Anna, is pregnant, and dad-thoughts are big on his mind. He'll actually *be* a dad in three months or so. And he's watching this guy love-nibbling on his kid's tiny little hands. And the baby's making faces up at him, writhing around, kicking, and all those future-dad-worries that have been needling at Nick for months just float away, and Nick thinks, *Yeah.*

Yeah, that's the kind of dad I'm going to be. Just like that guy. Loving that baby up. A good dad.

It's an affirmation and an inspiration, and it rocks Nick's soul gently, like the calm bob-weave of the train through the ground.

Nick's stop comes, and he leaves the subway feeling good. Bright and simple and good. Swinging the grocery bag, humming a little. He'll go home, throw the bag on the counter, and hold Anna tight until she kind of laughs and says, "You okay?"

"Mmhm," he'll say. "I just love you, is all."

"I love you, too, babe . . . They had chocolate mint?"

"Yes, ma'am."

"*Yes.* Ah. You're so *good* to me."

Then they'll kiss. Bliss. Anna is so happy she could die. Nick is so happy he could die. They'll eat dinner, and make love, and fall asleep tangled in each other like limp spaghetti. And Nick will dream of that man loving his baby up. That cute-talking, love-gnawing man, cherishing his child on the southbound G . . .

When Nick gets off the southbound G, the man keeps nibbling. As the train roars on, he keeps nibbling and nibbling until the child's fingers disappear. He swallows. He works his way down the arm. He sucks on the muscle. Eats the shoulder, cleans the ribs. Takes a long time chewing the lungs, which are tough, still gasping air when he reaches them, trying to work up a scream.

He exits the train at the last stop. He walks to a dumpster in an empty alleyway and dumps the little bones inside. They clatter out of the duffel bag in a big white heap. He walks to the back door of an unmarked building. He sits against the wall. Waits. Fidgets with the duffel bag, which was stamped long ago with bright brass initials, faded now, and grimed: *W. G. H.* He's forgotten what these letters mean, or how they're supposed to make him feel. All he feels these days is hunger.

Eventually, a woman emerges from the back door, carrying a small bundle. The man stands. He zips open the duffel bag, offers its mouth to her. She places the bundle inside. It cries a little. The man zips the duffel bag shut. The woman thanks him profusely. He can't speak. He just walks away.

The man gets back on the G, heading north. He zips open the duffel bag, takes the baby out, lays it across his lap. He begins nibbling at its fingers. They are the juiciest, sweetest part of the entire body. He can still taste the womb on them.

"Yum," he tells the child. Muttering. Smiling. Shaking his head. "Yum yum yum."

He takes the train all the way north, to its final destination. And slowly, he devours the entire child.

From: Rachel Durwood <radurwood@bhs.org>
To: tom.durwood@gmail.com
Re: The Stain

No one ever claimed the Renfield house. They had no other family outside the county. It stood for years before it collapsed, another mass of decay in a forest already populated by dilapidated buildings, unplanned communities carved into hills, ramshackle slipshods, forgotten concrete things, and other rusting shards of civilization.

For a while, the house remained almost exactly as it had been the day everybody in it died. Right down to the food Adelaide had been making: half-cut vegetables left on the counter, a pudding cooling in the fridge. Everything frozen in time. Including the stain across almost the entire floor.

The first things people stole were the shotgun shells. The police took only one and left the rest behind. Not much of an investigation was needed—Lawrence was just *there* in the barn, all bloody, when the police came, walking lost in circles. He was already muttering a confession as they cuffed him. So when people later broke into the house to gawk and prod, there was a significant amount of evidence just lying around. And those shells were the first to go. Then went the splinters and the buckshot from the bathroom door upstairs, and the broken hinge from the back door. Then the entire back door. People took salt shakers and furniture. Utensils, dishes, towels. Pictures off the walls. They took May's diary and books from Henry's room. They stole Robert's toys and Lawrence's razor. They stole the pudding out of the fridge, knickknacks off the shelves. The mailbox. Somebody dug Lawrence's fingernail from the painting of the giant in the barn.

Where these souvenirs have all gone is difficult to say. A friend of mine at Edenville College had a Renfield towel she got from her grandmother. She never used it, but whenever she touched it, weird blisters appeared on her hands. One of my teachers at Bent High (you never had Mr. Blake, did you?) had a Renfield doily framed on his wall. His classroom always had a bad vibe. Just being in there gave me a headache. Plus he was a total dick. He made me *hate* math.

Correlation? Causation? Don't know.

And, of course—Mom had a souvenir, too. But we'll get to that.

For almost an entire decade, people whittled souvenirs away from the Renfield house, until it was nothing more than an empty shell.

And then, in the spring of 1936, it collapsed.

Cheers, Tom. Pick up your phone.

SO MY COUSIN KNEW THIS GUY

(BEST SERVED OVERHEARD AT A VERY LOW-KEY BACKYARD HANG IN BENT: SUMMER NIGHT, CRICKETS, FIRE SMOKE, CORONA IN HAND, DON'T FORGET THE LIME)

Bill was just starting to get into meditation. Trying to relax a little, you know? He was a managing editor or something, over at *Lillian Journal*. They were always rushing issues to print, so it was super fuckin stressful. Like every day, this guy Bill had some big new problem show up on his desk that he had to look at. Shit like: The front page would be organized all wrong, and if Bill didn't figure it out, the issue would go to print and everybody would buy this wrong page. That's gotta be nuts. *Super* stressful. But then Bill sees this thing on Facebook about meditating and clearing your mind and shit. So Bill figures he'll pick it up. Half an hour before bed, every night. Lower his blood pressure. Easy.

He's got himself a pretty good setup, too, from what my cousin tells me. Has a space cleared in the middle of his living room, a nice rug all laid out. He sits down on the floor with his legs all crossed, this expensive candle burning. Little pillow, cuz he's got this thing with his lower back (happens). He puts his hands in his lap, palms up. And he closes his eyes, and he breathes. He does that for, like, twenty minutes.

But he has trouble focusing. I mean, everybody does when you start out. But Bill has a short attention span, he's *super* impatient, so he really has trouble focusing. And after a few weeks, Bill just gives up.

My cousin says Bill goes to a mutual friend of theirs who's been meditating for years. I think he even owns his own yoga studio or something, up in Lillian. I know, bougie. My cousin and Bill both live up that way. It's fuckin nice.

Anyway, Bill asks the guy for advice. Something to help him focus. And the guy's like, "Just . . . stare at the backs of your eyelids." And Bill's like, *Holy shit*. That's *exactly* what he needed to hear. Because he realizes that's his problem—he needs something to *stare* at.

All day long, he's staring at layouts and copyedits and shit on his computer. And then at night when he goes to meditate, suddenly his eyes are closed and he's not staring at *anything*. That's why he can't focus. His brain needs something to look at. He'd try focusing on his breath, his body. My cousin says he even told Bill to focus on his butthole. The, like, deep center of your fuckin body, you know? But nothing is working. So when this yoga guy is like, "Well, just *stare* at the backs of your eyelids," Bill's like, *Duh*.

So that night, he sits down to meditate. Gets himself all set up with his candle, his little pillow. He even adds some incense this time because he figures what the hell. He gets this shit that's supposed to activate his root chakra, but it just makes him sneeze, so he snuffs it out and throws away the whole pack. Then he sits down again, shuts his eyes, and he just . . . stares at the backs of his eyelids.

And he does that for, like, twenty minutes. And it *kind of* works. He feels calm. He feels good. His brain is pretty much empty. All the stress from his job and his life just floats away.

But then it starts to freak him out. Because he realizes, *Oh my god. I'm always seeing things.*

So think about it. When you close your eyes, you're not seeing anything. Right? Not true. Your eyes are still working. Still *seeing*. They're just seeing black because it's your fuckin eyelids. It's all dark. But your eyes are still *on*. Still sending data to your brain, even if that data is just static or, like, those little patches of color you get when you close your eyes too hard.

This whole idea freaks Bill out. Drives him nuts. Every time he closes his eyes, he thinks about it. No matter what—whether he's at work or home or even asleep—he's *still* looking at stuff. He'll *never* be able to turn it off.

Well, it drives him up the goddamn wall. He can't even sleep that night. Just keeps staring at the backs of his eyelids.

So he goes back to his yoga pal, and he's like, "Look, the staring thing didn't work."

And the guy's like, "Why not?"

And Bill's like, "Well, I just want to shut my eyes *off*. I mean, I want to be totally zen. I don't want to see *anything*. Even my fuckin eyelids." Except I don't think he said *fuckin* because my cousin says Bill's kind of a goodie-goodie. Like, tightly wound, you know? Total neat freak, borderline OCD. Probably why he freaked out so much when he couldn't get zen, you know? He's *used* to being in control.

So the yoga guy thinks about this for a second. And he goes, "You want to shut your eyes off."

And Bill's like, "Yeah."

And the guy goes, "Well. Once you transcend your physical

body and enter a complete meditative state, the physical plane presented to your eyes is—"

And Bill's basically like, "Oh, fuck you." Or whatever he says. And he walks away.

So a couple weeks go by, and Bill can*not* focus. He tries again *every* night. He puts his little pillow on the floor, lights his fuckin candle. Sits there with his legs crossed. And he stares at the backs of his eyelids, trying not to think about it, focusing on his butthole.

But he does think about it. He can't *stop* thinking about it. About how he's still seeing something literally *all* the time. He can't sleep. Can barely blink. And work is getting insane. Too many fuckups going on, too much for Bill to look at. Dude's losing control. In fact, he's thinking of quitting. He's got enough money saved up from this trust fund he had. He could take, like, five years off and be okay.

I know. Everyone in Lillian's fuckin bougie.

Anyway, something about all that—about how pissed he is that he can't focus, how he's thinking of quitting his job, and this ulcer he's getting—I mean, he is just *not* zen—this makes Bill think, *Well. Why don't I just get rid of my eyes.*

Now. My cousin's a doctor, right? Actually. Dylan. You know Dylan. You met him at that thing with the . . . Stacy's thing? Last summer? You remember Stacy.

Yeah, the hair.

Anyway, Dylan's, like, a surgeon. And Bill comes up to him and he's like, "Listen. Dylan. I want you to take out my eyes."

And Dylan's like, "I'm sorry . . . what?"

"I want you to take out my eyes."

And Dylan's like, "No fuckin way, man. You're crazy."

But Bill says he'll pay him. A lot. And he'll owe him a *huge* favor.

But Dylan says, "I'm not gonna take out your eyes, man. Why would I do that?"

Well, Bill gets this weird look on his face. Like his eyes are on fire. Heating him up from the inside. Melting his skull from their sockets. Burning Bill's brain. And he goes, "I *just* want to be zen, man. I haven't relaxed since I was, like, twenty." And he's about forty-five now, so that's a long time. "For once in my life. I *just* want to be calm."

It's kind of sad, dude. He lives by himself. No pets, no girlfriend. Dylan says he doesn't even know if Bill has a lot of friends. He just has his job, and his job sucks. And now he wants to be able to meditate. I mean, he's desperate. Dylan feels bad for the guy.

Which is why he agrees to cut out his eyes.

They do it in the hospital Dylan works at, late at night, when nobody's really around. I mean, there are nurses on duty and shit, but they don't notice anything. Bill and Dylan just pop into one of the surgery rooms in one of the smaller, like, wings that people don't really go in. Bill hops on the table. Dylan sanitizes his hands. And they go at it.

Dylan says the procedure didn't take that long. First, you use this special kind of forceps to hold the eyelids open. Then, you take these tiny scissors and snip away the membrane that covers the eyeball. You move in curves around the pupil and cornea, just taking tiny snips. The jelly is apparently super thin, like that part in *Goodfellas* when they're in jail and cutting garlic with razor blades. So you just slide the scissors up and down super careful, sawing off thin slices from the front of the eye. Then, there are these, like, rectus muscles all *around* the eyeball, which you have to kind of hook into. There's four of them, and they take the longest. Dylan said he just sawed at them with a scalpel. Blood spurting up at him and shit. Dylan didn't *exactly* know what he was doing because he's mostly, like, a foot surgeon, and he doesn't really "work" at the hospital, he works next door. But he says it was easy enough to figure out. He just had the forceps in one hand, and he was looking at diagrams on his phone with the other. I mean, he went to school for this shit, so.

After you get those rectus muscles, you have to sever these other two muscles. Gotta shift the eye to the side to reach them. Dylan says he just sort of squished it with his thumb, popped it out. You yank these other two muscles up with a different hook and snip them, too. You're supposed to leave something called, like, a hemeostat in there for a while so they don't bleed out, but Dylan forgot, so there was blood everywhere. It got into Bill's mouth, and he woke up for a second, choking. He started screaming, twisting his hands around, making these little fists, just moving his fingers. It took Dylan a whole minute to put him back under.

You imagine? You wake up and you have shit in your face like that? Little scissors and hooks swinging around out of your eyes?

Yeah, *hard* pass.

Anyway, once that's all done, you wiggle the eye back and forth with some more forceps until you find the optical nerve. Cut that, cauterize with a little torch (Dylan just used his Bic), and yank the whole thing out.

Dylan put the eyes in a jar of pickle juice. He strung a wire through it, popped a shade on top, turned it into a table lamp. He keeps it in his living room, on a side table by the couch. He thinks it's the funniest shit. Bill watching him while he does paperwork.

I saw it once. It was weird.

When he told me all this, I asked Dylan why. Like, isn't that super fucked up? Eyes in a lamp? But he just laughed and said, "Wait, wait, it gets better."

And it does.

After the surgery, Bill says he didn't feel a thing. He woke up from the gas and everything was black. His face ached, which is no fuckin surprise. But other than that, nothing.

Crazy, right? You wake up and you're just blind for the rest of your life? Think about what kind of person you gotta be to make that choice.

A few weeks later, Bill's almost totally fine. Of course, his sockets are still healing. They're throbbing and itching and shit. So Dylan finds these eyedrops at a pharmacy in Tinker's Falls. They're experimental—new on the market—and Dylan warns Bill that there might be some weird side effects, but they *should* help.

I know. You never buy "experimental" products from the Falls. My mom always said Falls candy would give you cancer. But Bill's face *aches*, so he's like, "Whatever, I'll take the drops."

Dylan started laughing when he told me this part, too. Like, knee-slapping belly laughs. He said something like, "The dumbass just took the drops! I couldn't believe it!" And—

Huh? Oh, why was he laughing?

Well . . . Dylan's always been . . . weird. When we were, like, seventeen, he killed his neighbor's cat. Did I ever tell you that? This little girl we used to know. She was super nice, and he killed her cat. He said it was possessed. And the girl *thanked* him when he killed it because he'd *convinced* her the cat was demonic. That's the thing. He was always telling her the cat was evil. Pointing out all this normal cat shit it was doing and saying, "See? That's not normal." And this was her first cat, so she didn't know. He worked her for *weeks*. He was her babysitter, so he was at their house all the time. And all the time, he'd talk about this cat and how he knew it was bad because he studied demonology (which was true—he had a *lot* of books). By the time he was done workin her, she was *begging* him to save her soul and kill the cat.

Fucked up, right?

That's why he told me all this. About Bill. He thinks it's hilarious. Just wait. You'll see.

So Bill takes the drops. Gets himself a nice pair of sunglasses. And he quits his job at *Lillian Journal*. They're bummed to see him go, of course, and everybody asks what happened to his eyes. He just says it was an accident, but it means he can't work anymore. They're all like, *No no, we'll get you a braille keyboard! You'll be fine!* But Bill says, "No, I'm fuckin out of here. Good luck!"

Dylan tells him to take the drops twice a day, which he does for, like, a week. And as soon as his sockets stop throbbing, Bill gets back on the floor with his candle. Fumbles around, manages to light it. Gets his little pillow. Sits cross-legged. Breathes. And he tries, once again, to meditate.

At first, it's great. He isn't seeing *anything*. And finally, his mind shuts off. Not a thought, not a feeling. Nothin. He is totally, totally blank. Maybe the calmest dude on the entire planet. For the first time in his *whole* adult life, Bill is completely, utterly zen.

But get this.

Slowly, at the very edge of his awareness, Bill starts seeing things again. They sort of slip into view. That's the word he used. They *slip* between cracks in the darkness, and start floating around, in this totally dark, blank space that's now Bill's world. These floating things, shimmering into view from . . . somewhere else.

These things are big, and they have horns.

He said it started as shapes. Like, shoulders and the outlines of legs, arms. Horns. But the longer Bill sits there, the more they come into focus. They float inward, from a distance, moving toward him.

As they get closer, they get clearer. Bill can't tell if he's making it up or if they're in his head or what. Maybe he's hallucinating. But something in his gut tells him this is real. He doesn't know how, he just feels it.

They're almost like people, but they have bright red skin and big, gleaming yellow eyes. They have beefy arms and legs, and horns that go from the top of their head, around the sides of their jaws, and then down and across like hooks. Like mandibles. They have more horns coming out of their thighs, covering their crotches, so he can't tell if they have, like, genitalia. They don't have wings or anything either. They just . . . float.

There's about fifty of them. Floating around in the dark, all of a sudden. Like they've just glided through from some other plane.

When they come into focus, they're turned away from Bill, like they're talking amongst themselves. And he just watches them. Obviously, he's freaking out. He can feel his heartbeat in his sockets, pounding. But he doesn't want to move. He doesn't know what to do. He figures he *must* be making this up. Screw what his gut tells him. This *must* be in his head. So he thinks maybe more drops will help. Maybe it'll flush out the nerve endings or something, who knows.

He gets up, starts moving slowly toward the bathroom, but he kicks the candle over. Luckily, the wax pours out and snuffs the flame so his place doesn't burn down. But when he kicks the candle, it makes a noise, and the things hear him. The very second that candle topples over, all of them turn and face Bill.

Bill says he just froze. His vision is filled with these floating things. And they're all looking at him. Pointing their big bug eyes right at him.

He says they started cocking their heads. Like dogs, trying to understand. Or like people at a fancy party, standing around with glasses of champagne when, suddenly, they're interrupted. Like in *The Shining*. They cock their heads like they're saying, *Oh. Hello. Who are* you? Except they're not saying anything because they don't have mouths. Just the eyes. The horns. But they seem . . . curious. Cocking their heads. Back, and forth.

They start moving, closer, moving fast. Swarming him. Bill turns around, and he sees them everywhere, all around him in the black. He's scared fucking stiff. He can't tell if they're going to hurt him, but they're coming closer. Closer. Floating toward him through the void. Cocking their heads.

Bill bursts out of his house and runs into the street. Dylan lives just down the road, which is how they know each other. So he starts running in the general direction of Dylan's house. But the things follow him. Even outside, he can see them all around. Coming fast through the void. And what's worse? They're freaking *multiplying*. More and more of them, coming straight up from under Bill's feet, swooping down on top of him. Every direction he turns his head, he sees swarms in the darkness. Hundreds of them. Floating right at him. Cocking their heads.

Luckily, Dylan is home, so Bill stumbles into his house and tells him everything that's happened. Dylan listens to the whole thing, nodding (which, like, obviously, Bill can't see), and Bill's freaking out, crying blood (because his sockets are still fucked up), and he's sweating and yelling. Dylan makes him some tea, which helps Bill calm down a little. Then Dylan asks him if he can see the floating things right now.

Bill's like, "Yes! They're everywhere!" He holds his head in his hands. "They just keep cocking their heads at me. I can't even cover my eyes with my fuckin hands, because it doesn't matter! I don't know what to do."

And Dylan's like, "Mmhmm, mmhmm. Can you feel them?"

Bill hesitates, then sticks his hand out, reaches around. He shakes his head.

"So they're not hurting you."

"No, man, but they're *terrifying*." Bill's waving his hand in front of his face when he says this. Like he's trying to wave away a bunch of bees. Bill's practically having a heart attack, right there in Dylan's living room. So Dylan's like, "Okay, okay. Everything's cool. It's fine. I know what they are."

Bill lowers his hand. He takes a big gulp of tea, and he says, "You . . . you do?"

"Yep. They don't have a name, as far as I know, but I know *what* they are."

So get this.

Apparently, these things are a specific *kind* of demon. And of course, Dylan knows all about them, because he loves demons. He tells Bill they're called "engineers." They're from some other place *between* places. Apparently, there are walls between worlds, and they live *inside* these walls. In a realm without sense, without solidity. A void that they just float around in, like ghosts stuck in purgatory. They get bored, Dylan says, so sometimes they manage to slip into our world and . . . explore.

They're relatively harmless. Mostly. They're just curious. What they *really* like to do is figure out how solid things work. Solid things like people. Sometimes they pick people apart without them ever realizing. Just slide into someone's mind and start pushin buttons, flickin switches, digging in with their horns. Sometimes, for whatever reason, people manage to see these things. And that's, like, *really* exciting to them. So if Bill's not careful, they might manage to glide right into him and pick apart his soul with their horns. Piece by piece. Just to understand why he can see them.

"Do you *want* them to take apart your body just to see how it works?" asks Dylan.

Well, Bill is super really scared. So he says, "Absolutely fucking not. Please help me, please."

And Dylan's like, "Okay. What you gotta do is send them back to *their* world."

So Dylan knows all about this ritual for getting rid of the engineers (because of course he does). What you do is offer up a piece of yourself. That way, they have something they can study, and they're . . . happy, I guess. Their curiosity is, like, met, and they go back home. Dylan explains all of this, and Bill takes it in stride, sipping his tea. Then he says, "Okay, okay . . . What do I need to do?"

Dylan explains that any piece is totally fine. It can be a hand, a foot, an ear. But the more interesting the piece, the more likely the engineers are to leave you alone for good. What you need to do is cut off that piece yourself. *You* have to be the one to cauterize the wound (these engineers have very specific rules, apparently), and you leave the piece by your bed overnight. You go to sleep. In the morning, the piece'll be gone, and you'll be left alone.

I know, it's like a weird urban legend. But I swear I'm not making this up.

Anyway, Bill shakes his head. "No way, man. I'm not losing any more of my parts for this shit."

"Well, then you're gonna die, dude. But if you want, we can do the ritual right here. Tonight. I'll help you. It's super easy. Just hack off an ear. Get it over with. I'll help."

So Bill thinks about this for a while. Drinks his tea. He stares into his lap, and Dylan can imagine the engineers floating there, in his lap, in the void. Bill doesn't want to cut himself up any more.

I mean, who would? But he doesn't know what else to do. And it's kind of sad, dude. I mean, he's desperate. He's losing control again. He can't handle it . . .

So he agrees to hack off an ear.

They get everything set up. Dylan gets a paring knife from the kitchen. He sanitizes it, gets out his lighter. He puts down some newspaper on the floor in the living room, gets a candle burning. Bill's just kind of standing around while he does all this. Just staring toward the floor, trying not to look at all the engineers. They're as close to him now as they can be. Cocking their heads. He can almost feel their horns touching his skin, ready to slice into him. All around him. Horns on every side of his body. Poking at him. They're all cocking their heads. He can feel it coming. He's practically numb, he's so scared.

He starts trying to make small talk, to make himself feel better. Saying shit like, "This feels like a nice rug."

And Dylan's like, "Yep."

"Is it new?"

"Yep."

"Hm. Nice."

"Yep."

Dylan's about to sit Bill on the floor when Bill says he needs a little pillow, cuz he's got that bad back thing, remember? So Dylan goes into the bedroom to get him a pillow, and when he comes back out, Bill's got his hands on the lamp.

Yeah. *The* lamp. The one with his eyes in it.

For a second, Dylan just freezes. He watches Bill run his hands over the big glass jar. Watches him feel the shade. From inside the lamp, Bill's eyes watch, too. Bobbing around in the green fluid.

Bill says, "Is this a new lamp?"

And Dylan's like, ". . . yep."

"It feels nice."

"Yep."

"Where'd you get it?"

"Walmart."

"Is it glass?"

"Yeeep."

Dylan's super nervous. Sweating and shit. But then he remembers: Bill can't see what's *inside* the lamp. He doesn't know. It's just a coincidence that he's holding it. So Dylan relaxes. Bill takes his hands off the thing. Dylan gives him the pillow. Starts helping Bill sit down again.

But then Bill frowns. Stops. Turns his head around the room. Turns back to the lamp. Puts his hands on it again.

Dylan's like, "What is it?"

And Bill goes, "They're all gathering around the lamp."

And Dylan's blood goes cold.

Bill tells him that all the engineers are staring down at the lamp. All around him. They've stopped moving. Stopped cocking their heads. They're watching his hands move over the glass. He knows something's up with the lamp.

"What's up with the lamp?" he asks.

And Dylan doesn't know what to say. Should he lie? Make something up? But what if the engineers try to do something? What if they turn on *him*?

Eventually, he just shrugs and says, "It's your eyes, Bill."

Bill gives him this look. This shocked, crazy look. Mouth open. Blood starting to leak from his sockets again. He can't believe it. I mean, *I* wouldn't believe it. It's nuts. It's his eyes. In a lamp.

And before Dylan can stop him, he's yanking the lamp out

of the wall. There's this big pop of electricity and the room goes dark and the last thing Dylan sees before everything's black is Bill holding the lamp over his head and yelling, "Take *this*, assholes!"

Dylan runs across the room to the light switch. He turns on the main light and you know what he sees? Bill's hands are empty. The lamp is gone. Even the lampshade is gone.

Bill turns to him. He's grinning. He looks insane. He's bleeding out of empty holes in his face. But he also looks blissed-out. Totally zen. And he says, "They're gone. It's . . . it's all empty. It's all . . . blank again."

And they stand there for a second.

Dylan opens his mouth to say something, but Bill's on top of him, shoving him against the wall and *demanding* to know why Dylan took his eyes and put em in a fuckin lamp.

Well, Dylan just starts laughing.

So Bill starts punching him. Just whaling on him, and Dylan keeps laughing and laughing. Just lets Bill go at him. Lets him lose control. Then finally, he's like, "Alright, man, alright. Stop. Here. Let me show you something."

Dylan leads him into this back room. This closet behind the bedroom. He guides Bill in there. Then he takes Bill's hand and lifts it to this shelf. First, he lets Bill feel the shelf, and Bill can feel that the whole *wall* is shelves. In fact, he goes around this whole back room, and the entire thing is covered in wooden shelves. Floor to ceiling. Then he starts feeling what's *on* the shelves, and it's jars. Jars and jars and jars. They're all the same. These big glass mason jars with little lampshades on them. Bill's like, "What's in these?" And of course, Dylan says, "They're eyes, Bill."

In every jar, there's a single eyeball. Staring out from yellow-green formaldehyde goo. I've seen this back room. It's weird. He's even got half an eye that he claims he bought at an auction. Says it belonged to Adelaide Renfield. He's also got this big slab of Renfield oak hanging on the wall of his living room, right over the mantel. Very spooky.

Anyway, Dylan tells Bill he's been doing this shit for years. He's done the same thing, over and over, to almost a hundred people.

"It's the drops," he says. "I don't know how it works. But they are a literal gateway drug. They allow you to see the unseeable."

Dylan says he bought the drops for the first time back in college. Says he'd been getting roofies from a guy who got busted, dried up his supply. Of course, I knew him when he was doing that whole thing, too—buying roofies on the reg. He's always been fucked up, like I said.

I mean, I'm not gonna *report* him. Why would I? He's my cousin. He's a surgeon. He's got a career and shit. I don't want to mess with that.

Anyway, his supplier got busted. So he gets hooked up with this new guy from the Falls. *This* guy offers him something he says is top-shelf. And it's these drops. The guy says they make you see shit. Not like shrooms or acid. They don't *alter* your mind. They *open* it. They show you other worlds, and allow other worlds to see you back. The guy called it "diluted spinal fluid," but when Dylan asked what that meant, he didn't really explain it. Just said, "The spine of the *universe*, my friend. The fluid that connects our plane to worlds further up, further down, and those that float between. Some people say we live in walls. But really? It's like floors on an elevator, man. Take a drop—and *see*."

Dylan was like, "Cool, man, I'll take twelve bottles."

What he usually does is slip the drops in people's coffee at work, or at cafés. He does it to people he meets online, at bars. Everywhere. He gets them to trust him, takes them back to his place, makes them tea, and convinces them to remove their eyes during the ritual, which he kind of read about somewhere but also kind of made up. It genuinely seems to work, though. The ritual, I mean. He says he knew it would because *he* took the drops once (of course he did). I don't know what piece *he* offered the engineers, but he swears it worked. Anyway, after the ritual, people fall asleep (because of course there's drugs in the tea), and while they're sleeping, Dylan leaves one eye for the engineers, but takes the other to make more lamps for his collection. You know. Trophies.

At this point, as he's telling Bill all this, he's chuckling. "But, Bill, you asked me to take your eyes *for* you. I didn't even *plan* for you. That was awesome. Seren-fuckin-dipity. My *best* lamp. So I had to come up with some other shit when I decided to give you the drops. I thought maybe an ear would be cool. Or your tongue."

He's telling Bill all this in that back room, surrounded by eyes. Bill's about to pass out, of course, because he drank the drug-tea. But before he faints, he says, "Dylan, man . . . You're evil."

And that makes Dylan *really* laugh. Laugh until he cries.

"You believe that shit?" he asked me. "Dude called me evil. What a dick."

I asked him what happened to Bill after Bill passed out. Dylan said he went for a swim in the lake. Which I know is, like, a euphemism for when somebody's dead. I mean, nobody *actually* goes swimming in Bartrick Lake. So I figure, while Bill was passed out, Dylan carried him to his car, drove out to the lake, and . . . fed the fish. I mean, I *hope* that's not true. Really, I just hope that wherever he is now, that dude Bill is totally, totally zen.

He deserves it.

And that's it. That's the story.

Yeah, creepy as hell. You imagine? Whole room full of eyes in jars. Just floatin around. Hundreds of them. Just staring at you. Forever. And all these people walkin around blind who have no idea . . .

Dylan swears the engineers are real. He says they really do come from in between everything. They float around the air all the time, like radio waves, or the internet. Just waiting. They really are just curious, he says. They do just want to learn. Dylan said he gets it because he's the same way. Just curious. And when you're curious, you gotta be a *little* evil. Right? What's science without a few dissected frogs? To learn about something, you gotta tear it apart. And I guess that makes sense, but still. I didn't sleep right for a *month* after he told me that story. Just kept staring at the backs of my eyelids. Thinking about what was floating around behind them. Waiting . . .

Oof. Freaky.

Anyway, I'm just sayin. If you're gonna start meditating, be careful, is all.

You never know.

From: Rachel Durwood <radurwood@bhs.org>
To: tom.durwood@gmail.com
Re: The Stain

Hey. I called. I texted. I know you're just on your couch. Are you really that mad at me? It's *really* gonna be the silent treatment?

Well, fine. Fuck me? Fuck you, too. We don't have to talk. But I will keep emailing you. So deal with it. Cheers, dick.

Listen:

When at long last the Renfield home finally collapsed, in the spring of 1936, people were poorer than they'd ever been. This was the Depression, after all. So they took the collapsed wood and repurposed it. The Masons tried to tell people not to, but no one listened. The wood was stripped from the Renfield ruins and sold, or just taken. It was fine wood. Good, strong cedar, oak, and pine. It went into sheds. Into fences and patios. It went into chairs and coffee tables and tobacco pipes. All over the county, the wood spread like a weed.

And on it, continents of bloodstain remained.

You can see stripes of stain behind wallpaper, in crawlspaces, in garages and toolsheds. You can see it on stools and tv stands and porches and butcher blocks. You can see it on bookshelves and picture frames and matching sets of knives. You can see it splashed across the lacquered wood of things at the flea market. You can feel it worming its way through time, through everything, scrabbling up and along the spine of the entire county. Searching, digging, latching on. Feeding, growing. Unkillable. Unquenchable.

It's rare that an entire piece of wood is stained. Typically, you see only a bit of dark red or brown, rippling over the middle of a board, or tinging its edge. But these remnants are everywhere. The stain is all around.

According to a special "Spring Style" issue of the *Lillian Journal* printed in 1956, for a while in the forties and fifties, one of the things you'd ask if you were buying secondhand wood in Renfield County was "Is this Renfield wood?" If the answer was yes and you still wanted it—if you were too poor for anything else—then you had an even more important question to ask: "Is it from the house? Or the barn?" According to local superstition, only people looking for trouble bought wood from the barn.

As time went on, however, interests changed. Attitudes shifted. People acquired more exotic, morbid tastes, especially during the eighties. And the barnwood spread freely into the world. Into basements and attics and porches. Classrooms and cafés and bars. Even hanging in one huge, unsettling swath in some guy's goddamn living room, where he uses it as decoration.

It feels wrong to say, but fuck it, I'm drunk, I'll say it: The spread of the stain is . . . almost admirable. Don't you think? If the evil in that blood is, indeed, sentient and full of some kind of life, even after it's been dry for decades, then you have to admire its tenacity and ingenuity. I mean, I certainly . . . Well, idk. Sometimes, late at night, ever since Mom died—I feel like I do. I admire the stain.

I mean, look at everything it's made. Everything it's accomplished. You have to admire its creativity.

ALLISON'S FACE

As a rule, Brin hated orientations. They were usually synonymous with torture. All those circles you had to sit in. Rapidly thinking of fun facts and what you'd be if you were a breakfast food. Making dumb things that the Freshman Guides (the sophomores in charge of all the freshman orientation bullshit) would hang in the common spaces or on dorm room doors. Brin hated arts and crafts. She didn't have any fun facts. And all she ever had for breakfast was Cheerios. Not even Honey Nut. Just bland, regular cereal. Bland, regular Brin. Who wanted to be that?

But as far as orientations went, this wasn't bad so far (knock on wood). There weren't any circles yet. No games. She hadn't had to tell everyone she'd be Cheerios if she could, and she wasn't being forced to make anything. They were all just *mixing*. Milling about Haywood Tower's ninth-floor common room.

The Tower was home to most of Edenville College's freshman body. It loomed over the quad from the east, nine stories tall, so that the entire quad was wreathed in shadow until the sun finally crested over Haywood's peak at noon. Gargoyles sprouted from each of the Tower's four sides, right around the base of the ninth-floor windows. Instead of snarling down at the rest of campus, they turned inward, and gazed into the Tower windows. Brin could easily look outside and lock eyes with a large stone moose-thing, with the fangs of a wolf. Tongue lolling, eyes wide and blank. It leered at her as she chewed a baby carrot. Its massive antlers, and the smaller horns along the bridge of its snout, were crusted over, white and green. Pigeons cooed on its shoulders. Far past it, Brin could see the bright yellow smear of sunflowers bordering the campus, and the waving sea of them filling the western end. She'd heard somewhere that the sunflowers had a mind of their own. That sometimes they curled around students walking by, ushered them into their rough green leaves, and vanished them forever. They were one of Edenville College's prominent features, but she didn't plan to go anywhere near them.

Really, this was all fine for an orientation. Brin *loved* gargoyles. And she was good enough at small talk to fend for herself, but making friends was always weird. Always left her feeling . . . tight inside. But there *was* a snack table. So Brin hovered there awkwardly, picking at carrots and cherry tomatoes, until hopefully enough time had passed that she could slip back to her room unnoticed.

Not too bad.

She popped a tomato between her teeth and sucked down the juice, thoughtful and relatively content. She scanned the room. People floated through it so effortlessly, so fluid. So loud and good.

Brin popped another tomato.

At an orientation talk earlier, one of the Guides had said, "Remember: college is a chance to reinvent yourself. So start thinking about who you want to be here." Well, Brin had been *thinking* for hours now, and it just didn't seem true at all. So far, college seemed like pretty much just High School Plus. Nobody seemed to be acting any differently from how they'd probably acted six months ago. She'd only been here less than a day, true, but that didn't change the fact that Brin could already see right through it all:

There was the popular blond girl with perfect-tan legs a thousand yards long. Beautiful. She even had a perfect little beauty mark (*ugh*). She stood in the middle of the room, soaking it up, laughing. She probably played lacrosse. Or would, at least. Her name was Allison. Brin watched Allison say something high and quick— the punch line of some story. The people orbiting her laughed and applauded loudly. She drank from a Nalgene water bottle, lips quirked in a smile, eyes moving keen around the circle. Watching for the next bite of attention.

What did it take to be that person? The one in the middle of the circle? Whatever it was, Brin didn't have it. She'd watched those girls throughout high school. As their clothes had gotten tighter and sleeker, Brin had shrunk further into baggy sweaters, plaid, loose jeans, oversized shirts for bands like Radiohead and Muse. In fact, she was wearing a supermassive Muse shirt right now, to hide the person whom the people like Allison never went to prom with. Never paid attention to. Never liked back.

Bland, regular Brin.

She swept her fingers through her hair, tugging on the ends, as the applause around Allison died. Brin's hair was her safety blanket. She could always tug at it if she felt nervous or out of place, like now. It was also the one piece of her appearance she took care of religiously.

She had a vague memory of standing in a church bathroom at a funeral when she was eight, looking in the mirror. She couldn't remember who'd died, or anything else about the funeral, really. But she remembered staring at herself in this mirror. Her face was pale because she was a reader, not a sporter, as her dad always put it. And it looked even paler this day, floating above her black dress. Her long ponytail rippled down over a shoulder, bright brown-red against the dark void of the dress. Her mom called the color auburn. *Auburn.* Brin loved that. It reminded her of autumn, the color of fallen leaves. *Auburn.* She said it to the mirror, "Auburn," and smiled. "I am Brin and my hair is auburn." She stroked the ripple of reddish brown, tugging lightly, the way you'd pet a cat's tail. "I am Brin and my hair is au-burnn." She drew it out, *au-burnnn.* The feel of it in her mouth like that—the way Brin's face hummed as the word purred across her tongue? Nothing had ever felt more true. More her. *I am Brin and my hair is auburn. I am Brin and my hair is auburn and I am content to stand here in the corner by the snacks. If nobody else is going to "reinvent" themselves here, why should I? How could I? Who would I even be? I'd rather just be Brin. Bland, regular, plain-Cheerio Brin. That's just fine with me.*

She bit into a carrot.

So there was Allison. And over *there* was Ryan, the cool nerdy guy surrounded by girls because he, you know, *listened* and *had smart opinions*. Just past Ryan, hanging out with some of the other Guides, was Brin's own Guide, Olivia. Olivia was short. Dimples. Very cute. When she'd introduced herself that morning, throwing out a hand for Brin to shake, that hand had jangled, covered in bracelets and rings. Brin had shaken it, her own hand silent, bare, and pale. When she'd said her name, Olivia had said, "I like that. Short for anything?"

"Brianna." She'd always gone by Brin, for reasons she couldn't remember now. Sometimes she thought about changing it, about adopting a new self. But now that she was eighteen, she felt like she couldn't really go back on it. She'd almost explained that, but Olivia had just shrugged like she already knew. "Brin is better. It sounds like burn. And it goes with your hair." Brin had blushed full and deep at that, feeling like her cheeks might *burn* right off her body.

She wondered now if Olivia even remembered her name.

Beyond Olivia, in the corner with a group of other dudes, was Joshua. Jock type. Thick arms and shoulders. He probably played . . . rugby, that was her guess. Her real guess was actually football, but Edenville College was a small liberal arts joint (read: no football), so. It was all the same, anyway.

Edenville College was widely considered a relatively quiet spot in Renfield County. It was far from Bartrick Lake, and the rumors and superstitions that floated thick around that area didn't *quite* stretch here. The town's few streets were lined with antique stores, ma-and-pa shops, an ice cream joint. The campus was classically pretty: brick buildings, an old church, a clock tower that gazed down upon all from the college center. There wasn't ivy, it wasn't *that* cliché, but it was nice. You could sense the calm as soon as you stepped onto the grassy quad. There was warmth here. The second Brin walked into Haywood for the first time, she could feel it. The weird stories and rumors she'd grown up with back home in Bent—they didn't live here.

But then . . . what did?

Because despite the warm vibe, Brin still felt severely out of place. She felt, as always, like she was behind glass. She chewed peacefully on her carrot as she surveyed the scene of bright, bubbly freshmen. At least in high school, you could sit in a row and be a number, be forgotten. That wasn't so bad. Not as bad as seeing the center of the room and knowing you weren't in it, like *this*. That's why she hadn't gone to prom. Not because she didn't have anyone to go with! It just . . . wasn't her scene. No scene was her scene. Life was scenes on a screen, and she just *watched*. She just—

She blinked. Somehow, she and Olivia had locked eyes. From all the way across the room. And before Brin knew it, Olivia was smiling at her. Olivia was walking over.

Brin froze. She stared straight ahead. She chewed the rest of the carrot, swallowed it. It went down as a dry, hard rock. She coughed.

"Hey hey," said Olivia. "Guarding the carrots?"

Brin swallowed pebbles. "I think someone should guard them from me."

Olivia gave an easy laugh. "Nice. You meeting people?"

"Oh, I . . ." She cleared her throat. "I don't . . ."

"We've got some cool people in our hall." Olivia gestured around the room. "Allison seems nice. And Ryan is pretty chill."

"Right."

"Oh!" Olivia put a hand on Brin's shoulder, just for a second, as she remembered something. Out quick, then back, like a scorpion. Her eyes went wide and she started explaining, but Brin only heard half of what she said. She was too stunned.

When Brin liked someone, there was no single element she particularly liked. Bodies were nice (and Olivia's was *nice*), but it was never exactly that. It was always just an impression. A kind of *wave*. She could never say that she liked someone's smile or their hair or anything specific like that (except this girl *did* have an awesome mass of short, curly hair). It was just the way people *engaged* with you. The way they held themselves. If they looked at you and it made you feel warm, that's what it was. That's what she liked. Olivia was like Edenville College. Her aura, her whole deal, was warm.

"So?" Olivia asked.

"Sorry, what?"

Olivia laughed again, and that was warm, too. She was probably used to people getting distracted by her. Brin wondered what that was like.

"I *said*," said Olivia, "do you want to check out the *house* tonight? It used to be the biology department, back in the day. Now it's just this fun . . . kind of spooky abandoned house, right off campus? It'll be chill. I've already got a little group from the floor. We can ditch the orientation thing tonight. I approve. It's just making door collages. Your door'll be blank. I hope you don't care."

Brin ran her hand through her hair, giving it a gentle cat-tail tug. She fluffed it so that a long rush of it fell over the shoulder. She couldn't be sure, but she thought she saw Olivia's eyes dart toward it, just for a second. Falling quick, then flicking back up. Scorpion-like.

"Yeah, I'm down," said Brin.

"Right on." Olivia made a fist, gave it a quick pump. "I'm stoked. I've never been to the house. It's nothing special. People just sit on the porch and drink. But you can see the stars *really* well. No lights or anything around. So. I thought it'd be a good group thing."

"Yeah, sounds fun." Brin smiled. Her first day of college, and she'd already made a friend. Maybe she could be somebody new here after all.

"As long as there aren't any arts. Or crafts," she said, popping another tomato between her teeth.

Past the southwestern edge of Edenville's campus, beyond a ten-foot-tall wooden fence, there is a large field. The slats of the fence are so tight-packed you can't see through them. And the gate of the fence only opens about a foot before it jams against the ground and refuses to move any farther. At the end of this field, if you can get past the fence, slouched along the bank of a small hill, is an old, abandoned house. A two-story Victorian-style monster. The whole thing bends rotten at an angle, the second story leaning far forward over the moldywood porch. Green paint chips and shingles scatter the porch. The walls are chipped in large chunks, peeling off in long, maggoty rolls. The columns on either side of the porch are cobweb-cracked enough to snap in half at any second. The windows on the front of the house are boarded up.

It is, in short, a spooky fuckin place.

It was once home to the old biology department on campus, before rumors began to circulate about the cruelty of one of that department's professors—all the bizarre underground experiments she made her fieldwork students perform. That professor was let go, the department was rehoused elsewhere, and the house was allowed to fester.

Students do visit it from time to time. It's a good place to bring a six-pack and see the stars. To sidle up next to someone for the first time, make a move in the humid cricket heat. To carve your name deep and eternal into the rotten wood. A good place to escape to on a night like this.

Except tonight, Brin was kicking herself.

I should have known, she kept thinking. *Should have fucking guessed. Stupid Brin. Just stupid.* Of *course* Ryan, Joshua, and fucking Allison were the only three from her hall who'd agreed to go to the house. The three biggest douchebags. She'd *wanted* to give them a shot, but they'd basically ignored her since leaving the dorm. Clearly saw her as some weird Other. And of course, of *course* Olivia was talking more to them than to Brin, especially Jock Joshua. She'd just invited Brin to be nice. Thinking Olivia was her friend was like thinking waiters are your friends. This was her *job*. And now Brin was stuck bumming along to the spooky house (which she hated) to drink beer (which she hated) and look at the stars (which she hated) with people whom she now hated. She held some hope for Olivia, but Olivia'd said, what, three words to her since they left the dorm? Just yukking it up with Joshua while Brin trailed along behind.

A scorpion indeed.

Stupid. Should have known, she repeated to herself. Life had been like this since second grade. The only parties Brin got invited to were the ones where parents invited the entire class. Pity invites. And this was no different. She could tell.

It took them a few minutes of walking through the quiet sidewalks of campus to reach the fence. The sunflowers on the western end of campus followed them as they passed, turning their heads and rustling their leaves. Brin waved to one, and it rattled a leaf in return.

Once they arrived at the fence, Jock Joshua led the charge through the big wooden gate. He was the biggest, and he figured if he could squeeze through, they all could.

"Be my guest," Allison told him. She cracked one of the beer cans Olivia had brought. Her hair seemed to glow in the light of a nearby lamppost. Even her beauty mark glowed. She *glowed*. Fuck her.

Olivia offered a can to Brin. "Brin? Want one? No pressure."

"Sure," said Brin, not wanting one. She cracked it open and sipped at the froth boiling over the top of the can. She looked across the parking lot at the wall of sunflowers. One cocked its head at her, and she stuck her tongue out at it. The flower tilted its face to the sky and shook, as if laughing.

"Cheers," said Ryan. He held up his own can. She clapped hers against his, and they both drank. She grimaced. It wasn't the first time she'd had beer (Dad had offered her one or two at barbecues and picnics), but it was still gross. It tasted like carpet.

"Not bad," said Ryan, smacking his lips.

"Yeah, thank you, Liv," said Allison.

"My pleasure, you guys," Olivia smiled.

Pfft. Liv.

Joshua squeezed himself through the gate, no problem, and called out from the other side. "Come on through!"

One by one, they followed into the field beyond. Past the fence—the edge of the world.

Brin's mom floated into her head: *We don't live in a town where you're entirely safe wandering around at night.* Her dad, too, nodding in agreement: *There are . . . weird things out here, Brin. You—*

"Hey, Brianna," Allison hissed from the other side of the gate. "You're the last one."

Brin realized she'd zoned out. She was the only one standing on the campus side of the fence. Her chest went tight. She poured half her beer onto the grass, then shoved herself through the fence. Its splinter-teeth dug into her ribs, her spine. Pressing her back, *don't go*, until she popped through. On the other side, she stumbled. Something tore at her bare legs. The grass was much taller here. Much sharper. The others stood in a half circle, running their hands over it, looking at her. The air was humid, her hair stuck to her forehead, and she slicked it back, and said, "It's Brin."

"Sorry?" said Allison.

"It's Brin. Not Brianna."

"Oh. Sorry."

"It's alright."

Allison pursed her lips. She sipped at her can. Over the rim, her eyes flicked to Ryan, and in the moonlight, Brin could see her eyebrows jerk once. Ryan held back a smile, hiding behind his own can. Brin ran a hand through her hair.

"Come on," said Olivia. "This way."

The field was some kind of tall wheat grass. None of them knew what it was, but it was high enough to whisper against their palms as they walked through it. Ryan suggested they google it, but there was no service there. Nor was there any real light. The moon was suddenly missing, and the stars were dim. The only reliable light was, more or less, the swerving, slicing dance of everyone's phones, shooting out bright white beams across the grass. The grass itself was a stark beige wall in all directions. It seemed to stretch on forever. Even when Brin turned, hoping to see the fence behind them, she saw only the grass. Waving in their wake.

She paused. Ran a hand through her hair again. She turned back and saw that the group had already moved on. *Figures.* She pushed to catch up, and when she did, Olivia smiled at her, but it seemed a little fake. Like she hadn't even known she'd been gone. Nobody else said anything.

After nearly five minutes of walking, they saw the house.

They stood in a small cluster in front of the porch, Joshua still in the lead. Brin at the edge. Allison at the center, as always. Brin could see their breath steam upward in the lights. It made the house a hazy-fog nightmare.

Joshua looked back at them. Lifted his eyebrows. "Sick."

"Now what?" asked Allison.

"Well, we go up to the porch," said Olivia.

"Are we technically still on campus?" asked Allison. "Nobody's, like, died here, right?"

Olivia shook her head. "Nah, we're fine."

The house creaked. Groaned. The wood shifted and whined. As if it, too, was answering.

"You hear that?" said Ryan. "Fucking spooky. Creaking in the wind like that."

"I hate the wind," said Joshua.

Brin gazed out at the field of grass. The still and silent grass.

"What wind?" she said.

Of course, no one heard her.

"Come on," said Ryan. "Let's do it."

As they started walking again, something cold wormed its way over Brin's shoulder. She turned. The grass seemed to shift back as she did. Like it'd reached out, stroked her, then moved away. She could almost feel it giving her a pointedly innocent look. *Not me. Nobody here but us grass . . .*

And this was the last thing she remembered before the basement. Standing in the field, hating everyone and everything around her, with the unmistakable feeling that she was being hunted.

Brin was the first to wake up. Slumped against the wall on the cold dirt floor. She looked around, blinking in the dim. No windows, dirt floor. The air wet-cold. Bootsteps thumped overhead, dropping small shafts of dust through the ceiling beams. Night-lights were plugged into outlets all around the walls. Flickering tiny orange flames. About four of them. There was a table-ish thing near the center of the room. A large butcher block. Wooden stairs in the far corner. And pipes. Many pipes. Thick tubes of rust running down from the ceiling and walls, at odd angles, all around the room. In the glow of the night-lights, the pipes seemed to writhe. To breathe. Like mambas creeping along the concrete walls. Five of these pipes, she saw, had bodies strapped to them. Her, Allison, Ryan, Joshua, and Olivia.

Brin tried to scream, of course, which is when she felt the dull, cold numb. It was like screaming through mud, like in a nightmare. She could barely even move her jaw. She tried to move her arms, too, which is when she felt the twine. Bound tight around her neck and her wrists, keeping her locked to the pipe. She worked her fingers, pawing at the cold flaky metal of the pipe. She twisted, turned against the pipe. She tried to move her head, but the twine around her neck seemed to tighten with every move, strangling her against the pipe. There was no escape from the pipe. But her joints weren't sore, which hopefully meant they hadn't been here that long. And she was, at least, surrounded by people she knew. Or . . . sort of knew. So that was something.

From a certain perspective, things weren't that bad yet.

Suddenly, noise erupted all around her. Slumped around the edges of the room, the others were waking up. Gasping, gurgling, too numb to scream. They kicked weakly against the floor and the pipes. Bodies like limp, wet noodles, heads rolling around. Their voices and movements made the pipes echo and ring. Brin could feel them vibrating up through the ceiling. And they must have been connected to something up there, some sort of signal, because a moment after everyone woke up—the woman in the apron arrived.

Brin heard her before she saw her. Heard a door open somewhere above the stairs. Heard it shut, heard the *thhhunk* of a deadbolt that must have been a foot long. Then came the sound of thick boots on wood, and seconds later, big black workboots came into view on the stairs. There was the sound of sliding metal, back and forth. When the woman's waist came into view, Brin could see that she carried a metal tray filled with tools. Brin could see them winking at her in the dim light. Scalpels, dentist's picks, a silver bonesaw, and larger curved things. They slid this way and that as the woman walked. Rasping in gleaming metal waves. The woman carried the tray to the butcher block. She reached up, clicked on a bare bulb dangling from the ceiling. In its light, Brin could see everyone around her mouthing things. Trying to scream around the invisible nightmare mud. Squirming against the drugs and the twine. Olivia bucked against her pipe, kicking her heels limp against the floor. Ryan moved his mouth in pitiful, pleading silence. Joshua strained his big arms against the twine. Allison just sat there, breathing through her mouth.

The woman ignored them. Simply stared down at the tools on the tray for what seemed a very long time.

Then she picked up the scalpel, turned to Allison, and Brin could no longer tell herself things weren't that bad. In fact, moments later, as Allison screamed so loud Brin thought her ears would explode, things seemed pretty fucking bad indeed.

The woman in the apron took Allison's face first. She rolled the skin slow off Allison's bones and carried it to the butcher block in the center of the room. She placed the bloodied scalpel carefully on the metal tray on the block and held Allison's face to the light. It drooped over her hands like pizza dough, and Brin could see how perfect the cut was. She could see the light bursting through the perfect lidless eyeholes, the perfect mouth. The face looked like it was exploding from the inside out. Like it was vomiting the sun.

She fussed with the face for a while, her back to Brin. Allison cried dull in the corner by the night-light. Tears running down the big open wound of her cheeks, her lips, her chin. Pinking up the front of her shirt with a frothy bloody drool.

Brin couldn't see what the woman was doing. But she heard scissors, a wet *flap*, the *pop* of thread through material, and suddenly, she knew. She knew exactly what was happening. And when the woman in the apron turned, holding Allison's face to the light again, lifting it by the strap of twine now tied around its back, Brin was surprised that she wasn't surprised at all.

She understood: The woman was making masks.

She wondered how the woman had gotten such a clean cut. How she'd managed to maneuver the muscles and the subtle outlines of Allison's skull. Especially with Allison blubbering, moving her mouth, squirming around. Even as scared as Brin was, she couldn't help but appreciate the woman's skill.

Or perhaps she wasn't thinking clearly. The woman must have injected them with something. It was the only explanation for the stiff, numb sensation blanketing Brin's entire body. She didn't feel paralyzed, just . . . lazy. Like she was exhausted and covered in ice. They must all be feeling the same, or Allison would be in shock right now, wouldn't she? Instead of mewling softly, all the muscles in her face exposed and glistening.

Brin also wondered if she was just telling herself that as an excuse. A reason for the fact that none of them, including her, seemed to be fighting back. To be struggling harder to break free. They *must* have been drugged. They must have. That's why they were just sitting here, watching this woman work.

Rattling. Brin looked up and saw the woman shaking a small silver-white can. She pressed a thumb down on the can's nozzle, and a wide arc of crystalline spray came out. She sprayed the Allison mask on both sides, then walked over and sprayed the weeping open wound of Allison's face. Allison squeezed her eyes shut. She coughed, let out a small croak, twitching against the spray. The woman ignored her.

Some kind of preservative, thought Brin. *Keep the skin fresh.* It was probably something she'd gotten in the Falls. Maybe even the same stuff she'd injected them with. Maybe she made it herself.

After spraying it down, the woman in the apron smoothed Allison's face flat on the butcher block. She picked up the scalpel, and carried it over to Brin. She loomed above Brin, looking down at her. They stared at each other for a long time. It was the first chance Brin had really had to look at her, to soak in the details, and she didn't want to squander it.

She was a giant. She was pushing sixty-five. She had tight white curls surrounding her head like steel wool. Her face was gray slate. Her jaw clenched, lips a near-invisible line. Her eyes were black holes. No matter how she turned or where she went in the room, they avoided the light. They were always in shadow. But all the same, Brin could feel them boring into her. Like twin fists revolving, turning, pushing deeper into her body. The apron reached down to the woman's knees. It was sky blue and had a crayon-drawing of a field filled with daisies plastered across its front. Over the flowers, a bright yellow sun and fluffy clouds.

What made the image so bad was how cheery it was. How un-even all the lines were, and the coloring. How the picture warped at the edges where the apron curved around the woman's waist. It looked like the woman's grandkid had drawn this and she'd blown it up, printed it on an apron. Like she was baking cookies.

The woman leaned down, breaking Brin's train of thought. She reached for Brin's head. Brin squirmed back and forth, but the woman dug her fingers into the back of Brin's skull. Her nails bore into some kind of pressure point. Digging into her brain. Fireworks blew behind Brin's eyes. Hammers beat at her where the woman dug. She gasped, stilled, and the woman began carving Brin's face from her head like a jack-o'-lantern. Brin tried to keep her eyes open. Tried to watch everything. And she saw, as the woman's hands moved, that there was a fine white line along the knuckles of her right hand. A scar, but different somehow. Grayer. Slightly sluglike.

An identifying mark, thought Brin. *To tell the police. If we can get out of here, we can—*

The knife curved under her cheek. She heard it, felt it, tasted it scrape against her bone. She felt her cheek rasp and rip. She felt the knife sawing at it, pumping up and down. Slicing into her. She felt something inside her sigh, give way, and for the next several minutes, there was nothing but dark, and the hot white star gliding over her face.

I am Brin, she told herself. *And my hair is auburn.* A cool, calming mantra. Centering herself. Gathering herself into a small, secret corner far away from the knife. *I am Brin and my hair is auburn.* Over and over. *I am Brin and my hair is auburn. I am Brin and my hair is auburn. I am Brin and my hair is auburn. I am Brin and* . . .

Having her face removed was like someone pouring hot glue all over her, then tearing it away in one long roll. Slow and tedious. Not exactly painful, but *hard.* She could feel the woman's fingertips digging at her, working the skin off her. Like the tiny mouths of maggots eating her face. She felt the muscles pop around as the woman worked. She could hear the *slick* as her edges came free. And after, the frigid air of the basement stuck to the open wound. She twitched, each movement stinging all over from her forehead to her chin. It throbbed and throbbed, and she could feel it leaking in thin lines, pattering soft onto her shirt. It was like staring into a freezing, unending wind. It stung *so* bad. Thank god the woman had left her eyelids alone; Brin could not imagine how much more terrible this could be. But the worst part was hearing herself bleed, slow and steady, onto her shirt. She *liked* that shirt.

She couldn't imagine what this would have been like if she weren't so numb.

She watched the woman in the apron carry her skin to the butcher block. There came the same sounds as before. Scissors, twine, spray. The woman turned, held up Brin's face so it basked in the din from the night-lights and the bulb overhead. Brin looked up at herself. Her empty, bleeding eyes. The ragged, wide-open gap of her mouth. Looking at it made something in her stomach tighten. She felt like her brain was sliding out the back of her skull.

She closed her eyes.

Brin listened as the woman in the apron smoothed her face flat again on the butcher block. She listened as the woman stomped back to her corner. She listened as the woman sprayed her, and she felt the hard sandpaper rip of cold spray on her already freezing, cracking flesh. She listened as the woman walked away, leaned over someone else. She listened to the wet pop of skin. The *scrrrape* of steel on bone. The dull, numb groan of horror and the sawing of the knife.

She listened to all of this twice more.

Her fingers itched for the comfort of her hair. For the cool glide of it over her palm. *This is all fine*, she told herself. *She can take my face. She can take all of our faces. But I'll fucking kill her if she touches my hair.*

The woman had a hard time removing Joshua's face. His was last. Brin had opened her eyes by then, and could see the woman tugging at it, trying to get it all off in one clean sheet. A long chunk tore across the forehead, clinging to Joshua's scalp in thin strings. He writhed against the pipe, jaw working uselessly. The strings of skin wobbled. One snapped, and the face came away in the woman's hands. Joshua howled. A deep, bellowing wordlessness, all vowels. He coughed, choked, twisted against the twine. The woman remained bent at the waist, looming over him. She turned the face over and over in her hands. Then she stood, holding the skin gently between her fingertips. She carried it to the butcher block, placed it alongside the others. She smoothed it out. Examined it. Smoothed it again. She tapped the tip of the knife against her chin. Finally, she shrugged and sewed up the torn forehead, sprayed his face with the can, and it was good to go.

Five masks now, all in a row.

Allison was mumbling to herself, blubbering bubbles onto the bare muscles of her chin. Brin watched her. The membranes and muscles of Brin's face were beginning to dry, and it was painful now even to blink. When she moved at all, parts of her cracked, began to ooze.

The woman in the apron stood still by the butcher block. Thinking. After a moment, she lifted a face from the block, held it by the twine strap, and carried it to Olivia. She bent, slipped the twine over Olivia's head, fitting the mask to her face. Olivia didn't move. Just stared straight ahead. The woman stood back. Brin's chest twisted into a small, tight knot. Olivia's eyes continued to gaze and blink, blank and empty, from their sockets. But they weren't her sockets anymore. They were Ryan's. Ryan's cheeks, lips, forehead. Floating atop Olivia's body. A perfect mask. But more than that. Somehow, the skin curved neatly onto Olivia's bones. As if it belonged there.

The woman cocked her head. Analyzing the fit. Then she went back to the butcher block, picked up another face, and moved across the room to Ryan. Ryan cried as the woman slipped Brin's face over his flesh. As the woman clomped away from him, Ryan looked desperately at Brin. Maybe even apologetically. Brin couldn't tell. She was too busy staring at her own face.

That's my skin, she kept thinking. *That's my skin that's my skin.*

The woman in the apron distributed masks all around the room. Joshua and Allison got each other. Allison cried. Thick tears pouring from the ripped, broken sockets of Joshua's face. He kept trying to talk. Allison's lips trembled over his mouth as he did.

The woman did Brin last, giving her Olivia's face. She slid the twine over Brin's ears, and the skin held, sticking to the wet muscle. Brin was too scared to move, too numb. The woman adjusted the edges of the mask, rolling it flat against the bloody ooze of Brin's head with the ball of her thumb. Parts of it didn't fit quite right.

Olivia's head was a different size. But then, all of a sudden, it did. It felt like her face. It felt like *her* skin. Seamless. As if it wasn't a mask at all.

She looked around the room, meeting everyone else's eyes. They all blinked at each other.

The woman stood back. She wiped her hands on the apron, dragging a bright red rain across the daisy field. She stood akimbo, then relaxed, dropping her meaty hands. Her lips tightened just a little, so the edges of her mouth wrinkled like cracked glass.

She's smiling.

The woman moved to the center of the room. She turned in a circle, staring at each of them for a long, long time, arms like thick logs hanging at her sides. She angled her head over her left shoulder. Gazing at them the way you might look at something in a museum. As if from a great distance away.

Brin started to feel itchy. Started to crave the touch of her hair between her fingers. Some small comfort. The itch grew and grew until finally, after an eternity, the woman stepped toward Allison. Brin felt a surge of relief. The woman wasn't walking toward her.

The woman slipped the Joshua mask off Allison's head, and the relief evaporated. Allison screamed. A high tea-kettle pain. The woman carried the mask to Ryan, slipped his off, and replaced it with Joshua's face. He screamed. She took Brin's face from Ryan and gave it to Olivia, and one by one, she removed their masks and switched them around the room, and everybody, every fucking time, screamed.

Again, Brin was last. *Figures*, she thought, with a kind of sick humor. By the time the woman came to her, the room was filled with a jangling major chord of screams. When the woman slid the mask off her face, Brin understood why. She could feel a wet *pop* as the mask parted from her. Cords snapped between her and the skin, and then the *cold*. The cold burned. She found herself pleading, begging, *Give me a mask. Please, God, give me a mask . . .*

And the woman did. She gave them all new faces. Trading them all around the whole room. The relief was unbearable. As soon as Brin felt the new mask slip onto her, felt it fuse with herself, covering her, she began to cry. She was so grateful, and mad that she was so grateful. She cried, and worked her tongue over lips that weren't hers.

Once more, the woman stood back, examined her work. Angling her head. Turning. A tourist in a museum. Then she did it again. Clomping around the room in her big black boots. There was the pain, slicing searing cold, followed by the comfort of a new face. A new mask. And again the woman stood back, studying her work.

Then she did it again.

And again.

And again.

For hours.

Brin wore everyone's face at least once. She tried tracking the order, but there was no pattern to it. She tried tracking the others, too, but it was all nonsense. Olivia wore Allison's face three times in a row. The woman would slip it off. Look at it. Slip it back on. Securing the twine tightly in place each time. Brin kept beating her brain against the arrangement of the faces. If she could find some solid, meaningful facts, she might feel better. She even tried analyzing the scar on the woman's hand. Every time she came close, Brin would study it. Try to notice something new about it, something meaningful hiding in the little gray-white line. But nothing came to her. Nothing at all. Then the woman would remove her mask, and the pain was too huge to concentrate.

She wished, so hard it hurt, that she could touch her hair. Just run her hand through it once. Just a finger. Just to remind herself it was still there. That she was still okay. But no. Her wrists ached. The twine was fire against her skin. The pipe dug into her shoulder blades.

And her face. She had to keep pressing it from her mind. It throbbed so bad during those few minutes it took the woman to exchange masks. She hated being raw and open like that, and she loved the feeling of having a new skin pressed onto her, of becoming someone else. But those few in-between minutes ached *so* bad. Made her whole body scream. She craved the mask. She hated that she did, but she did. She yearned for that warm, sweet pressure. Each time, she begged, *Put it back on me. Cover me up. Please, cover me back up.*

Every so often, she and Olivia would lock eyes and stare at each other for a long time. Breathing together. Sometimes they stared at each other from the sockets of the other's face. Brin found herself sliding into a fantasy when they looked at each other like this. They'd get out of here. They'd have shared trauma. They'd have each other. They'd get their own faces back, their own lips. They'd lie in bed together, just themselves.

If they got out. And even then, who knew.

Some fucking Guide you are, Brin told her in her head.

Olivia just breathed.

Auburn, Brin tried to say to herself. *Auburn*, the way Mom used to say it. But her jaw was still too tight. Too numb. It came out as a muffled groan, "Awurr." She thought about trying again, but she figured it'd just make her cry.

I am Brin and my hair is auburn. I am Brin and my hair is auburn. I am Brin and . . .

* * *

The woman stomped toward Allison for the millionth time, then stopped. Paused. Stepped back. And did something new. The thick log arms—shook. A twitching, jerking dance. Again, the mouth cracked into a smile-web. The black eyes crinkled.

She's excited, Brin realized. *She's fucking excited.*

The woman slapped both hands against the apron. Blood spattered over the daisies, the clouds, the sun. She shook her arms in the air, waving her hands, and Brin could feel drops raining on her. Then the woman turned and went to the butcher block. Brin looked around. Allison was wearing Brin, Brin was wearing Ryan. If there was an order, it had ceased to matter long ago. They all stared at the woman in the center of the room. Brin leaned forward, straining the twine, pushing forward with her whole being. The woman raised a hand, gave it a flick like a chef, and let it hover above the tray of tools. Fear flooded Brin like boiling water. She watched the woman's hand, floating there above the tray. The fingers danced a little. Thinking. Ready to pick up the scalpel again. Or something bigger.

Everyone watched. Leaned forward, jaws slack. They couldn't speak, but they could watch.

Finally, the woman decided. She flicked her hand again, riffled through the contents of the tray. Metal clattering on metal, scratching in echoes across the room.

She didn't go for the knife. Instead, she picked up something heavier. Brin heard it sliding up over the tray. Rasping and then singing as the woman hefted it into the air. Brin could see the dark square of a cleaver. It glowed. A foot-long patch of dim fire.

The woman walked around the block to Ryan's corner of the room. He watched her through Olivia's face. The woman stood above him for a moment, cleaver gleaming in her fist. She reached around him, and began to undo the twine around the pipe, binding his wrists. Ryan's eyes turned manic. He shifted on the floor. His whole body coiled back, ready to spring at her, get loose, go for help. Everyone tensed. The air seemed to drain from the room. The woman worked at the knot for several seconds. Finally, Ryan's hand popped free. Immediately, he lunged at her, and snapped back, banging the back of his head against the pipe.

The other hand was still tight in place.

He tugged at it, tried to get it loose. He jerked back and forth, reaching for the woman with his free hand. But she was just out of reach. She watched him, cleaver at her side. He tried the knot again. Drool flew off his chin in long lines. He worked and worked, and when he couldn't get loose, he lunged at her again, fingers stretching, reaching for the apron, and she whipped out a hand, caught his wrist. She pulled his arm taut and, with one clean sweep of the cleaver, hacked through the limb at the elbow. She gave her hand a sharp twist, and Brin could hear the crack as the joint popped, came free. Brin squeezed her eyes shut, but she couldn't squeeze out the scream. It made all the pipes in the room sing.

When she opened her eyes again, the woman had moved across the room. Ryan's arm lay on the butcher block like a big sausage. The woman stood now above Olivia.

Ryan sat staring at his stump. It wasn't bleeding very much. No spurting black puddle like Brin expected there to be, like on tv. Just a slow trickle. The jagged ends of broken flesh and bone. He gaped at it, not understanding.

Olivia wept and tried to press herself back against the pipe. It didn't matter. The woman reached around her. She undid the knot with one hand, holding the dripping cleaver in the other. Suddenly, Olivia's arm was free. She wrapped it backward against the pipe, shaking her head. The woman shot out the hilt of the cleaver, cracked Olivia in the ribs. Olivia jerked on reflex. Her arm came up. The woman darted forward, grabbed it, swiped the cleaver through its middle. She twisted the wrist, *pop-crack-snap*, and the arm wrenched loose.

Two arms on the block now. Nice and neat. And two small shadows spread across the dirt floor, leaking in slow brooks from the stumps.

The woman placed the cleaver back in the tray. She hovered there again, standing statue-still in her big boots and apron. Then, she picked up both arms. They flopped, fingers dangling limp as she turned from the block. She walked to Olivia, who didn't even look up. The woman knelt, getting stiffly onto one knee. She hefted Ryan's arm and (Brin couldn't, didn't believe it) rammed it onto Olivia's stump. Olivia's eyes went wide. Her body rigid, shaking. As she shook, the arm stayed in place. Stuck to her. Even more (Brin couldn't believe this either), the arm shook *with* her. The fingers twitched and danced. Like they were her own.

The woman wasn't even watching. She was already across the room, jamming Olivia's arm onto Ryan's body. Ryan convulsed, too, and the arm moved with him. He screamed, staring at the small painted fingernails at the end of his arm.

The woman moved back to the butcher block and turned. First one way, then the other. Examining the two new bodies she'd made.

Then she picked up the cleaver, and moved around the room. She went to Joshua, Allison, then Brin. When she arrived at Brin, the room was filled with the copper stink of blood, and Brin could think of nothing else to do except cry and plead, and the woman's eyes bored into her, and she grabbed Brin's wrist and the cleaver came down and Brin went somewhere else.

* * *

I am Brin and my hair is auburn. I am Brin and my hair is auburn. I am Brin and my hair is auburn. I am Brin and my hair is auburn. I am Brin and my hair is auburn. I am Brin and my hair is auburn. I am Brin and

Joshua's arm was wider at the elbow than hers, but she could feel it bend and shift, wrapping around her stump and becoming one with her. It cracked and popped, throbbed for a second, and there were pins and needles, as if Brin had whacked her funny bone hard. The seam between him and her was a ragged red line, but she could feel the fingers move as she flexed them. She tried watching the hand at the end of this arm move as she moved it, but it was too awful. Made her head turn upside down, made the room swim. Brin looked away, and saw Allison wearing *her* arm. Brin watched the chipped nails of her own hand flick at the dirt floor as Allison cried through her mask, and that was awful, too.

Everything was awful now.

When the woman took Joshua's arm from Brin, it felt like someone sucking part of her out through a straw. It wasn't the raw, exposed feeling of losing a mask. Just tight and cold.

As with the masks, the woman lined up their arms on the block, studied them for a moment, then made a new arrangement. She brought Brin Allison's arm, which fit better. Brin stared at its perfect-paint nails. She flexed her hand, and she watched her own arm mold itself to Olivia across the room. She wondered what Olivia thought of her arm. Wondered if she liked it. Because personally, she found herself flexing her fingers again. Found herself gazing down at the lacquered nails with something that . . . Something that wasn't quite horror.

When the woman had gone all around the room again, she stood in its center and examined her work. Then she shook her arms once more, flicking blood across the room, onto the night-lights, into Brin's eyes so they stung and Brin had to blink it away. She took the can of spray, and brought it around the room. She came to Brin first, shaking the can and loosing a huge dose of silvery spray on the seam between Brin and Allison's arm. The spray was death-cold, as before, and Brin flinched away from it. But when she looked down, she realized the woman had actually healed the wound. There was now no distinction between herself and Allison, aside from a drying, thin, grayish white scar. Just like the thing on the woman's hand.

Understanding hit Brin in the gut like a bullet. She didn't know why, or for what, and as far as she was concerned, it didn't fucking matter. But the woman was making something specific. Something like herself. Brin understood that now. And she understood, just as suddenly, that the woman wouldn't stop torturing them until she was done with her arts and crafts.

When the woman was finished spraying their arms, she took their arms back, which was a sad surprise. Brin had hoped they were done with that part. It was the same straw-suck sensation, but significantly lessened now, and no more blood. Whatever that spray was, maybe it wasn't just a preservative. Brin thought, *Magic glue?* But that sounded too childish and . . . fun. *This* was not fun.

In the dark light of the night-lights and the bulb overhead, Brin watched the woman return their arms to the butcher block. She stood there, thinking.

It was time, once again, for something new.

The woman took a smaller tool from the tray. Another blade. Not quite as small as the scalpel, but not as large as the cleaver. Curved slightly, like a scimitar. She examined it in the light for a moment. Then took an arm (Olivia's) in one hand, the new blade in the other. And she came toward Brin. She jammed the arm onto

Brin's stump—*I am Brin and my hair is auburn I am Brin and my hair is auburn I am Brin and*—and stepped back. Brin swallowed down the hard popping feeling, the pins and needles. The woman angled her head. The blade turned in her hand. Brin stared up at her. Those eyes, those black holes.

The woman reached down. Brin thought maybe she was going for the mask. That she was going to start changing their faces again, too. But no. Instead, the woman reached higher. Instead, she worked her thick, bloodstained fingers into Brin's hair.

No.

The woman wormed her hand over Brin's head. She tangled herself up in the auburn hair.

No.

She scraped her nails across Brin's scalp, gathering a fistful of rich red-brown.

No no NO!

She tightened her grip, lifting Brin's head back. She brought the knife to Brin's forehead, ready to slice across the scalp. An image slammed into Brin's mind. Her hair, bloodied and tangled. No longer perfect auburn. Sitting on Allison's head. And Allison's own thin blond mop, bloody and squatting on Brin's scalp.

Absolutely fucking not.

The knife pressed into her skin, right above the mask she wore (she couldn't even remember whose it was), and Brin made good on her promise: *I'll fucking kill her if she touches my hair.*

She jerked her (Olivia's) hand up, catching the woman in the stomach. The woman gave a grunt, a quick puff of surprised air, but she didn't move. She was too solid, her boots too firm on the dirt. But Brin had caught her by surprise. For just a second, the woman wasn't in control.

It was enough.

Brin grabbed at the woman's wrist. She could feel something there (another thin white scar, maybe), but ignored it. She grabbed, held, twisted. The woman's boots were planted to the ground, but the rest of her fell forward. Brin let her go and grabbed at the curved knife. She managed to wrench it free and brought it around to the woman's throat. The woman caught Brin's hand, twisted. Fingers dug into the skin and Brin gasped. It must have been another pressure point. The woman must have known all of them. Brin almost appreciated this, too, but she didn't have time. The knife fell into the dirt between them. The woman punched Brin in the gut. Air whooshed from her body, making her cough and wheeze. The woman reached for the knife. Brin grabbed the wool of her hair, pulled down. At last, the woman fell, splayed out into the dirt, a big cloud puffing out around her. Brin grabbed at the knife and brought it down into the back of the woman's neck, burying it to the hilt. She yanked it free. Buried it again. Again. Again. No blood came. She realized she was hissing through her teeth. Not a scream exactly, but anger boiling out of her like steam. She gave the knife a twist, *fuck you, you Franken-bitch*, and left it there in the neck.

She leaned back against the pipe, panting. She looked down at the body, ready for it to move again. To rise and continue hacking them apart. She looked down on this woman and, suddenly, could see dozens of scars. Thin gray-white lines all over her neck. Down her arms. Everywhere. She must have been working on herself for a very long time. Switching around her parts with . . . who?

Brin yanked the knife free, twisted her arm around, and hacked at the twine still holding her other hand. She sawed, desperate, and felt something snap. The twine loosened. Not much, but enough to squeeze out her hand. She sawed at the cord around her neck. Gasped. Retched. She scrambled up to her feet. Her legs were beyond weak, but she managed to limp to the butcher block. In the tray, there were hundreds of tools. Blades of every kind. Small bent ones. Big flat ones. Knives as long as her arm.

Her eyes moved to the surface of the block itself. A long strip of dark, stained wood ran down its length. Brin ran a hand over it. Something whispered in her ear, the syllables popping wet and salivating. She jerked her hand away, shivering. Wiped her hand on her pants. Stories flew into her head. People doing evil, twisted things. She'd always thought the stain was bullshit. But now . . .

Hell, now she didn't care. She just wanted to go home.

She limped to Olivia and sawed through the twine. She helped Olivia stand. The Guide's legs wobbled. Olivia held out her hand. She licked her lips, and to the surprise of both her and Brin, the drugs were wearing off. She spoke.

"Gimme the knife," she choked. "I'll let the others out. You go get help."

"You sure?" Brin choked back.

Olivia nodded. "Yeah."

They glanced at the dark form of the woman in the apron. She was still.

"Here." Brin gave Olivia the knife. Without another word, she moved to the stairs. Her legs were more awake now. A tingling, stabbing ripple went up them with every step, making her wince.

Olivia started to limp to Joshua (*of course she's freeing Joshua first*), then stopped. "Wait."

Brin turned back.

"Do you want your arm back?"

Brin blinked. She hadn't even realized Olivia was wearing it.

"No," she said, and it was the truth.

"Well . . . Can I have mine at least?"

"We don't have time." She turned away, and pounded up the

stairs. The door at the top was bolted with a giant medieval-looking bar. It took her both hands to crank it open. Both hands to shove the door, to burst out into a small hallway. No doors. No windows. Dark. Wooden floor. A light green wallpaper, no design. Endless green. A single night-light in the middle of the hall, near the floor. Flickering.

We're in the house. In the field. It's gotta be.

Brin limped down the length of the hall. She tried to hold her breath, but her heart was beating too hard, so she took in short stabs of panicked air. There was movement at the end of the hall. Footsteps. She approached the doorway, leaned in, and stopped. Her blood went cold.

Surrounding a wide woven rug in the middle of what looked like a small, quaint living room (grandfather clock, hard furniture—the kind her grandparents owned), were almost a dozen people. Standing in a large circle. All middle-aged or older. Men and women. Dressed in slacks, jeans, button-downs, suspenders. They stood unblinking, unmoving. Staring at some point in the lower distance. All of them slouched slightly forward, birdlike, their shoulders hunched. She could see, in the dim light, that they were all covered in those thin white lines. All over their arms and hands and fingers, even their faces. Riddled with scars, or seams, just like the woman in the apron.

Brin wondered if she'd been stupid to think the woman was the only one.

No one moved. The grandfather clock ticked. If Brin had been more industrious, more interested in local lore, she might have noticed that every piece of furniture in the room once belonged to the Renfields. That there were still splashes of stain across the legs of the sofa, the chairs, the clock. That one of the chairs still possessed a wide, ragged Henry-hole. If the stain were, indeed, a wriggling, radioactive madness, then being in this room would be the equivalent of standing smack-dab in the center of Chernobyl in 1987.

Brin drew back. She examined the room, scanning for a way out. There were no windows here, either. More night-lights in outlets, all around the room, tossing rippling shadows across the ceiling. And there was a door, hiding in the far corner. No way could she get to it without being seen. She tried to memorize faces for the police but found it impossible. Everyone's face shifted and melted. They wouldn't stick in her brain, and the harder she looked at them, the more her head hurt. None of them had eyes, like the woman downstairs. Just black, empty things.

Before she could decide what to do, a man stepped into the center of the rug. He waited. The grandfather clock ticked away several seconds before a woman stepped forward to face him. The man lifted his hands to waist height, palms up. He held them there, as if miming carrying a large box. It all seemed very measured, very performed. Like an experimental play.

Brin didn't know how long she could watch before they saw her. She edged closer. Maybe she could make it to the door. If she was fast, maybe she could—

The man turned one hand over, wrapped his fingers around the opposite wrist. There was a loud crunch, and he popped off his hand. Held it out in front of him. Waiting. The woman echoed his movement, lifting her hands waist-high. She turned one over, wrapped her fingers around her wrist, and, with a short, sharp sound like the cracking of a peanut shell, she, too, removed her own hand. She held it out. She and the man exchanged hands. Popped the new ones onto their wrists. Wriggled their fingers. Looked at each other. And stepped back to join the circle.

Brin gripped the doorjamb, trembling. *Holy shit. Holy fucking shit.*

Maybe these people had started in the basement. Maybe the woman had worked on them, worked on them, until they'd graduated up to the rug, switching around their parts themselves. Moving around their bits at the seams. Maybe the woman was part of a cult. Brin wondered how long they'd been here. How many years. They were so pale.

Holy shit.

The woman with the new hand stepped forward again. A sick fascination gripped Brin, and she leaned forward again to watch. The woman rolled up her pants leg. She twisted, wrenched, and popped off a leg at the knee. She wobbled, balancing on one foot, holding the leg out like an offering. Another woman stepped onto the rug and removed her leg as well. They traded. Again, that sick tissue-paper crunch. The two looked at each other. The one who'd offered her leg stepped back, leaving the first woman alone on the rug. She stood there, waiting.

The circle burst into applause. The woman on the rug put up her hands and turned in a slow, luxurious circle. Showing off. The applause roared. As the woman turned, Brin could see that almost all of her pieces were different. Mismatched. One leg had darker skin, one arm was longer than the other. Her head didn't quite match the size of her neck. But somehow . . . it worked. Somehow, she gave off a wave of completion. Of warm, stunning peace. She looked wonderful. Beautiful. She beamed. The group applauded, loud, and the last piece of understanding clicked into place. The woman in the apron wasn't trying to hurt them. It wasn't for her benefit. She was trying to make them something *better*. Helping them be the best they could be.

As Brin realized this, something deeper than understanding hit her. Something bordering, again, on appreciation.

Someone new stepped into the center of the circle. The applause died, and the woman they'd been clapping for stepped back. This person placed his hands firmly on either side of his head, lifted upward, and that crunching, cracking, tissue-paper roar filled the room once more. There was a pop. He held his head there, a foot above his neck. Blinking. A second man came forward onto the rug. Removed his head. And they swapped. The second man stepped back, and the circle applauded for the first man. He turned, smiling. Arms raised. They all clapped. Another well-made combination. All of them beaming. All of them proud, and warm.

Brin was in awe.

She watched them for another minute or so. Two more combinations were made in the middle of the rug. Two more people turned, slow and luxurious, and were applauded.

It seemed easy. An easy, accepting group. They were just helping each other. Really, that's what it was. Helping each other be better-made. Giving everybody a chance in the middle of the room.

Brin felt something shift inside her chest.

She eyed the door across the room and chewed her lip, realizing it wasn't her lip at all. But it *felt* like hers. It felt natural. And when she ran a hand through her hair, she couldn't feel the twine holding the mask to her head anymore. She felt like herself. She felt light. She felt . . . right.

As someone else turned to the sound of the applause, Brin ran a hand through her hair again. She watched. She watched. She watched.

Then she turned and headed back down the stairs.

Olivia was still trying to saw through Joshua's twine.

"I can't fucking get this," she said. "I'm sorry. Can you—"

Brin kicked her in the jaw.

* * *

Joshua's arms seemed like the logical choice, since they were the strongest. She popped them on pretty easy, one after the other, *pop pop*. She left Allison's arms on the block, but took the hands. Had to saw the wrists herself. She sprayed them and held them to the light. They looked good at the ends of Joshua's muscles. One of the fingers, though, was a little bent. Unattractive. Had a weird wart on it. She traded it for one of Olivia's fingers. Had to saw that off herself, too. She gave herself Ryan's feet, kept her own legs. And she'd be keeping her own hair, that was obviously nonnegotiable. She sprayed it all with the can, feeling the seams mold themselves onto her body. Feeling those thin gray lines settle into her flesh. Feeling herself breathe into the new pieces. *Her* new pieces. Her "reinvented" whole. And then, at last, she slipped Allison's face over her own. She felt the skin seal itself to her. Felt her muscles and bones form themselves to Allison's lips, Allison's forehead, Allison's cheeks. She reached up Allison's hand and felt the beauty mark. That fucking beauty mark. She poked it, and *felt* the finger there, as if the mark were her own.

And really, it was.

She left the others on the floor. The numbness had worn off completely now, and two of them were dead. Allison was no more than a limbless, headless log, spurting from all ends. Joshua she'd had fun with, ramming Olivia's legs onto the stumps of his arms and Allison's arms onto his legs. He'd kicked and flailed and tried to walk on the hands, and then he threw up and he died. Ryan and Olivia lay there in pieces, crying. Olivia's severed head sucked sobs through its open throat, the hole farting like an anus as she gasped.

Brin came back up the stairs and down the hall. She didn't try to be quiet this time, and the circle of people turned as she entered the room. She felt their eyes on her. Felt her skin crawling with their attention. Buzzing with it. She felt all her parts throb with life.

The circle parted, accepting her without a word, and she stepped into its center. The rug was cool and soft against her feet—grass after rain. She stood, put her arms above her head, and turned. A slow, luxurious three-sixty. She smiled to herself, then to the room. She threw her head back. The auburn billowed around her like brilliant, blazing wildfire. She beamed, spun again, and again, and waited for the applause, and when it came, it was loud, and euphoria washed over her like a wave. A warm, warm wave. Someone embraced her, circled their arms about her neck, then slipped down to her waist. They fiddled with something behind her back. They stepped away, and Brin looked down, and she was wearing the apron, but it was clean, fresh, with a different design. Someone shoved a tray into her hands, and the tray was filled with tools. They pointed her to a door, and she saw now that there were many, many doors, to many, many basements, all around the room. She could choose any one she wanted, be anyone she pleased, and the applause was loud, loud, loud, and good, fucking *good*.

From: Rachel Durwood <radurwood@bhs.org>
To: tom.durwood@gmail.com
Re: The Stain

Mere hours before he was hanged at Bartrick Prison on March 3, 1935, Lawrence Renfield agreed to speak with a reporter for the *Lillian Journal*. He had not agreed to any other interview up until that point, so this was big news. The reporter asked him what he would have done if the police hadn't caught him. Would he have killed anyone else? Tried to hide the bodies? What would have happened if Edna Mason had not seen Lawrence dragging his son into the barn and run for the authorities?

A direct quote: "Well, I . . . would have become . . . something *better*. For the giant men, above the mist." When asked to elaborate, Lawrence just shook his head and stared at the wall, his eyes "sharp but distant."

These would turn out to be his final words. Even when they put the hood over his head, he remained silent.

From later in the article: "It seems to this reporter that Lawrence believed the kick in the head he suffered four months before the incident in December '27 did little to scramble his sanity. Rather, Lawrence believed it knocked loose something important. Something that had been waiting there for a very, very long time . . ."

It took Lawrence Renfield three minutes to die. The same amount of time he'd been unconscious in August, after the incident with the mule. The same amount of time it took him to murder five people.

If that's not some divine fuckin bullshit, then . . . Well, Tom, then I just don't know what to do with myself. I don't know what to do with myself. I don't know what to do. I don't know what it means. I don't know . . .

Look, I'm sorry. I really am. But it's time to call me back now. It's been hours and I'm really trying to be cool, but I'm so drunk. I'm so drunk now I don't care. Why aren't you picking up? This is beyond being mad at me. I can *feel* something is wrong. Are you okay? I feel like . . .

Fuck, this is so stupid. I'm sorry. I know. I *know* I've done this before. I vanish for weeks and then I reemerge and flood you with apologies and bullshit, and the irony is I've ignored *your* calls plenty of times. So fine. You're mad. As the older sis, I needed to be there after Mom died, and I wasn't. I suck. You're *allowed* to not be here tonight.

But Tom, why can't I *feel* you anymore? I *always* feel you, but all of a sudden, I . . . feel like I'm by myself.

Where are you?

AND EVERY THURSDAY
WE FEED THE CATS

Cal is losing weight. It's his second Thursday working at Harv's, and it's weird that he's skinnier than when he started, because he's not eating any less. In fact, he's eating a *lot* of Harv's food, which is greasy, heavy, usually fried. He should be *gaining* weight, if anything.

But here he is, brushing his teeth on Thursday morning when he notices something strange in the mirror. He can see his sternum much better than he could before. He turns, examines his profile. Frowns. Finishes brushing, spits, and steps on the scale. Sure enough, he's dropped a few pounds. He frowns at the number. Tries the scale again. It gives him the same thing. He picks it up, shakes it (maybe the mechanism's fucked), and tries again. Again, it's the same number.

Cal thinks about this as he gets ready for work. He thinks about it during the whole fifteen-minute drive to Harv's Diner. He thinks about it all day as he's handing out food to Harv's regulars.

Why the hell is he losing weight?

Maybe he's overthinking it. Maybe it's just the day. Thursdays have been hard, after all, these last few years.

But still.

When he takes his lunch break, hunkering down at the bar with a burger and a yellowed paperback (Cal *loves* fantasy novels, and maybe that's making him paranoid, too—thinking about black magic and wishing the world was more adventurous than it really is), he gives himself a few extra fries. He eats them fast, makes sure they stick. He can feel them sitting in his stomach.

Every Thursday evening, Harv has him put out a tray of food for the strays behind the diner. There are supposed to be cats back there, but Cal's never seen them. Regardless, they eat well: a big metal tray full of people food, every week. He leaves it for them on the back stoop. Burgers and chicken and fish sticks. Today, Cal flips a chicken breast. He watches it sizzle on the grill. He puts a hand on his stomach. Takes a breath. Feels the air swell inside him.

His first Thursday at Harv's, Cal put down that tray of food and felt good. He felt like he had a purpose, feeding the stray cats. Taking care of something. It was his favorite part of the week.

But feeding the cats came right before going home. And going home meant walking through that living room. Walking past that perpetual tv, and Mom in her chair. Thursday was payday, and that meant her stopping him to ask for his paycheck. It meant her cool, thin smile as she purred, "I'll take care of this for you." Which she won't. She only leaves him money for gas, and the rest of it's supposedly going into Cal's savings account.

Supposedly.

As Cal scoops the chicken onto the tray for the strays, his thoughts turn back to Douchebag Darren—the whole reason he's working here at Harv's in the first place. Cal remembers Darren standing there in his dumb fuckin hoodie. His skinny jeans. His backpack filled with all those stupid little baggies. *Just hold it for me, man, don't be an asshole* . . . And for a second, Cal forgets where he is, and the chunks of chicken he's plopping onto the tray are actually bags of weed. Big bulging sacks of stinking nugs. Smoking up at him from the tray. He can smell it. Thick, cloyingly sweet skunk. The tray is covered with it. Piles and piles of it. He blinks, and it's gone.

It's just chicken.

But he can't shake the feeling that, somehow, he's covered the tray with something other than food. Something . . . more.

This feeling follows him for the rest of the day. It sits on his chest as he lies in bed, trying to sleep. *Something weird*, he thinks, *is happening at Harv's*.

Harv's Diner is off a winding little woods-road that's not quite dirt but not quite pavement. Deer like to hang out there. If you're not careful around the turns, you could end up stranded, antlers stuck through your windshield. A buck lying on the shoulder, screaming. Or something worse.

Harv's is across the road from Babylon, the rust-shack trailer park many of the Falls's lower class inhabit. All of Harv's regulars (his only customers, really) live there. It's a short walk for them and they mostly pay cash, which Harv appreciates because then he doesn't have to file it all.

The diner itself is a big white box carved into the side of a slope, just at the base of a giant granite hill. It looks like it might even be just another Babylonian trailer. A metal and concrete behemoth built by someone focused on function rather than fashion. There's a vestibule sticking out of the front end, surrounded by glass, with two cement steps leading up. There's a long wheelchair ramp on the side. Through the glass of the vestibule, you can see an old skill crane. Flashing yellow carnival bulbs run up and around the face of the machine, lighting up the cracked plastic eyes of the plush things jammed together inside. The claw doesn't close right (Harv loosened a screw a while back), so the animals in the pit have been lying down there for ages. Some of them, on the bottom, have been there since Harv opened the diner years ago. Sometimes Harv jokes that they've rotted down there. That you could win a prize of maggots and filth if you dug hard enough. He laughs when he says this, but there's a part of him that isn't entirely sure it's a joke.

There's a gumball machine in the vestibule, too, but the gumballs are all old as shit. They shatter into shards between your teeth, and the flavor saps away within minutes.

Just like life.

The slope behind the diner sweeps up and away, steep into the woods, right up to the hilt of that massive granite blade. This is shit woods, too. Covered in trash. Beer bottles with torn, faded labels. Plastic ex-containers of detergent. Pillows, a table leg. Used condoms. All of it peeking up through layers of fallen leaves. It's not inviting, per se. Not the kind of trees you'd want to wander through on a sunny day. They're always reaching, always scheming. The kind of trees that tap against your window at three a.m., just lightly enough so when your mom tells you it's the wind, you almost believe her, you fuckin idiot. They're not branches. They're tentacles. And they spread over the roof of the diner in long, gnarled weeds, cracking through the air at odd angles. The buzzing neon letters on Harv's roof (DINER) blare against the underbellies of the branches, shading them a deep crimson. When it rains, the limbs of these trees appear to bleed.

This place sucks, thought Cal the first time he saw it.

Which is . . . yeah, a more concise way to put it.

It was eight o'clock at night when Cal first arrived. The end of June. The dark was hot and wet. Heavy. Full of mosquitoes and moist. He'd driven through fading ink to get here, the sun already hiding behind hills. It's only about fifteen minutes from his house in Bent, but when you're cruising through ink, that's, what? An hour?

As he pulled into the parking lot, Cal noticed the floodlights first. Three on each side of the gravel-crusted sprawl before the diner. They're utilitarian, almost dystopian. The blinding white beams exploding out of them, shooting down into the gravel, look like wide, rectangular arms. Holding back the dark of the woods beyond. And that's probably why the light is so strong—there's a *lot* of dark to hold back. With the floodlights, Harv's Diner reminded Cal of a military outpost. A bunker cut into the trees and rock. The thought made Cal's scalp itch. But even though the light in the parking lot was the first off-putting thing Cal noticed about Harv's Diner, it would be far from the last.

It'll be another week before he realizes he's losing weight.

He parked his car (a hand-me-down Toyota Corolla from Grandpa) right under one of those military spotlights. They looked even more dystopian up close. All buzzing metal and sharp edges. Cal turned off the car, stepped out. The heel of his sneaker made the ground crunch. The gravelly sound echoed through the branches above, signaling Cal's arrival to the birds and the night. He zipped up his hoodie, put his hands in his pockets. Squeezed his shoulders together and wondered why he was shivering if it was so warm. Was it because this was his first-ever job and he was nervous? Or . . . was it something else?

Poor kid. In he went. Wearing his little V-neck and hoodie. Old faded Vans. He started walking to the diner, wondering if he was going to get hacked up and eaten, which is exactly the kind of thing he should have been wondering. He climbed those two cement steps, opened the vestibule door with the old brass bell (silent, missing a hammer), and met Harv for the first time.

You know, it's hard to know the moment that officially dooms you. Was it answering that Craigslist ad for a job at a diner? Was it buying weed from Douchebag Darren in the first place? Was it this, was it that . . . Whatever it was for Cal, by the time he met Harv, it didn't matter anymore.

He was already fucked.

Cal's first impression of the man was of an angry bee storming around a hive. He buzzed from the diner's kitchen to its tables and back, carrying food and shouting at no one in particular. Cal stood just inside the vestibule, waiting politely to be noticed. He watched Harv carry plates from the kitchen, to the kitchen, and around the wide carpeted space of the diner, for almost five minutes before Harv even looked at him.

Cal took the time to notice what he could about his new digs: The carpet is a burnt red. Small cigarette holes polka-dot it. All the tables are this faded blue Formica. There's half a dozen or so tossed around the middle of the room, and maybe ten booths lining the walls. All the chairs and booth seats are thin red pleather and black metal. The walls are all white. Mirrors in every corner. On the far wall, opposite the front door, there's a bar with a bunch of red-cushioned stools bolted to it. Next to it is the kitchen door, and a long, thin window looking in.

There were five people in there that night, but the emptiness was so palpable it felt like a sixth customer. Cal could tell right away they were all local, from the trailer park. They were wrinkled and dry, and they moved slow, like the air was mud. He'd always heard people from the Falls were weird. The air there "feels bad," he'd heard. And now that he saw the people who breathed it 24/7, he understood.

Overhead, speakers in the ceiling played some slow eighties

love ballad. As Cal stood there, "Take My Breath Away" by Berlin burbled on. Cal doesn't have any strong opinions on music, but he found himself desperately hoping the speakers would play some other kind of thing sometime soon.

A fool's hope. They never would.

Harv burst out of the kitchen carrying a patty melt and a pile of fries.

"Here's your fuckin meat, you cheap shit," he said, literally dropping the plate on a table. The couple sitting there (man and woman in their forties), jerked back as drops of grease spattered over the Formica.

"You're lucky you make a mean patty melt, asshole," said the woman. The man was wiping at his shirt, mumbling to himself.

"Thank you," said Harv. And at last, he turned, faced Cal, beamed, and stuck out his hand. "You must be Cal. Craigslist guy."

What surprised Cal about this was that it was all one fluid motion. Like it was just another step in the dance Harv had been doing for decades. Cal had expected him to turn suddenly, surprised to see him standing there. Instead, he was part of Harv's ballet.

"You . . . saw me?" he asked dumbly.

"Was I not supposed to? Sorry about the wait. I had orders. Shake my fuckin hand."

Shake is the wrong word, because what really happened was Cal stuck out his hand, and Harv crushed it between a bunch of iron sausages. *Sausages* is the *right* word because Harv's a big, forty-six-year-old kind of sausage-man. His fingers are sausages, his legs are sausages. All his limbs are like tree-trunk meat tubes, patched with scars and burn marks—the stains of working in a kitchen for ages. He's bald. His face is hardened leather. Deeply cracked and shot through with burst veins, broad acne craters. His torso is a big hard ball, and if you look at him from a certain angle, it looks like someone rolled a bunch of Play-Doh nice and tight into logs, and jammed them all together onto a doughy sphere. He is thick, solid, and somehow swelling outward in all directions, all the time. Like when he dies, he won't *die* so much as *rupture*. One day, all those burst blood vessels on his cheeks and nose, the bulge-cords of muscle in his neck and forearms—all those bits that look like they're pushing out against his skin—will pop, and he'll fly around the diner, whining out air, until he drops.

This was Cal's take on him, anyway. Maybe it's all the fantasy novels he reads instead of having friends.

"You answered the ad real quick," said Harv, releasing him.

"I needed the job," said Cal, rubbing his hand.

"You planning to work five days a week? Open to close?"

"I . . . I guess, if that's what you're—"

"You don't have school?"

"Just graduated. Like, a week ago."

"Uhn. Congrats. So you're starting college in the fall."

Cal started to answer, but Harv was already walking away, going toward the kitchen. Which was fine by Cal because he didn't want to answer anyway.

"Your job's simple," Harv said over his shoulder, flying toward the kitchen window. Cal followed, moving fast to keep up. "Tell me who needs what through here." Harv stopped, patting the windowsill. "I'll make the food. Hand it through the thing. You bring it to whoever bought it. Ring em out on the thing." He waved a hand at the register, a stained metal box squatting at the end of the bar. "Cool?"

"Cool." Except Cal wasn't totally sure it was cool yet. He was just trying to keep up.

But Harv was buzzing away again. Over his shoulder: "Here's the register." He planted himself in front of it, gestured for Cal to

stand next to him. Cal put his hands in the pockets of his hoodie.
He carried a lighter in one pocket—a Bic with a flying monkey
on it. He turned it around in his hand. Figured that was un-
professional. Took his hands out of his pockets. They wavered
against his thighs, unsure.

He wanted to go home. To bury himself in bed with a book. To
stare at the ceiling above his bed and listen to the traffic.

Poor kid. Poor fucked kid.

"Very simple," Harv was saying. "You enter the . . . fuckin
thing . . . pop the . . . thing." He slammed knuckles into buttons as
he talked. The buttons were all so yellow and faded Cal couldn't
see what they said. Then Harv hit a big one at the bottom of the
keypad, and the cash drawer yawned out.

"Ya like math?" Harv asked. He beamed at Cal, and Cal noticed
his teeth for the first time. They're bright. Too bright. Pure, crystalline, almost impossible. And long. Like uncarved dominos.

"Uh, yeah, I guess," said Cal. "I'm not a big fan of, like, parabolas,
but . . ."

Harv waved this away. "That's high school shit. Total waste of
time. I'm asking about *life* math. *Change.* You know change. Everybody knows change."

Cal nodded. He used to be in charge of the cash at the garage
sales he and his dad would throw every so often. Selling Cal's old
toys. His dad's old VHS tapes and records. Mom helped sometimes, but . . . Dad was always the fun one.

"I know change," he said.

"Great," said Harv. He snapped his fingers and pointed, dismis-
sively, at the cash in the drawer. "Change. Great. Now, to close
it . . ." He slammed the drawer shut, locking his fingers inside. His
body jolted, eyes bugging out. The cords in his neck bulged. He

gasped. Cal leapt in to help, but Harv was already laughing. A wet, hard sound, like someone shaking moist pebbles in a paper bag.

"I'm fuckin with you," he said.

Cal could hear the locals around the room laughing, too.

"Go easy on him," someone called.

Harv whirled around. "Eat your fuckin meat!" He beamed at Cal. "So. Got the register?"

This fucking guy, Cal thought. "Yeah. Got it."

Overhead, the eighties still pumped through the speakers. Cal wished somebody would just take Berlin's fuckin breath away already.

"You ever had a job before?" Harv asked.

"No," said Cal, a little relieved this was out in the open now.

"Some people would have you believe that service jobs require *experience*," said Harv. "Exper*tise*. Maybe some do. Here, there's only three things. I can do all three myself, but I like having two people working on em. Better ratio, you know what I mean?" He bared his teeth again.

"I do. The three things are . . . ?"

Harv ticked off on his sausage-fingers. "Ya make the food, ya serve the food, ya ring up the food. *I'll* make the food, like I said, so you just carry it. Pour drinks, I guess. Soda fountain's . . ." He waved at the bar. Before Cal could see exactly where the fountain was, Harv was saying, "Look, it's not that much, you know what I mean?"

"What about dishes?"

"Hah?"

"Doing dishes. Isn't that a fourth thing?"

"Uhn. Right. Uh . . . Well, I don't fuckin . . . You want to switch off? Every other day?"

"I mean, I'm not gonna say no."

Harv laughed again. "Well, how about I take Mondays, Wednesdays, whatever. You can just do Tuesdays and Th—" Harv clapped his hands to the sides of his head. His eyes bugged out. "Jesus! I almost forgot! Come on." He jerked his head toward the kitchen and started walking. Cal followed, already tired.

Harv felt like an illusion. He moved so fast, talked so loud. All of a sudden, he was saying *this* over *here*, then he was laughing over *there*. Like there was a blur between each point of movement. He reminded Cal of the Flash or something.

"This lettuce tastes like sweat," someone called from a booth.

"Eat it, you cheap fuck!" A blur, and suddenly they were in the kitchen. Cal blinked, head reeling.

"There's *another* fourth thing," said Harv. "Pretty simple. Only happens once a week, on Thursdays. Every Thursday, we feed the cats."

Harv reached up. He slid down off the shelf above the grill a metal lunch tray. The kind you'd see in a very terrible high school (like Cal's), or a prison. *Militaristic*, is the word that came to Cal's mind. It reminded him of the lights outside. Made him shiver again.

"I keep it tucked behind some spices," said Harv. He held it out. Cal accepted it in both hands, wary. He could immediately tell, just off the vibe, that he was holding something sacred.

"We've got a bunch of strays around here," said Harv. "Stray cats, I mean. Some wander over from the trailer park. Some, I don't know. They hang out in a little fuckin *colony* up the ridge there." His eyes moved up and down between Cal's face and the tray. Worming over him. Gauging Cal's reaction to all this. Cal didn't know what to do. In a way, it appealed to the fantasy part of him, like he was accepting an ancestral sword. He hefted the tray in his hands, making a show of it. Of this thing Harv was, like, passing on to him. It felt like a duty. Everything else Harv had talked about was a *job*. But this was a *duty*. Cal could feel it in the way Harv spoke. His voice was more measured, more hushed and slow. Harv is the kind of guy who talks just to talk, but as soon as he handed over that tray, he was *saying* something.

"You foster them?" Cal asked. "The cats?"

"Foster's a strong word. I just put out a little food every Thursday. Keeps em happy for the week. Couple cheeseburgers. Some meatloafs. Fish sticks. They love fish sticks. You just pile it up on the tray and set it outside on the back stoop." He jabbed a thumb over his shoulder at a small back hall Cal hadn't noticed before. Lit by a dim bulb in the ceiling, making everything glow electric orange. The walls were paneled wood. There was a door with a small window, covered by a thin blue curtain. It was dark back there, cave-like. It didn't even feel like part of the same diner. And lining the door were nine thick deadbolts.

Cal ignored another shiver.

"So," he asked, "you, uh . . . cook for them? Can't you just put out, like, raw meat or something?"

Harv's face darkened. Behind him, the back hall seemed to expand. The tray seemed to gain a couple pounds. Cal felt his arms suddenly straining with the weight. Everything was swelling.

"They like *cooked* food," said Harv. He stepped forward. "That's important. You notice the lights in the parking lot? Sometimes, cats aren't well-fed enough, they get rowdy. Cause mischief. Light keeps em at bay. Food keeps em happy. Mostly, they hang out up the slope there. You feed em, you won't really see em."

"What if I want to? I like cats."

Harv grinned again. Those clickity-clean white teeth. Cal could almost hear the sparkly *ding* they gave off as they shone. "Like I said. You probably won't."

Harv reached out and plucked the tray from Cal's hands, holding it delicately between two fingers. He slid it back on the shelf, behind the spices. Turned, and clapped his hands.

"Well," he said. "I'm excited to get you started tomorrow, Cal. Tomorrow's Thursday, so you get to feed the cats. *You* will *always* be the one feeding them."

Cal almost asked why, but he felt some small part inside himself say, *Don't*, so he didn't. "Alright," he said instead, an uneasiness growing in his gut.

Harv beamed. "Okay. Pleased to meet you, Cal." He shoved his hand out. Cal took it, and Harv jacked their hands up and down so hard Cal was amazed his arm didn't fly out of its socket.

"You too," he said, voice shaking as Harv pumped his arm.

Cal walked back out through the dining area. "Time of My Life" was crying through the ceiling now. None of the locals looked up as Cal passed. They stared down at the blue tables, chewing like lobotomized cows.

A minute later, Cal was in his car again. He leaned his head back against the headrest. Stared at the ceiling. Examined the odd shadows cast over it by the floodlights. Cal filled his gut with air and blew it all out, puffing his cheeks like a cartoon storm cloud blowing wind. He reached up and traced a line along the ceiling. He likes the feel of car ceilings. The way they rasp over his fingertip. It reminds him of being a kid. Of going to the drive-in in the Mill with his dad. Cal's mom wanted them to go by themselves. He remembers that. She came sometimes, but mostly told them to go have "guy time." To bond. So Cal's dad would take him to see things his mom wouldn't necessarily allow. There was one beautiful summer when they went to the drive-in almost every night. Cal was twelve. They saw *Iron Man* and *Tropic Thunder*, *Incredible Hulk* and *Wanted*. They saw *Dark Knight* three times. And after each of these movies, Cal would lie sleepily in the backseat, staring up at the ceiling as his dad drove them home, playing fantasy novels on audiobook so Cal's dreams were filled with magic. His small body wrapped up tight in a blanket. Warm, safe, and comfortable. Streetlights moving in dim waves across the felt ceiling, up there, in the sky.

Years later, sitting in front of Harv's, Cal considered hotboxing the car. He was down to his very last bowl. Maybe now was the right time?

Nah, he could wait until he got home. He'd never drive high. That'd be begging an accident to happen. And he wouldn't go like that. Not after Dad. It was just a fifteen-minute drive. Then he could sit in his driveway, get baked, play some music, go upstairs, and read Jim Butcher in bed until he couldn't keep his eyes open.

Good plan.

He ran his finger along the ceiling once more, breathed, and started the car.

Something behind him moved.

Cal spun around, looked out the window. A flicker of movement, darting through the trees behind the lights, at the bottom of the ridge beyond the diner. A long, pale limb. He saw it bend, spring, and run away. Two eyes flashing a bright animal yellow, then gone in less than a second.

Cal stared at the patch of trees. He felt the hot prickle-rush of adrenaline pulse, and fade. He shivered, shook it out, and pulled away from Harv's.

Later, sitting in his driveway, holding his little green glass pipe to his mouth, he thought about that limb again. It must have been a deer. The leg of a deer. Bending, and prancing away. He blew out smoke. His face got fuzzy and he sank into himself. He blinked around the car, at the dark neighborhood outside the windows.

He told himself there was nothing out there. Told himself he was being paranoid. And even if, *if*, there *had* been something, it was all the way up by Harv's, and Cal was now safe at home in Bent. A whole different town. A neighborhood guarded by lampposts and other homes.

But, of course, when he got out of the car, he walked quickly to the door. He made sure (three times) the door was locked behind him. Told himself again, as he curled up in bed, that he was being paranoid. *It's just the weed. Really. It's just the weed . . .*

But it isn't.

Harv's is less foreboding in the daytime. The floodlights are off, and Cal can see the edges of the lot in full. He eyes them as he walks up the two concrete steps to the vestibule. His hands are sweating, he's nervous for his first day, and as he walks inside, he's pocketing and unpocketing them, worrying about looking professional. He flicks the monkey Bic once at his hip, for good luck, then pockets it.

Harv is already there, of course. Heating up the grill in the back. The rest of the place is empty. From the ceiling, Bette Midler is wailing about the wind beneath her wings. Later, Cal looks up this song to confirm it's only five minutes long, because it seems to last all day.

"Cal!" Harv waves a spatula at him through the kitchen window.

"Harv!" Cal calls back. He thinks this is a good comeback, but Harv just grimaces. The fluorescents make the teeth gleam. Cal's not sure how to take that.

"You can just hang out until someone shows," Harv tells him. "Familiarize yourself with . . . shit."

"You got it." Cal gives him a thumbs-up.

Harv grimaces again. "Uhn." He turns back to the grill.

Cal spends an hour or so standing by the register, figuring out the buttons. More than once, he looks up at the ceiling and wishes he were somewhere else. Wishes he could reach up and graze a fingertip along the ceiling tiles. But then Bette Midler picks up again, and he looks away. Cal feels personally attacked by the ceiling speakers.

He stands around for nearly an hour before someone finally walks in. An old guy with Santa hair tucked into a worn-out baseball cap. Both the hat and the guy are fraying at the edges. He slips into a corner booth. The booth moans. Cal approaches, heart beating, all nervous.

"Hey, man," he says, trying to play it cool. "What, uh, what can I get ya?"

Slowly, the guy looks up. His neck creaks. He's a scaggy thing. Pocked with the deep dry wrinkles you just want to stretch and crack apart. He's no more than a bag of sticks in jeans. He eyes Cal all over. His voice is a cigarette: "You just start today?"

Cal nods. "I'm Cal. You want to see a menu?"

The guy snorts. "Menu. Tell Harv I'll have the usual." He turns away, digging at something under his thumbnail.

Cal lingers. "Is that, like . . . a sandwich or . . . ?"

"Harv knows." Not looking up.

"Okay then."

Cal goes to the kitchen window and tells Harv they've got someone asking for the usual.

"Who?" asks Harv. He doesn't look up either. He's making what looks like a potato omelette.

"That guy." Cal points.

"Uhn." Harv waddles over and sticks his head through the window. When he sees the scaggy Santa guy, he slaps his spatula on the windowsill. "Goddammit, Terry, don't give the new kid shit. You want a fuckin omelette, you ask for a fuckin omelette."

"I want a fuckin omelette," says Terry.

"I'm already workin on it." Harv vanishes back into the kitchen.

Cal lingers by the window. The grill hisses. Terry picks at his thumb. Picks. Picks. Picks. Pick. Pock. Pick. Pock. Pick.

Cal feels himself sinking into the carpet. The air is so dense, filled with grease and stale disinfectant piss-stink and love ballads. It presses him down. He tries looking at the ceiling to calm himself again, but now Joe Cocker's shouting down at him about being up where we belong, and it feels like a sick joke, so Cal looks away and then there's a blur and he's holding a steaming omelette on a plate.

It goes like that pretty much all day. All the customers are regulars, and all the regulars have usuals. A few hours in, Cal figures out that he can just explain it's his first day, and whoever it is will say, "Well, welcome, I guess. Tell the fat fuck in back Sally's here." Then Cal can just call through the window, "Sally's here," and mere moments later, he's holding a patty melt, chicken parm, whatever. It's so much easier than he'd thought it'd be. Cal even figures out the register in what must be record time. He memorizes all the buttons. Gets quick at giving change. After a while, he stops fussing with his hands and the pockets of his hoodie, and he's even bobbing a little with the music. Bette Midler's back on, and Cal's starting to learn the lyrics. Which he kind of hates, but.

About half an hour before closing, the last customer shuffles out the door.

"See you tomorrow, kid," she says over her shoulder. She taps a pack of Noxboros against her palm. They're striped blue and white and have a small fox insignia printed on the filter. Cal has always thought they taste like fresh mulch and ass combined. But to each their own.

She steps into the military-light-drenched lot. She stands outside on the top step for a moment, cigarette dangling. She scans the lot. Peers out at the sunset. *She looks*, Cal thinks, *like she's going to war*. Then she steps down, and it's over. His first full day.

Cal smiles to himself. Not so bad.

"Cal!" Harv calls. Cal follows his voice into the kitchen. Harv's wringing his hands on a rag. He flips it over his shoulder, reaches up, and slides the tray from the shelf above the grill. It grates. Cal feels that same sense of sacred duty that he felt the night before. Harv hands him the tray, making it seem, again, like a ceremony.

"Time to feed the cats," he says.

Harv explains each piece of the meal he wants Cal to set out, pointing around the kitchen to each in turn. "I put some burgers out *there*. Just fry em for a few minutes, slap on some cheese from the fridge, put em in a bun. Fish sticks, *there*, you can nuke in the microwave. There's some meatloaf *here* in the fridge you can nuke, too. Make sure you got a nice little mountain of loaf on the tray before you set it out. Okay?"

"Okay." It seems like a lot of food, but Cal doesn't say anything.

"Great. Come here."

Cal follows Harv down the back hall. It's so dark here. Even the little window in the door doesn't offer much light.

Harv points to the bottom deadbolt. The ninth one in the line.

"This one's broken," says Harv. "Turns the other way. See?" He turns the knob so it's facing the way it should if the bolt were home. But as he turns it, Cal can hear the bolt retract, the lock click open. Harv turns the knob back, and the bolt slides into place. "Got it?"

Cal nods.

"Alright." Harv claps his hands. "I'm gonna close out the register. Holler if you need me."

A blur, and Cal's alone.

At first, he feels alright. He finds the fish sticks in the freezer, the burgers on the counter, everything else in the fridge. He nukes the meat. He's doing good. He's feeding some strays. He's always liked cats. Never got to own one (Mom's allergic), but he feels like kind of a stray himself. So it's all good. It's nice.

But then he starts frying the burgers. And as the meat hisses and pops on the grill, his mind wanders, and a memory slips into him like a splinter. Something he'd almost forgotten, or made himself forget:

Standing at a grill in the backyard. A long, strong arm around him, guiding his hand. Dad's voice, explaining how to tell if the meat's cooked yet.

Cal sticks a hand in his pocket, turns the Bic around in his palm. Massages the wheel with his thumb, careful not to spark it and set himself on fire. That memory swims around and around. Choking him.

The poor fuck.

By the time the burgers are done (perfectly grilled, the way Dad taught him), he's feeling the absolute opposite of alright. He feels despair. And he feels himself filling the tray with that despair. Dumping the memory onto the metal, not wanting it anymore, slapping it down with all that meat. Each *slap* of the food onto the tray is a big cathartic punch. He's gritting his teeth against the memory, and he feels almost like he's grilled it right into the meat. Like it's branded there in the beef.

As he works, he doesn't look up at the ceiling at all.

He carries the tray down the hall. It's heavy, and the hall is so dark. Cal feels like he's carrying an offering to a great, unseen god. A barely benevolent being hiding just beyond the curtain covering the window. He undoes all the locks, balancing the tray on one palm. He tries to open the door, but it sticks and he almost drops the tray, stumbling back. Then he remembers the last bolt, turns it back the other way, and the door slides open like butter.

Outside is a small concrete stoop, a wide patch of dirt, and then the steep rise of the woods. A mountain of scrub and trash and thin, scraggly trees. The granite wall beyond.

He also notices a tall chain-link fence topped with razor wire, running from both ends of the diner's back wall, up the slope, vanishing amongst the trees. How did he not notice this before? It's got signs plastered all over it. Big red circles covering hands touching wires. There's a giant *electric* fucking fence running up the slope, surrounding the backside of the diner.

Why?

There's another shiver. One he can't ignore. He places the tray on the stoop and moves quickly back inside. He slides all the bolts in place, all eight, and then the ninth, turned the other way. He moves the curtain aside with a finger, trying to catch a glimpse of the cats. He stands there for a while, but nothing comes. He swallows a shard of disappointment.

Cal walks back through the diner. Thankfully, the ceiling is quiet, the love ballads done for the day. The silence is a warm blanket. Cal feels lighter, walking through it. Feels that despair from before bleed away.

Harv is counting bills at the register. He waves as Cal passes.

"Good job on your first day," he says. "Tomorrow, bright and early!"

"Sure thing." Cal waves back.

This time, Harv grins. Gives him a thumbs-up. The picket-fence teeth shine.

When Cal gets home, he watches the moon shine through the

window with the same silk-alien glow as Harv's teeth, and in the morning, Cal's pants are just a little bit looser, just a bit, and as he zips them up, he thinks, *Weird*.

As the Thursday sun sets and Cal drives home, a swarm of bodies descends upon the tray. They shove and claw at each other, fighting over the food. Tearing it apart, ravenous and angry. Within seconds, the food is gone. Scarfed up by dozens of hungry, hissing mouths. The bodies scurry away into the night.

Harv waits until they're done, until they've retreated back up the slope. He turns the ninth bolt in the door. It's not a deadbolt at all. It controls another door entirely. The door that keeps the strays where they belong. He's wary about this other door, always keeps it closed. And he knows that if anybody *does* manage to slip through, the fence will keep them in. Their only way to go is down to the lot, under the lights. The lights are good security. He can see the escapees quite well. Can blow their brains out their ear with the rifle under the grill, which he does every time. He's a good shot. Has been since the navy. Then he'll scoop up the body, grind it, and serve it as meat the next day. That doesn't happen a lot, but sometimes the animals aren't that passive. He likes the passive ones. He likes Cal.

When the strays are back up the slope and locked in tight, Harv collects the tray. He licks it clean. It tastes like loss.

Cal never considered dropping out of high school, but he never really saw the point in excelling either. He knew he *needed* school, and he kind of knew he needed college after that. Jobs, more or less, relied on that kind of thing. But Cal was what his math teacher Mr. Blake called "a shrugger." He never understood why people went out of their way to get into the Honor Society. Why they broke their backs to be in the school musical or throw a ball around a field. He just liked to read. To dive into other worlds like Westeros or Earthsea, Middle-earth or whatever. He found them to be kinder than Renfield County. Things happened for a reason. Heroes prevailed. And evil was obvious.

Halfway through his senior year, Cal wrote an essay for a scholarship to Edenville College. He and his mom didn't have enough money to pay for a nice school, and he'd pretty much resigned himself to not going anywhere. But then he realized you could *apply* for money, which was sort of a novel concept. So he wrote a little treatise on the importance of fantasy literature and the "relaxed exploration of universal human truths" offered by works such as *Lord of the Rings*, in which war and death and casual racism could be explored in a relatively safe environment, and could eventually lead to real conversations. A few months later, just as Cal was beginning to forget about it, the essay won him the Spirit of Edenville Scholarship. A totally free ride. Reading his acceptance letter, Cal's eyes began to burn. He felt hope blossom in his throat. This was the only way he would have ever been able to attend a school like E.C. Especially since Cal's mom didn't work and his dad died a long time ago.

See, before Cal was in high school, the weekly routine in their home revolved around Thursday nights. After dinner, every Thursday night for Cal's whole life, his dad would get his keys off the hook in the hall. He'd come into the kitchen, where Cal sat doing his homework at the table. Cal's mom stood at the sink, washing dishes.

"You want to come this week?" Cal's dad would ask, every Thursday. Swinging the keys round a finger. Catching them in his palm. Swinging them round again. Round and round.

Cal's mom would look at him and smile. "You go for both of us, hon."

After a second, he'd smile back. A crooked, warm thing. "Alrighty then, party people. Smell ya later." And he'd be gone. Swinging his keys out the door. Several hours later, he'd return, smelling like stale Noxboro. Sometimes, once a year, he'd come home with a poker chip. He'd show it to Cal's mom. She'd *ooh-ahh* and say, "We did it again." Though, really, she never did anything.

When Cal was ten, his mom explained it to him, what those Thursdays were about. And one night, a few months after Cal's fourteenth birthday, the man never came home. They searched the woods for a long time, but neither Cal's dad nor his car were ever found.

"Lot of swamps around here," said the police. "He must have gone over the shoulder, got sucked in. Sank. The muck can swallow you whole."

Muck. When the police left them alone, Cal's mom said it over and over. *Muck.* She stared at the wall for days, saying it. *Muck.* Letting it hum and then snap.

One Thursday not long after, she went to the store. Came back with bottles. Sat in her chair. Turned on the tv. And never stood up again. As if all the despair had sapped the life from her. She'd never left the house much before, usually relying on Cal's dad for things. But now she got skinnier and skinnier until she was just part of the chair.

She still cared for Cal. Asked him about his day when he moved through the living room. Asked him what he wanted for dinner. Still listened to his answer, even though her response always ended up being, "Well, that sounds good. Whatever we can have delivered. There's money on the counter." When Cal was a bit younger, the money on the counter was a magic thing. He didn't know where it came from. Over time, he put together that some of it was life insurance. Some of it was donated from Dad's old group. Some of it was savings. Then all of it was savings. And then there was less and less of it each time.

With all this in mind, Cal often wonders if his passivity is genetic. If it's no wonder he floats. No wonder he drifted lifeless through the halls of Bent High, just like his mother floats lifeless through the channels of the tv. Just like his dad floats lifeless somewhere else.

But we already told you about Cal's dad. How he died. You already know that story.

Don't you.

During his first two weeks at Harv's, Cal discovers his mom is like the sun. She wakes with it, goes to sleep with it. Slides lazy through the day with it. If he comes home after sunset, he doesn't need to see her awake at all. So he stays with Harv until after close. He drives back to Bent through humid buggy night. He slinks past Mom, snoring wet sounds on the chair in the dark. He can even pretend, sometimes, that she's dead, too. Rotting there in front of the tv. He can spend his whole day drowning her out in the bright lights of Harv's Diner and the sticky, glossy music honeying out of the speakers in endless drools. Working at Harv's, Cal can pretend he's living in a stagnant dream at the end of the world. It's easier that way. Especially now that he's sucked up his last bowl. There's no more weed left to smudge out Mom at home. Sometimes, under the constant eighties barrage of Harv's speakers, he wishes badly he had more. But Douchebag Darren won't talk to him anymore. Not after the Great Backpack Incident. He just left Cal high and dry.

They weren't really friends. In fact, Cal barely knew him, but they rode the same bus. Darren sat in front of Cal in ninth grade health, the year Cal really began to shrug his way through school. One day, when the bell rang after a lecture on the perils of drugs, Darren turned to Cal and said, "Yo, you want any?"

Cal blinked at him. They'd only spoken a handful of times before, so he was surprised. "Do I . . . You mean . . . drugs?"

"Yeah, bro. You smoke?"

They'd just sat through an *entire* lecture about how weed was a terrible gateway drug. Drugs in general were serious business in Renfield. A few senior kids had just lost their minds taking some kind of eyedrops they'd bought in the Falls. But Cal's dad had been dead for just over four months. The lecture was lost on Cal.

"Yeah," he said. "Yes please."

"Sick. See you on the bus."

Cal bought his first eighth on the back of that bus. Darren taught him how to breathe deep, hold it, and let the smoke work into his blood, flooding out all other feeling. Darren sold him his little glass bowl and even threw in a free lighter—a little Bic with a flying monkey on it. Pretty soon, that lighter became Cal's closest friend. Not that it had a lot of competition, but still. He kept it at his side while he read, high out of his skull. Twirled it between the fingers of one hand while he turned pages with the other. He loved the oblivion and the way his attention would narrow to a single word at a time. He loved that swimming-through-sand feeling. He loved the way it broke time.

For a couple years, Darren and Cal lived a peaceful existence. Cal would steal some of Mom's counter money, sit next to Darren in the back of the bus. Darren would open his big backpack, root around the many baggies inside, and hand Cal an eighth of Butcher Kush or Sour Shembels, or some other of the many strains that grew around Renfield.

Then came the last day. The day some front-of-the-bus nerd ratted on them. Cal never even knew what was happening until it was too late.

After school, he was at his locker when Darren rushed past,

chucked the backpack at him, and said, "Hold this for me." Next thing Cal knew, he was on the bus by himself while a K9 unit sniffed its way down the aisle.

"Got a report," said the school officer, his big fist clenched around the dog's leash, "that somebody on this bus . . . is a *criminal*."

And there was Cal. Big backpack full of drugs just sitting on his lap.

Poor, poor dumbass. He never knew what hit him. It wasn't until that dog started snorffling around his crotch and barking at him that he realized he'd been played.

Cut to Cal's long conversation with the guidance counselor and the principal. *Conversation* is actually the wrong word—they talked *at* him. Asked him why he smoked. He looked at the ceiling. Where did he get the pot? The ceiling seemed so far away. Was he planning to sell? Cal wished he could reach up and brush the ceiling with his fingertip. He wished it would drive him home and tuck him into bed. He wished he could wake up the next morning and pick the movie-theater kernels from his teeth.

"Cal," said the principal. "I asked you a question. What are *you* doing with *this* much marijuana?"

"I don't know," he said, lost in the tiles of the ceiling.

They let him finish school, which was fair. He only had about a month left. They kept him on probation, though. Mandatory detention every day, so he always took the late bus, never sat next to Darren again. And Darren started ignoring Cal in the hallways, even when Cal yelled at him, "You're a douchebag!" Darren had a business to protect, after all. So the few nugs still hiding under Cal's bed were all he had left. Maybe forever.

"Really," said Cal's mom one night, "you got off light. Don't you think? Drugs hurt, you know."

He sat on the couch across from her chair. He picked at the

lining of the armrest. Next to him, the tv droned. Always droned. He didn't look at her. Just kept picking.

"Well, as long as you learned your lesson," she slurred. "You should get some sleep now."

"It's five o'clock."

"Is it?" She squinted at the digital clock on the cable box. "Huh. Well. What do you want for dinner, then? We can get something special. I'm in the mood for delivery. I was *just* thinking a burger would go good with this." She jingled the glass of bourbon and Coke at him.

The next day, Cal walked down the driveway, opened the mailbox, and out fell a letter from E.C. Warmth pumped through him as he scooped it off the ground. He figured it would be something about freshman orientation. Something to look forward to. He needed something good right now. He ripped open the letter in one hungry, ragged tear. He started to read: "Dear Calvin. We're sure you are a bright, promising individual, and we're happy to offer you a place among our rising freshman class. However, while you are still welcome on campus in the fall, in light of recent events reported by your high school, we unfortunately can no longer offer you the Spirit of Edenville Scholarship. We believe you no longer reflect the impeccable values of our institution, and . . ."

He had to stop. He couldn't see the words on the page anymore. He melted, slumping against the mailbox, unable to catch his breath. He gasped and gasped and the world swam around him and he cried and he cried and he cried.

When finally he calmed, he opened the letter again. Read its opening a second time. Further down, they said that if Cal could pay tuition in full by the deadline in two weeks, he could still attend. In other words, he couldn't attend at all. Because there *was* no money. Where was there money? Mom was drinking it all. He'd never go to college. Never do anything.

Useless.

Cal's life began to truly ache. A gnawing, blooming blackness in his throat. An oblivion more real and more crushing than any short sweet thing weed ever could have offered him.

He rationed the remaining under-bed weed as best he could. Sometimes, he just sat in his room in the dark. Stone sober, flicking the little flame of his lighter on, off. Lighting up the room, plunging it into ink. Pretending to be high. Pretending to be dead. On, off. On, off.

When he sat down to look at jobs on Craigslist, leaning over the laptop perched on his knees on his bed, there was only one thing available for miles. It'd appeared just that morning. Just in the nick of time.

Service job, it read. *No experience necessary. Call Harv to set up interview.*

"It's perfect," Cal told his mom. "And it's out of town, so I don't have to run into anybody from school."

"A miracle," said Mom. The word came sideways and slow, like everything she said.

Harv's felt like a perfect fit. It felt, finally, like something to actually kind of look forward to. It felt like purpose. It felt like a glimmer of something good.

Suffice it to say, that feeling didn't last.

On Cal's third Thursday at Harv's, there are sloppy joes. Harv makes a big vat of them on the stove. It boils and steams throughout the day, filling the kitchen with a thick saucy stench that Cal almost gags on every time he gets a whiff of it.

"Jesus," says Harv, the ninth time it happens. "If you're feelin sick, go home."

"I'm alright," says Cal, holding his nose.

"You sure?" Harv runs his eyes over Cal's face, which is getting bonier every day.

"I'm sure," Cal mutters. He moves away. He can feel Harv's eyes squirming over his body, and it makes him feel greasy. Like the sloppy joes are on him and inside him now, too. Like the whole world is sloppy, sloppy joe.

It's been a week since Cal saw those bags of weed on the tray instead of chicken, and his skeleton is getting more and more visible under his skin. Every morning, he's been analyzing himself in the mirror. He eats a little more for breakfast, for lunch, for dinner, but nothing seems to be working. He can suck in his stomach and see the outlines of his ribs. That's new. That's bad.

The regulars all recognize him now (they come every day). They're not exactly warm, but they tolerate him, which Cal appreciates. No matter how small, it's still more affection than he gets at home.

That evening, Cal slides the tray out from its place on the shelf and starts filling it with sloppy joe. He can do this with one hand, so the other hand takes out his phone and starts scrolling idly through Instagram. Since he doesn't really have any friends, his feed is just people he knew at school. He listens to Harv laughing outside the kitchen with some old wrinkle-bag as he scrolls past dozens of pictures of people he's only spoken to once or twice. They're all laughing, too. Laughing on boats, in cars, on beaches, in pools. Everybody's laughing except Cal. Even Douchebag Darren is on Instagram, posting about his last few weeks before college starts, smoking in the park and playing video games. In almost every picture, he's spewing huge clouds out of his mouth. And yet,

Cal's the one who's stuck here in the goddamn kitchen, scooping shit onto a tray. Spoonful after spoonful of goop, slopping onto the metal with thick, sucking burps. Cal keeps scrolling, feeling angrier and lower, and the sound of the slop gets worse—spoonful after spoonful of dribbling, greasy black muck, dripping off the sides of the tray and—

Cal shouts, jerks back. He drops the ladle into the vat. The tray is heaped full of sludge. Not sloppy joe, but dark, dark ooze. Black mud. Swamp mud.

Muck.

Harv bursts into the kitchen. Sees Cal standing there, all numb. "The fuck, kid? You scared the shit out of me."

Cal doesn't know what to say. He's breathing hard. Staring at the tray. The tray, of course, is filled with sloppy joe.

"You sure you don't need to go home?"

"I'm fine," says Cal.

"Uhn." Harv clicks his teeth, considering. His eyes worm over Cal's body. "Alright. Well. Hurry up. I'm hungry."

There's a blur, and Cal's alone again.

Maybe it's because Harv's never changes. Maybe that's why that brief sense of purpose Cal had is fading so fast. Everything here just *is*. Always the same. The plush critters in the skill crane will always be there. The regulars will always be there. The stray cats will always eat the food. And Cal will just keep working here. Forever.

Maybe, he thinks as he carries the tray to the back door, *it's just Thursdays.* Thursdays have always been hard. Thursday is when Dad died.

Cal sighs as he slides the deadbolts on the back door. He does the ninth one first, before he forgets, then works his way up. He puts the tray outside on the concrete stoop, then goes in, slides all the locks back. He stands there for a moment. Looks up. The ceiling is about nine feet tall. Just out of reach.

On the way home, Cal stops by a gas station. He goes into the little store. He uses some of the money Mom leaves him for gas to buy three bags of chips, a microwaveable thing of mac and cheese, two cans of onion dip, four sticks of beef jerky, a block of cheese, a box of crackers, a huge bag of mixed nuts, and eight candy bars. He eats all of it in bed, reading Dad's old copy of *Fellowship of the Ring*. He's read it before. But he likes the part at the beginning where the Hobbits have simple lives, before they're called on an adventure. He likes when Bilbo describes himself as feeling spread thin, like butter over toast. Cal reaches the end of that part, then reads it again. He likes the prologue, too. The twenty pages that just describe Hobbits in general. All sedentary and kind. When finally he sleeps, the pages of that section are smudged with chocolate and grease.

Cal wakes up the following morning to discover he's dropped another pound. He gives the scale the finger. The food was a test, and his body failed. He explores himself with both hands. Feeling around the new hollows and emptinesses. There are so many now. It makes his hands shake. He doesn't know what to do. He doesn't feel full, but he doesn't feel hungry.

He just is.

On the fourth Thursday, there's a wake. Terry (the Santa Claus, Cal's first customer) is fresh in the ground. Heart attack. Poor bastard.

"Makes sense," Harv says when he tells Cal what happened. "Guy ate nothin but potatoes."

"He seemed cool, though."

"He was." Harv nods solemnly. "But hearts don't give a shit about cool."

Some of the regulars are gathering in the diner to toast Terry's farewell. Harv ushers them all in, holding the door open for about twenty people. They're all wearing black. Not suits, but black shirts, black jeans, simple black dresses. A few black ties. They're all carrying big trays of food and deep casseroles. They start dragging several tables together, raking long marks across the carpet. Cal helps them assemble one long table, spanning almost the entire width of the diner. A few of them mumble their thanks. One guy whose name Cal has never learned pats Cal's shoulder, gives him a dead look.

Cal feels like he should say something to Harv, who's having trouble looking up from the floor today. He racks his brain for the things people said to him after Dad died that he actually appreciated.

He can't think of anything.

Harv tells him, "You can go home if you want. Everybody brought their own shit."

Cal weighs the torture of home versus the torture of the ceiling love songs. He watches the regulars pop open their various Tupperware.

"If I stay, can I read?" he asks. "I'll just sit at the bar and—"

Harv claps him on the shoulder. "Sure, kid. I'll let you know if we need anything." A blur, and he's in the kitchen.

Cal sits at the bar with a yellowing Anne McCaffrey. From the ceiling, Supertramp squeals down at him. The seat feels weird under him, and he realizes it's because his ass is skinnier.

"Goddamn," says one of the regulars. "This was Terry's favorite. Fuckin loved the Tramp."

"It's a sign," says the dead-look guy. "He's with us."

Harv reemerges from the kitchen with a stack of plates and cups. He carries it all back to the table. There's the pop of champagne, and the fizz of it draining into a slew of plastic cups.

"To Terry," says Harv.

"To Terry," they all echo.

The cups slam together. Cal hunches farther down. He can't get his elbows comfortable on the bar. They're too knobby now. He moves to a booth in the far corner. He reads a hundred pages, just sitting there. Leaning back. Listening every so often to the regulars tell stories, laugh, mourn, and shout, "To Terry."

The day becomes one long blur.

Eventually, Cal looks up. He blinks. The sun is setting. Some of the regulars have left. Some are dozing in their chairs around the table. There's leftover casserole and torn-apart bread, scooped-out dip and demolished blocks of cheese. Plates and glasses and empty bottles everywhere. Harv is at the end of the table. He looks planted there. All his big limbs and his meatball body are stiff. Immovable. Cal can almost hear the metal chair sweating under his weight.

Harv is getting bigger every day.

Cal rubs his eyes. He's exhausted. He stands, stretches, gets himself ready to slip out for the day. Then he remembers somebody has to feed the cats.

Cal sticks his hands in the pockets of his jeans (*way* too loose now). He shuffles over to the table. Harv is talking to one of the regulars (Sally). Sally leans over the table, nodding as he speaks.

Cal clears his throat. "Harv?"

Harv turns, slow, and blinks at him. "Yeah?"

"It's Thursday. We have to feed the cats."

Harv blinks at him again. "So . . . do it."

"We didn't make any food today. The grill is cold."

"Uhn." Harv looks around the table. He grabs a large dish of spaghetti and meatballs. Holds it out. "Give em this."

Cal takes it. It doesn't look like enough. Certainly not as much as Cal's been putting out every week. He doesn't want the strays to get mad. Cause trouble, as Harv put it. He wonders if he should say something.

Sally pats Harv's shoulder. She taps a pack of Noxboros against the table. Slides out one and puts it between her lips as she stands.

"Headin out, Harv," she says softly.

"Have a good." He waves her away, closing his eyes. He rests his hands on the balloon of his stomach.

Cal remains for a moment, uncertain. Then he carries the spaghetti to the kitchen. He puts it on the grill and slides out the tray. It shrieks as he takes it out. The sound makes him wince. He shovels the food onto the tray with a spatula, spattering sauce onto the floor. As he's shoveling it, for a second, the pasta turns into something else. Loose strips of paper. Crumpled and steaming. The meatballs are spitballs. Dripping, pooling around the tray.

Cal blinks, and it's pasta again.

He digs the heels of his hands into his eyes. Poor kid. He thinks he's going crazy.

He carries the tray to the back door and it feels heavier than ever. Feels like it weighs a million pounds. Or maybe he's losing muscle now, too. Maybe the thin sticks of his arms don't have any muscle *left*, and three pounds feels like three hundred.

Maybe he's dying.

Cal unlocks the door and leaves the tray on the stoop. He sees something move up on the slope, in the long shadows stretching out from the sunset. He squints at it, but it's gone. Whatever it was, it was larger than a cat. He can tell that for sure.

Cal comes back inside, locking the door behind him. When he

goes back out of the kitchen, everyone's gone except Harv. Dozing in his chair. A big, bounceless ball. Cal goes to him, tries shaking him awake by the shoulder. "Harv?"

"To Terry," says Harv, eyes closed.

Cal pulls out a chair, sits. He stretches, his back throbbing. He sighs. Poor Cal. He just sits there, worrying. Not sure what to do. He pulls at his loose jeans. Wonders what's happening to him.

He sits there for a while, listening to Harv breathe. He's about to just go home when Harv reaches out and pats his knee. It's a genuine, avuncular pat. The hand doesn't linger. There's nothing else in the gesture. Nothing weird. It just is. Cal can feel the warmth of it after it's gone. He stares down at his knee, feeling a knot cinch in his chest. Harv says, "You're good, Cal."

"Thanks." His voice is quiet.

"Good employee."

Cal nods. "Thanks."

Harv's eyes are still closed. "My last guy, before you? Kind of a lazy-ass. But not *you*." He wags a finger vaguely in Cal's direction. "You're very good. Very . . ." He trails off.

Cal looks down into his lap.

"What's your plan, Cal?" says Harv. "What are you doing after this, I mean? College?"

"I kinda got kicked out," Cal mumbles.

Harv clicks his teeth. "Uhn. Happens. What about your family? Anything to . . . go home to?"

"Don't really have one. Just my mom."

"Happens . . . What about friends? What do you do on the weekend?"

Cal shrugs. Stares harder into his lap. "Nothing. I just . . . work here and feed the cats, but . . . It's like . . ."

He pauses.

Fuck it, just say it: "It's like I'm losing something. Like every time I put out the food on that tray and carry it to the door, I'm carrying a part of me with it. Like I'm *emptying* myself. And I'm leaving myself out there for the cats to . . . gobble up. I don't know. Is that dumb?"

He looks at Harv. Harv still has his eyes closed. His breath is steady.

"Nah," says Harv. He shakes his head. Slow, side to side. "They don't gobble you up." His voice comes out in a low gravel purr. The sound of beans in a rain stick. "Nah . . ." His mouth curves upward at the edges. "I do."

A pause.

"Do what?" Cal asks.

"*I* gobble it up. I lick it off the tray when you leave. Slurp it up like . . . fuckin spaghetti. You can't shit it out, ya know. Just builds." He massages his gut like the swell of an unborn child. "But damn, the *taste* . . ." He runs his tongue over his lips. He bares those bright white teeth. They gleam in the fluorescents. "The taste . . ."

Cal stares at him. His blood is cold. He waits for Harv to say something else, but nothing else comes.

Cal stands, shaking. He waits for Harv to move. To grab him. But the man starts to snore.

Cal backs away, out the door. He walks fast to his car, sticking to the brightest parts of the lot.

As he drives home, his hands twist around the wheel. He keeps tossing this around in his head. *I lick it off the tray when you leave . . .*

He lies in bed for a long time, staring at the ceiling. Thinking. Flicking his lighter on and off. All that despair. That oblivion. That sinking, dragging feeling. He knew it. *Knew* it. He *was* dumping it all on the tray. Pouring it out of himself. Every week for an entire month. And Harv was swallowing it whole. *This* is where that weight has been going.

And is it so illogical? It sounds like something straight out of a book. Some kind of dark magic. Like Harv has cast some curse on him. It *sounds* unbelievable, but that's exactly why Cal *does* believe it. He's read enough fantasy to believe, tangentially at least, in magic. Besides, he felt cursed already. And Harv said it himself. He admitted it. *I lick it off the tray when you leave . . .*

Cal decides the strays aren't real. There are no cats at all. Just Harv, eating him off the tray. Gobbling him up.

He lies there, flicking his lighter on and off. Staring at its little flame for hours.

Harv isn't human. That's what Cal decides. Or not *fully* human maybe. A ghoul or something. The specifics don't matter. Cal keeps turning those words over and over in his head. *The taste . . .* Should he skip work tomorrow, stay at home? But there's nothing *for* Cal at home. Nothing for him anywhere.

He starts to think about running away.

He figures he should go somewhere without setting. Without time or place. Maybe he'll work on a farm and marry a farmer chick, like one of those dudes in *Of Mice and Men* or *O Brother, Where Art Thou?* His life abandoned him, so he'll abandon it back.

He has to get out.

He gets out of bed. There's a duffel bag in the basement. It used to be his dad's. The basement door is just off the living room, so he has to walk by Mom.

"Going somewhere?" she asks as he passes. There's humor in her tone, like she's almost encouraging him.

"Working on a project for Harv," says Cal. He's surprised at how easily the lie comes.

"I'm glad you're keeping busy," she slurs. Someone on the tv gets shot, drawing her attention. She sips at her drink. The rattle of the ice inside booms throughout the house.

Cal drags the duffel upstairs. He blows dust off it, wipes away an old, dead spider, and spreads the bag on his bed. He packs some clothes and some books. Three different hoodies, including the one he was wearing the day the K9 sniffed him out. It still kind of smells like pot, but maybe that's his imagination. The memory catches him off guard. Folds itself in with the hoodie as he folds it into the bag. So he unpacks the hoodie and throws it into the back of the closet to be forgotten.

Cal stands there, thinking. He stares into the black maw of the bag. It seems like it's speaking, mid-question: *Are you gonna do it?* Cal tries to think of an answer. Twirling his lighter between his fingers. Flicking it on and off. He can hear Mom downstairs, coughing. Wonders where he'll go. What he'll do. Suddenly, he's exhausted.

Tomorrow, he thinks.

He scrapes the bag onto the floor. Lies in bed for a while. Then drags the bag back up next to him. Curls himself around it. He falls asleep, hugging it to his chest.

The next day, Harv doesn't remember they had a conversation at all.

Cal doesn't go tomorrow. Or the next day, or the next. He keeps waiting for the courage. For "the moment." In the stories Cal likes to read, things happen neatly. Heroes have a call to arms. Someone important dies, or a major battle is lost, and the hero says, "No more!" Without this moment of no return, nothing would change. The hero would keep working at Harv's. Keep letting things get worse. Keep sinking into muck.

Cal's waiting for this moment, without realizing it's already come.

The poor kid.

For almost a week, he watches Harv and tries to figure out what kind of creature he is. A sausage-demon is the best he can come up with, and even that doesn't exactly make sense. He scours the little library in his room, looking for inspiration. Nothing comes. He even spends an hour flipping through this old book of Greek mythology he has, but he realizes he's barking up the wrong tree. Whatever Harv is, it's not Greek. It's not some well-known succubus. It's something unrecognizable. Something nameless. Something older.

Every day, Cal peers out the window of the diner's back door, trying to catch a glimpse of the "cats." Nothing comes. So he just keeps working. Carrying orders around. Listening to Harv and the regulars yell at each other. Listening to Bryan Adams wail about heaven—another song that seems to last all day.

Cal stands over the duffel bag every night. Flicking the lighter on and off. Watching it light up the room, casting shadows over the bag. He watches the light dance over the clothes inside. He reaches one hand up to the ceiling. Runs his fingers over the smooth surface.

Where would he go? He has no money, no plan. And would he ever be able to get himself back? Get back the weight he's lost? Or is it gone forever? Licked up by the sausage-man? That's part of what's keeping him. He's afraid he'll never get himself back.

He's scared from all angles.

One day, when Cal leaves for work, he checks the mail (as he always does), and waiting for him is another letter from E.C. A little needle of hope stabs its way into his chest (maybe *this* is his call to arms), until he opens the letter and starts reading.

The E.C. Student Accounts Office reminds him, basically, that he hasn't paid his tuition, he isn't enrolled, he shouldn't come, and he should probably just shoot himself in the eye. Something like that. The letter also reminds him that next Thursday is the first day of freshman orientation. "We remind you again not to attend."

Cal reads the letter three times. Then he smashes it into a ball between his hands and eats it.

"Goddamn," says Harv that night. "I didn't think I ate that much for breakfast, but I am fucking *full*."

"I'll bet you are," Cal mutters as he sweeps the shit-carpet. The diner is empty except for them. And Berlin, crooning overhead. Cal sweeps, and sweeps, and sweeps. He can't tell if he's breathing or if someone's already taken his breath away.

Later, Cal stands idle in Harv's kitchen. Harv is busy doing something else. Nobody's watching Cal. He eyes the knives on the counter, sitting in their little block. Cal thinks for a moment. He pulls one out. Stares at it for a second. Then he presses it down into his arm.

There'd been a rabid raccoon loose in Cal's neighborhood once. They'd finally cornered it (Cal's dad and a few of the other neighbor men), and someone shot it in the head. The thing had been so dehydrated it bled only air.

Cal runs the knife up his arm. He watches the skin pucker open. It hurts, but not that much, and nothing comes out but air.

Cal wraps the arm with a napkin. Something deep in his mind screams, *Get out get out get out*.

Every night, the duffel in his room is an open wound. Clothes bleeding out of it. He never moves the bag off the bed. It just shifts around, changing shape. Some days, it's solid and ready to go, until Cal thinks again, *But where? How?* And the bag drools out again. He hasn't slept with a stuffed thing since he was four, but he sleeps curled up with the bag every night now. This fact feels like one of his largest regressions so far. It's a solid lump of despair in his throat. He wonders what that lump would look like if he piled it onto the tray. *A potato*, he thinks. A potato that looks like a stone.

For dinner each night, Cal treats himself to a double cheeseburger with bacon, fries, and two slices of chocolate cake, all from Harv's kitchen. The next day, every day, he's lost another pound.

It's getting bad now. One morning, he's only 131 pounds. He stands there on the scale, and googles his BMI. It's fuckin bad. He looks at his ribs in the bathroom mirror. He sucks in, and his stomach turns into a canyon. He can see his heartbeat through the mountains of his ribs, like a worm trying to birth itself from under his sternum. He hates it. He breathes out so the beat of the worm squirms back inside him. He can feel it there. Sliding around. Pulsing around his skull, which he can see the outlines of now, too. He can see all of himself.

It's official, he thinks. His mother is drinking him. Harv is eating him. He's dying.

Poor kid.

And as he stands there, he feels it. Something boiling up inside him. He feels the passivity recede. He realizes the call to arms is never gonna come. It's time to make that call himself. It's time to go. Time to say *fuck* this. Fuck this life. Fuck being a shrugger, and fuck Harv's cats. It's time to get the hell out.

He steps off the scale, goes to his room, and finally zips up the duffel. Slings it over his shoulder. Breathes in. Nods to himself. He pats his pocket, makes sure the lighter is there. Looks around his room one last time. Makes sure there's nothing he's forgetting. He's good. He's got it all. He steps out into the hall.

Today is Thursday.

* * *

Everything's gray. Clouds brew overhead. It's ominous, and fitting, really. It always storms during these big moments.

Cal carries the duffel downstairs. It feels like it weighs a thousand pounds. Mom is already pouring bourbon in her coffee in the kitchen, holding her mug in one bony hand.

"You're leaving," she says. She cocks an eyebrow.

"Orientation starts today," says Cal. He shifts the bag to the other shoulder.

"Oh," she says. She stops pouring coffee. "I . . . I thought your scholarship . . ."

"I wrote another essay about my time with Harv and how transformative it was. They offered me a spot again." Cal surprises himself again with how smooth a liar he is. He'll make a good runaway.

"Oh." Mom nods, impressed. A cloud passes over her face. She puts her mug on the counter. Doesn't look at him. "Well, I . . . I'm not prepared."

"I'll be nearby. You can visit. It's, like, a half-hour drive."

"Oh, I . . ."

Never leave the house, he finishes for her. *Never have.*

"I'll miss you," she says. So soft, he can barely hear her.

Cal puts the bag on the floor. He goes to her and swallows her in a hug. She clings to him. He clings back.

"You'll be alright," he tells her. His eyes are hot and starting to water.

"I didn't . . . I don't . . ." says Mom, over and over. "I'm not . . ."

"I know," he says.

"You do?"

"I do, Mom. I love you."

"I love you."

They hold each other for a long time.

Cal is the first to let go.

When he starts to back out of the driveway, Cal sees something move in front of him. It's Mom. Coming outside. She moves onto the front porch. Her legs are stiff. She blinks unsure at the sky. She looks so old and thin. Sapped dry. Just like Cal.

Seeing her like that, he almost doesn't go. But he can't not. He can't. He let Douchebag Darren walk all over him. He let Harv eat him up. He let Mom drain his blood. It's time. He has to leave.

He waves to her. She waves back. He cranes around over the seat to see as he backs away down the drive. When he turns out onto the street, he waves again. She clings to the banister. Watching him go. Watching him leave her behind. Just like Dad.

Today, Cal's fifth Thursday at Harv's, it rains. He figures he should work one last day, pick up his paycheck, and then run. He's already got a full tank of gas, so he can go anywhere. Plus, he's taken Mom's credit card. We gotta respect him for that.

Cal watches the rain through the diner windows, turning the big gravel lot outside to rocky mud. Small rivers run down the slope behind the diner. Leaks creep in over the floor of the kitchen, through the back door. Harv slips at one point and catches himself against the fridge, which pops open, spilling vegetables. Cal and Harv laugh, and Cal thinks, *Awesome, we're bonding. I'll leave on a good note.*

He moves through the day in a fog. It feels good to just drift and know there's an end to it. That made high school bearable for Cal—knowing there was an end. It's also part of what made working at Harv's so hard. No end in sight. But today is different. He's coasting toward the finish line.

Harv's being his usual self. Shouting, banging around. His special today is meatloaf (again), so the cats (if there are any) will be getting a combination of that and fish sticks. Not a bad haul.

But as Cal slides the tray off the shelf, he stops. He looks at his arm. He can almost see right through it. There's nothing there. Just bones and skin. A slim bandage, sealing up the wound from the knife. Cal's been poking at it a bit. Folding back the skin, looking inside. He can see his muscle and bone. He can see his veins pump a weak, dribbling pulse.

If he feeds the cats one more time, he'll die.

The cats.

He goes to the back door, hoping one last time to catch a glimpse. It'd be a shame to leave with this mystery. He peers outside. And as he does, something scurries away through the mud. Cal can't be sure, but he swears it's that same pale limb he saw on his first day. Darting away between the trees. Except this time, he can tell it's definitely *not* a deer leg. He can tell by the way it bends.

He presses against the window, peering around, trying to see more. He shivers. His spine twitches like it did that first day. He looks down, and his whole body goes cold. There, in the mud by the stoop, are footprints. Human prints. It looks exactly like someone scrambled up to the stoop, looking for the tray, and then ran away up the slope.

I knew it, thinks Cal. *I fucking knew it.*

Whatever's out there, it isn't cats.

Quickly, he carries the tray back to its shelf. He slides it home behind the spices. It grates. Fuck the last paycheck. He'll figure it out. Right now, it's time to go.

A blur, and Harv is standing in front of him.

"Whatcha doin?" he asks. His teeth shine.

Cal stops. Swallows. "I . . . I'm leaving early today."

Harv's eyes flick up at the tray. They're like separate living things, those eyes. Like the heads of worms living in Harv's skull. They flick back to Cal. "Goin home?"

"Yeah."

"To what?"

"Sorry?"

"To *what*." The eyes are moving again. Wriggling around. Harv grins wider. The picket-fence teeth seem to grow. "*What* are you going home to?"

Cal swallows again. *Stupid.* He should have left before this. Now he's stuck inside with inhuman Harv. What if Harv makes him stay? He's too thin. One more feeding and he'll be done. He'll be entirely gone. He has to think of something.

Cal and Harv just stare at each other.

Finally, Harv laughs. "Jesus, kid. I was just asking you a fuckin—"

Cal bolts.

Harv is standing between him and the entrance, so he books it down the dim hall, toward the back door. Harv shouts after him, starts waddling down the hall. Cal throws back the deadbolts, tries to open the door.

It won't go.

For a blind-panic second, Cal's done. He's fucked. Until he remembers: the bottom lock.

He tosses it back the other way, and the door swings open.

A blur—Harv's snatching at his hoodie. Cal swings himself out of it, tearing his arms from the sleeves. As he struggles, he feels something wriggling up his elbow. Feels two long thin tendrils of something moving over his skin, and the only thing he can think of is Harv's eyes, wriggling out of the man's skull. He doesn't look, he just runs for the slope and the woods and the rain. The electric fence hums at his side as he climbs. There must be a gap in it farther up, by the granite wall. There *must* be, he figures. *Gotta* be . . . *please.*

The slope is steep. Cal keeps slipping as he tries to run. The rain beats at him. Pushing him down. Making him slip around in the mud and the gunk. He digs at the muck and the fallen leaves, cutting his knuckles and palms against the trash and fallen branches. He's panting, heart working overtime. He climbs and climbs and climbs. He's weak. So weak. He claws at a small branch on a young tree, using it to hoist himself up, and he realizes his arm is as small as the branch. A used condom sticks to his hand and he flicks it away. He clings to the thin trunk of the tree, panting. His whole body is throbbing. Weak, so weak. He feels dizzy, about to pass out. It's too much exercise for such a frail body. He retches, spits on the ground. He wipes the rain out of his eyes. He looks back down the slope. The door is shut. Harv isn't following him.

Cal lets out a little laugh. He thinks he's made it. He really does. The poor kid. We almost feel bad for him. And we hardly *ever* feel bad. For *any* of you.

He looks around. The sun is setting. The shadows are longer. It's already dim, with the rain, and getting dimmer. Dark is starting to slither over him, stretching across the ground. He looks down upon the diner, nestled into the crook of this curved hill. And all along the ridge is that electric fence. Tall and deadly. Blocking him in. There's no gap in it. Why would there be?

He's trapped.

As he stands there, catching his breath, there's an electric *clang* and the lights whoosh on. Flooding the parking lot below with brilliant white. Cal can see his car at the far end of the lot. He can see his duffel bag in the backseat. He can see everything from up here. And suddenly, he realizes why the place looks so militaristic: It's a pen. The diner is a guard outpost. Floodlights to catch escapees. It's a fucking prison complex. And he's just run right into the heart of it.

Stupid.

He licks his lips, looks around again. There's no way past the fence. The only way down is through the lot. Through the lights.

Or he can go farther up, toward the granite wall atop the hill. And the strays.

He looks up the slope. It's dark up there. Old plastic containers and bottles and random debris seem to glow in the dimming light and storm.

Cal should have just gone down into the lot. He should have gotten into his car and driven away. Harv might have let him, too, we don't know. He might have shot him. Blown chunks out of him with the rifle as soon as Cal stepped out the front door. Harv might have ground him up and fed him to the regulars as meatloaf, as cheeseburgers, as sloppy joe. That probably would have been better than what Cal chose. Quicker, at least. Because what Cal does instead is head farther up. Thinking maybe, *maybe*, there's a way out up there, hidden in the granite.

There isn't.

He works his way slow up the rest of the slope. Goes from tree to tree, trudging through heaps of trash and leaves. Kicking over old tires and laundry hampers, getting tangled up in garbage bags. A river of rain knocks him down at one point and he has to just sit there for a minute, catching his breath again. The world goes blurry. Cal blinks rapidly to stop himself from passing out. He makes himself stand. Knees shaking. He makes himself keep moving.

Somewhere in the back of his mind, he thinks of Mount Doom. He thinks of climbing the impossible, making it to the top, and getting swooped away to safety by the eagles. He thinks about falling asleep in their safe grasp. Looking up at the sky. Running his fingers along its perfect surface as he's driven home . . .

At last, he makes it to level ground. He bends over. Puts his hands on his knees. Breathes hard. He feels like his heart is going to break through his ribs. He puts a hand to it. Feels it kick at him. The world is swimming around him. He wastes several minutes waiting for it to slow.

It's full dark now. Cal takes the lighter out of his pocket. Flicks it on. Orange light spreads in a wide sphere around him. He can see the slope below him. The red neon of the diner bleeding through the trees. And, no more than three feet in front of him, the wall. A slick sheet of granite, jutting out of the ground and rising dozens of feet into the air. Plain and formidable. No breaks in its surface. Cal moves his hand around, pointing the light in both directions, but the wall doesn't end. It stretches on and on, all across the slope, right up to the fence.

Cal's stomach sinks. He was wrong. So wrong. The only way out is back down. Through the lights.

Cal gazes up at the massive expanse of rock. He hates it, hates himself. He should have just gotten in the car and left this morning. Gone apple picking out west for the rest of his life. Screw that last paycheck. Screw this stupid diner. And screw—

Cal spots a dark patch in the rock.

He frowns, gets closer. The patch reveals itself to be a small, jagged cave. About five feet tall. Carved into the face of the granite.

The lighter goes out.

Of course, Cal thinks. *It's finally out of fuel. Of* course *it's doing this* now.

He shakes it, listens to the soft slosh of liquid inside. There's still a little left. He lights it. It illuminates the mouth of the cave again. Cal steps closer. He hears something move inside. Rock clattering against rock. The slippery wet slap of skin against cave. Bare feet, padding around. He stops, listens. Silence. A full silence. The kind that feels shared. As if something is listening back.

Cal steps forward again. Broken glass crunches under his shoe. The sound echoes throughout the cave mouth. Cal dips his head. He steps inside the cave. It's cold in here, and silent. The walls are smooth, the floor and ceiling rounded together. As if someone has carved a perfect cylinder into the rock.

The lighter goes out and the dark swallows him.

Cal shakes the lighter, heart pounding. He hears something move deep inside the cave, and frantically, he rolls the wheel of the lighter with his thumb. It sparks, but doesn't catch. Movement again, closer this time. Cal tries the lighter again. A spark, then nothing. He shakes it again, and again there's the sound of feet padding against stone. Closer, and closer. Cal tries the lighter one more time, and this time the spark catches, lights up, and he's surrounded by faces.

Thirty of them, at least. Skeletal, pale, almost translucent. Cal can see networks of veins beating beneath their skin. Pulsing. Their eyes are wide hollows sunk back into their faces. Their hair is clusters of limp noodles. They squat around him in a wide crowd. Some of them hiss at the light, hold up their hands. Cal can see their teeth, or what's left of them. Rotted black kernels. And their hands—long, inhuman. Ghoulish. All of their limbs are like that. Slightly too long, too thin. Most of them are wearing loose, dirty, threadbare jeans and shirts, some kind of ragged hoodie or sweater. A few of them are shirtless, and Cal can see the worm of their heartbeat, just like his.

Just like him.

A blur—one lunges at him, knocking the lighter from his hands. Cal hears a crunch, and realizes, too late, that someone has crushed the lighter beneath their heel.

Next thing he knows, they're pawing at him. Digging into his clothes, gripping his flesh, or what's left of it. Their voices are strained, dry. Quick wheezes and gasps, wails and broken growls. First, they're complimenting him:

"Thank you for the fish sticks."

"We liked the fish sticks."

"Fish sticks."

"Fish sticks."

A chorus of snakes, smiling in adoration. Drooling at the thought. "Fish sssticksss."

Then, they're pawing harder, harder. Shaking him. Slapping him, shoving him, asking questions:

"Where's the food?"

"What day is it?"

"What's *your* name?"

"Have you seen my uncle?"

"Are my parents still alive?"

"Does anyone remember me?"

"What year is it?"

"Did we win the war?"

Cal screams, shoves them away. They hiss, clawing deeper. Their nails burrow into the skin of his arms, his shoulders, his legs.

"You don't matter," they screech. "You don't matter, you don't matter, they won't remember you, they won't care, that's why he *picked* you. You don't matter!"

Cal kicks out into the dark. His foot lands against something soft. He feels it snap. One of the things howls, and the grip of the others loosens. Just a little. Cal drives a shoulder into one. It screams, a high keening that nearly bursts Cal's eardrums. He drives the creature back against the wall, pinning it by the throat to the granite. It claws at him with all four limbs like a monkey. Other hands start pawing at Cal's back. One reaches under a shoulder blade, gripping the bone in its fingers. It pulls. Cal screams again as pain rockets through his body. It feels like his spine is being torn out, which it kind of is. He slams his head back, connects with something, hears a pop. More howling and wailing. Cal whirls around, makes a dash back to the cave mouth. He can make it. He can slide down the slope, into the light. Maybe Harv will let him go. Maybe he'll show mercy.

But Harv is waiting at the back door of the diner, rifle in hand. He hears Cal scream, up there in the cave. He grins—those long white dominos—and turns the ninth bolt. As he does, a door slams shut over the mouth of the cave.

Cal runs into it headfirst, forehead smacking against its surface. Stars explode behind his eyes. He falls back onto the ground. His head cracks against the rock.

And they're on him again. One of them sits on his chest, patting at his face with reeking, stinking, sticky fingers. The rest of them paw at his clothes, his hoodie. One digs into his pocket, takes out his car keys, crunches them between its teeth. Cal can see the little sparks as it chews.

Before he blacks out, they're asking him more questions:

"Do you know what year it is?"

"Do you know my aunt?"

"Are my parents still looking for me?"

"Is the high school still there?"

"Does anybody know my name?"

"Did we win the fucking *war*?"

Then laughter, like the sound of breaking glass, shattering throughout the cave. They press against him, pawing at his clothes. Tugging at him. Laughing at him. Covering him. They jump on him, stomping, flattening. Pressing him down. He feels himself break. Feels his ribs pop out of place and flatten. He feels his hips crack and shift as the strays crush and crush him flat. He feels them pounding out the pounds. Spreading him thin, like Bilbo Baggins. Crushing the last little weight out of him. Turning him into one of them.

They do it and they laugh.

Harv puts the gun back under the grill. He smiles to himself, licks his teeth. He takes out his laptop, and begins putting the ad back up on Craigslist.

We have to give him credit. He is a *very* efficient creature. And we like him because he always gives us the cars so we can scrap them for parts. The stuff in Cal's duffel bag—all those clothes and books and memories—Harv just burns.

Months later, when the new kid comes into the cave, skinny and scared just like the rest, Cal's teeth have rotted away. His hoodie is rags. His voice is the rasp of a whetting blade. He jumps at the kid with the others and asks, demands, *has* to know: "Did you see my mom? Is my mom out there? Have you seen my mom? Is she still alive? Did she ask about me? Does she wonder where I am? Is she looking for me? Do you know a Darren? What did *you* do? Why did he pick *you*? Are you a lazy fuck? Are you? You lazy fuck. Why did he pick *you*?"

The new kid screams, runs, slams headfirst into the door of the cave. Cal jumps on him, paws at him, tells him he doesn't matter. He eats the kid's keys. They taste like death.

He laughs with all the other strays.

From: Rachel Durwood <radurwood@bhs.org>
To: tom.durwood@gmail.com
Re: The Stain

Nobody knows what exactly drew the Renfields here in the first place, far north in the New York woods. The earliest record of them comes from the early 18th century, a time when thousands of Dutch and German immigrants were settling along the Hudson and in the Mohawk Valley. A fur tradesman named George Haywood passed through Renfield on his way south from Fort Frontenac, back when the county was nothing more than a sparse cluster of homesteads along the lake. In a letter addressed to his sister in Montreal, dated April 9, 1732, Haywood names two distinct families: the Renfields and the Bartricks. He calls them all "fine, strong folk" and claims that the valley is so peaceful, the "lake so inviting," that he might end up settling there himself. (Sidebar: I think it's ironic that Bartrick Lake could ever be considered "peaceful," but I guess it must have been. Haywood also describes the Bent River as "sanguine," which I think is *hilarious*.) Anyway, according to a marriage certificate between Haywood and one Lillian Frye from September 1733, he apparently did, he stayed here. He even built the Lillian Trading Co., which, of course, blossomed into the town of Lillian in 1752, just three years before Renfield County became an officially incorporated settlement.

What's interesting is that there's no record of the Renfields before Haywood stumbled across them. The Bartricks can be traced to a group of Dutch immigrants from New Amsterdam, but it's almost as if the Renfields just . . . appeared. So, like, why? How? Well, maybe something *had* been waiting. Maybe something old and cruel birthed them from the forest, the mist, and the pines, and simply bided its time until the right moment, yearning for centuries to be set loose upon the land. Through blood. Through Lawrence. Maybe all the Renfields before him felt it, too, they just didn't act on it. Or maybe they did—and history just refused to write it down.

This is, of course, all speculation. Nobody knows for sure. Not even Detective Walter Harren, with his pages and pages of notes and theories about the benefits of eating babies or whatever. *I* certainly don't know.

And that's the big problem: I. Don't. Know.

But here's a fact: When Lawrence killed his family, acting either on the whim of some sleeping giant or of his own accord, he made murder part of the county itself. He made it part of the name. Part of the land. He made it a part of everyone who lives here.

The people outside this valley don't know: Death governs here.

And if you weren't totally sure about that, here's one final piece of this history report:

At approximately 4 p.m. on Tuesday, July 17, 2018, Mom cut her wrists with a paring knife. You knew that already, of course.

But did you know that the handle of the knife she did it with was made of wood? Yep. A long piece of well-stained cedar. Did you know that the Renfields used cedar in their living room, in the floors and walls? Did you know that Mom bought *me* that knife at the Mill Flea Market? That I wouldn't take it? That she called me ungrateful and that it snowballed into this insane argument, all over text? That I texted her, "I don't want to talk about this anymore," and then three minutes later (*three minutes*, Tom), she texted me, "Goodbye then." Did you know that something *happened* in those three minutes? That somehow, in the same space of time it took Lawrence Renfield to kill his entire family, Mom decided to die, too?

Did you know that?

Did you know that's why this matters so much to me? Do you see *why* I need this to be Renfield's fault, not mine?

Did you know that I'm holding that same knife *right fucking now*?

Oh yeah. I can feel it hum. It burns, and it's cold. And I can feel it . . . I don't know how to explain this . . . I can feel it *tasting* me through my skin . . .

But at least I can feel *something*, Tom.

At least I don't feel alone.

GLITCH

Beer just made Tom more depressed. Chips, too. He knew that. But fuck it, this was all he was good at. Becca had made that clear enough. Not with any specifics. She hadn't said as much. In fact, she hadn't said anything, just "Goodbye, Tom." But the way she made him *feel* when she left like that? She didn't need to *say* anything. He was a fat, unlovable sack. The very act of her leaving made that abundantly clear. Otherwise she would have stayed, right? She would have said something. At least given a reason after four solid years together. But no. Nothing. That's what people did. They just left. Even his own *family*. First Mom and then Rachel. Though honestly, Rachel had been leaving off and on for a long damn time.

Rachel was one of those people who talk incessantly about their own issues, to the point that most of the issues begin to feel made up after a while. Like, how can you go from one boiling pot of drama to another *so* rapidly? How do people live their lives hopping from one catastrophe to the next? Can't they see that these catastrophes might not *actually be* catastrophes but mere episodes in a television show you've somehow made yourself the main character in? Always gotta create more conflict for another season, right?

Tom hated that energy. She'd grown into it over time, and he'd drifted from her because of it. Because how many times can you *truly* be too busy to text someone back? Such bullshit. And then, on the few occasions when the energy in the conversation was light enough, if she was having a calm-enough day, Tom would share some of his own personal pains, and Rachel would say, "I didn't know that was happening to you. I'm so sorry. You can tell me this stuff, ya know, you don't have to bottle it up. *Why* don't you tell me this stuff?" After years of this, Tom eventually just gave her this blank stare whenever she said that. A vacant gape he hoped said, *Please just leave me alone*.

So whatever she's texting, and calling, *and* fucking emailing him about tonight—it can't possibly be important. No matter how important she *thinks* it is. No, fuck her. Probably just being a manic bitch, as always. This wasn't the first novel-length email he'd ever gotten from her, so how was he supposed to have the energy to give a shit? Some bullshit about Mom had her freaked out, he figured. Whatever. Like he needed any more shit about Mom. Fuck her, too, in fact. She didn't love her kids enough to stick around for em? Fine by Tom. Good riddance. She was poison, too.

Please, he begs his phone. *Please just leave me alone.*

Really, who *cared* if he drank and ate himself to death in front of the tv like this? Who cared if this was how he'd spent the last two weeks? Nobody. And clearly it was all he was good at, so.

That was actually unfair. He was also good at tying his brain in knots, trying to figure out what it was about himself that made Becca leave. Trying to come up with a reason. Counting all the things it could have been, and hating himself for them, was something Tom was *very* good at. And burying those feelings beneath bags of chips and hours of Netflix was also something at which he considered himself pretty goddamn talented.

On this particular night, Tom was inhaling episodes of a dark and bloody sci-fi series Becca would have hated. A mystery with aliens. The main character was a robot, but he didn't know it yet.

Mysteries made Becca anxious. She'd even cringed when Tom had tried to talk to her about what happened with Mom. The unknown made her uneasy, and, aside from Instagram, she didn't really trust technology. This show wouldn't have been her thing at all.

Tom relished it. The darkness, the blood, the brooding robot protagonist. He kept the volume spitefully loud.

He reached down to the six-pack on the floor in front of the couch. He slid his empty into its old slot in the carrier and slid a full one out. He whacked it open against the coffee table. The bottle cap went clattering, lost, forgotten, somewhere across the hardwood floor, coming to rest in the dust with the four others Tom had already forgotten about since he sat down.

He was usually cleaner than this. Usually, he'd gather up the caps. He'd wipe his hands on a napkin instead of licking the chip grit off himself like an animal. But recently, he *felt* like an animal, so fuck it. He drank deep. Shoved a hand into the bag at his side. Scooped up a thick fistful of rancid salt and vinegar chips. He let them cut into his gums, the roof of his mouth.

The tv blared.

Yeah, this was him. This was all he was worth. Becca was right to cut it off, whatever her reason had been. Was it him, was it her, was it the fact that she'd had to go to the funeral with him and see his stupid hometown? Who cared. He didn't need her. Didn't need *anybody*. He had his beer, his tv, his chips. *This* he was good at. So fuck it.

Right?

Fuck it.

He ate.

He drank.

On the tv, blue-skinned things with tentacles for eyes shot at each other. One exploded. Another lost an arm. Bright yellow juice sprayed across the screen as the arm flew off at the socket. Tom lapped it all up. Becca would have made him turn it off. But the—

Something beeped.

He thought it was something in the show. Or maybe the tv glitched for a second. He didn't think about it. Took another sip of beer. More chips. He scratched at the stubble he was letting grow out. The stubble Becca hadn't been able to *stand*. The—

Something beeped.

Tom sucked the inside of his cheek between his teeth. Gnawing at it as he paused the tv and sat still, listening. Silence, except the sound of his blood pumping in his ears. He jerked his shoulders, dismissing it, and turned the tv back on.

Half a minute passed.

And then something beeped.

Tom paused the tv and sat up. He moved his eyes about the room, trying to catch the source. He sat there for a full minute before the sound went off again.

He sighed, stood. Walked to the center of the room, still holding his beer. He listened. Sure enough, another beep came. Just a short, sharp electric ping. Almost like a smoke detector, except he didn't have a smoke detector.

Tom walked in a small circle around the living room. Stood by the window. The tv. The couch. He stood by the doorway leading to the hall. But everywhere he stood, the beep sounded exactly the same. Never louder or softer, and always just slightly to his right.

"The fuck."

He walked into the hall. Listened. The sound came again, just as loud. He stood stock-still, counting the seconds. Sixty-three before the beep chimed again. Tom counted again, not moving. The next beep came after forty-five seconds. Then a minute and a half. Twenty-three seconds. Thirty-nine. Two minutes, one second.

"The *fuck*."

Tom peered down the hall, trying to hear if the sound was coming from the bathroom or the bedroom—somewhere else in the apartment. Even hidden, maybe, in the hall closet. After the next beep, he took a step forward. Listened for the next one. Then stepped back. Listened for the next. But it didn't change. It was the same volume, the same pitch. Still just a little off to his right.

He went into the kitchen. Listened. Put his ear against the fridge. Listened. Leaned over the stove. Fucking *listened*.

Nothing. No matter where he went, the beep sounded exactly the same, continuing at odd intervals.

Tom scratched his head. Nibbled again at the inside of his cheek. A hot, irritated wave rolled through his blood. He could feel the beginning itch of anger. On top of everything else, he was an idiot now, too. Couldn't figure out what should have been a relatively simple puzzle.

Stupid. Worthless.

He lifted his beer and started to take a long drag off the bottle when the sound exploded into his ear. He jerked his head back. Blinked. Held the bottle in front of his face. He waited. When it came again, the beep was very loud and very close.

Of course. The sound was coming from *inside* the bottle.

It made him laugh, it made so much sense. This entire time, the bottle had been in his right hand.

Of course.

He stared into the bottle. The glass was too dark to see if anything was floating around inside. But when he held it up to his ear, he could hear the beeping clear as crystal.

He brought the bottle to the kitchen sink and turned it over. He watched the liquid gush out of its mouth. Watched it froth down into the drain, sizzling and churning and gone.

But nothing else came out.

He tilted the bottle back and stared into its open mouth. It beeped again.

"Fucking . . ."

He put the bottle on the counter. Anger. Embarrassment. His cheeks burned, like Becca was in the room with him, judging. She was always judging. Maybe *that* was the reason: she'd run out of things to judge. His weight, his intelligence, his taste in music, movies, books . . . He could almost hear her voice, lurking in the corners of his mind. Judging judging judging. He needed to drown it all out. To sit back down, open another beer, pour more chips on top of her. He needed to bury her.

But this beeping.

He didn't know what to do. He stared at the empty bottle, hands at his sides. It beeped again. Definitely taunting him now. He ground his teeth into the flesh of his cheek, trying to figure it out. He scratched at the back of his head, and, for the second time, the beep exploded at him.

Very loud and very close.

Tom froze, hand still on his head. He stayed like that for a minute. Waiting.

It beeped.

Slowly, Tom moved his hand in front of his face. He stared at his palm.

It beeped.

Tom sucked a stab of air through his teeth. He blinked. His hand—he was positive it was his hand now—beeped again. He turned his head, put his ear against the back of his hand. It beeped instantly. Deafening, and slightly to the left. He moved the back of his hand around against his ear, listening to each repetition of the tone, until it chimed directly over his ear canal. He listened to it beep three times in a row, just to be sure.

He smiled.

He took his hand away. Stared at it. Turned it over. Flexed his fingers, like he might feel the thing beeping in there. When, of course, he didn't, he brought his hand close to his face. Inspected it. Listened to it beep another four times. Just to be double-sure.

He went back to the living room. Turned on the lamp. Moved his hand around under its light. Ran his fingers over the skin. Tried to feel something in there. Some lump or irregularity. He squinted in the light to see if anything was visible.

Nothing.

The entire time he was poking and prodding and moving his hand around, it kept beeping at him. Beeping and beeping.

The taste of blood bloomed in Tom's mouth and he realized he'd bitten through the flesh of his cheek. He realized how anxious the entire thing was making him. How desperately he needed to solve this. To have it be over. Because the longer he was away from the couch, the more solid Becca's voice became. It was starting to worm into his very bones now. He could almost hear her, like she was right there: *You fat asshole . . .* He knew the beer and chips made it worse. *Worthless sack of shit.* But fuck it, right? *Something's wrong with you.* Well, fuck it, if he was sitting down and distracted. But being alone with himself like this, probing himself in silence, and this fucking beeping? *I don't know how I put up with you so long.* No. This he could not abide. *This* he needed to be over.

He stood there by the lamp for a long time, thinking. He closed his fist. Opened it. He began to breathe quickly. Deep rushing gusts through his nostrils.

He went into the hall.

The X-acto knife lived in a basket of odds and ends he kept in the hall closet. He took the basket off the top shelf and pawed through the screwdrivers, light bulbs, other shit, until he found what he was looking for.

He carried the knife into the bathroom, holding it out in front of him like it might break or bite him. His hand beeped again as he turned on the bathroom light, making him wince. Its tones were piercing now. Nails driving into his head. He took a bottle of alcohol, tweezers, and a roll of gauze out of the medicine cabinet. Took the towel from the rack. Brought them all into the kitchen and dumped them onto the table. Stood there, staring at them. Breathing even harder.

He couldn't be sure, but he thought the sounds were coming more quickly now.

Tom took a moment to appreciate himself. He was being a man of action. He was going to find the solution to this puzzle. He was going to figure out what was making this sound. What was squatting inside of him that kept fucking beeping. He was actually *doing* something, for the first time in weeks. He just took a moment to be proud of that.

Maybe he wasn't so stupid or worthless after all.

Maybe he could even tell Becca about this. Give her a call.

Tom sat down. He took the knife in his left hand. Hesitated. Dropped it, and stood. He flapped his hand back and forth. Flexed the fingers. He unspooled his belt from around his waist. Sat down. Put the belt between his teeth. Bit into the leather. Bunched the towel up by the edge of the wooden table, around his wrist. Picked up the knife. He moved the slide up. Listened to it click twice. The blade was half an inch out. He knew that if he hesitated any more at all, he would never do it, and she had always chastised him for being indecisive, so without thinking he slipped the blade into the back of his hand and worked it down toward his wrist, careful to avoid the blue bulge of his vein, and feeling his teeth grind into the leather as long shanks of razor-wire pain clawed up his flesh and swam up his arm into his shoulder. It was hot and he ground his teeth into the belt. There was very little blood at first. It spread in two thin lines down the sides of his hand, onto the towel. But the pain made his eyes go wide. His skin was tougher than he thought, and he had to move the knife up and down, sawing as he went. Hacking at the muscle. He almost couldn't stand the sound it made. Thick, wet rip and hiss. Like cutting a ripe tomato. He thought he might faint. Collapse onto the table, twitching, bleeding out. But he didn't stop moving until he'd made a line big enough to push the tweezers in. When he had, he dropped the knife. Picked up the tweezers. He blinked several times, trying to keep his eyes open against the millions of burning needles shooting up his wrist. His shoulder screamed, but he couldn't stop. He drove the tweezers between the folds of skin and began to dig. He could feel the tissue, the muscle, sliding around across the metal as he pushed his way deeper. Deeper. His hand beeped again, but he could hardly hear it. The tweezers grazed against something hard and a shock went through the base of his body. Like the entire world was suddenly the teeth-break feeling of nails on chalkboard. Bone. He'd hit bone. He slid the tweezers back out, sending three new streams of blood spurting over the towel, the table. He picked up the knife again. He cut sideways this time, making a neat crosshatch in the center of his hand. The knife caught against a tendon, and another bright shock cracked through him. He wriggled the knife, pulled, tore straight through the cord, hearing it, feeling it *snap* against the blade. The pain was awesome. Blinding. Like it might split his skull in half, and he had to blink so many times to stop the table from rippling and swimming away. Something fell off his face, dropped into the wound, burned, and he realized he was pouring sweat. He let the knife clatter to the table, spattering blood onto his clothes. His hand shook as he took the tweezers again, and his hand beeped as he dove into himself once more. He worked the tweezers back and forth, rooting around in his flesh for something, *anything*. He hit bone again and again and again. His skull boomed. His ears howled a steady airplane-engine roar. His entire arm throbbed like it was filled with broken glass. The table swung to the side. The room burst into static. Tom began to slide off his chair. He shook his head, willed himself to keep going. The wound wept openly now, blood pulsing from all angles. He kept digging. Thought briefly about how Becca might react if she could see him now. If she could see his *drive*. Finally, he felt something catch around the tweezers. Excited, he pulled back, and the something popped. A deep pressure. The blood came harder. Dark red, almost-black rivers, gushing out against his skin. He ignored it. Dug deeper, until he could feel the ends of the tweezers jab through the skin of his palm. He'd gone all the way through himself. He pulled the tweezers back out. They came up caked in gore and empty, and he could see the pinpricks of light coming through his hand like eyes.

But other than that?

Nothing.

He picked up the knife again, and stopped himself at last. It was too much. He was shaking too much. Blood was cascading onto the floor in bright crimson waves. *It'll stain*, he thought. He wondered briefly if he could spread the Renfield poison here, to this apartment in Brooklyn. If you grew up around bloodywood and then *you* bled onto some *other* wood, would the effect transfer? Was it *in* him like that? Was *that* why she left him, could she *feel* it?

Oh man, listen to this. He didn't believe in that shit. And he wasn't going to find whatever it was, the beeping thing. He should go to a hospital. Check himself in somewhere. Get stitches. An X-ray. Psychiatric help. Seriously, *look* at him. He was probably dying.

But no. He could do this. He didn't need anybody's help. He'd figure himself out on his own, just fine. Then he'd patch himself up. The gauze and the alcohol would do. And he had thread somewhere, probably. A needle. No, he didn't have a needle, now that he thought about it. Fuck it, a toothpick would be fine. He'd tie a thread around the dull end and just grit his teeth.

He could do this.

But his hand was still shaking too hard. He dropped the knife. Let his fingers go limp. He leaned forward. Moved his head around, examining the insides of the crosshatch. Trying to see among the torn flesh and muscle, the oozing veins and white bones. Bones. He could see his own bones.

But other than that?

Nothing.

But there *had* to be something. Didn't there? Otherwise he wouldn't be beeping like that. There had to be a reason. Had to be *some*thing. The very act of the beeping made that abundantly clear. He just didn't know what that something was.

He sat there, pulsing onto the table. Staring into himself. Lost. Alone.

Something beeped.

"Fuck it."

Tom picked up the knife, clicked the blade up another half inch, and tore at himself relentlessly until he was gone.

From: Rachel Durwood <radurwood@bhs.org>
To: tom.durwood@gmail.com
Re: The Stain

So that brings us to today: September 22, 2018.

Whew. I'm trashed, man.

Well, just write back, "Fuck you, Rachel!" I've totally earned it. This is what I've been doing instead of reaching out? Researching a ghost story? Insane, I know. And not fair to you. Sorry. You're totally within your rights to write back, "Fuck off."

Just please write *something*.

You know, an ex of mine (remember Ryan from the Mill? The guy who disappeared when I was a freshman at E.C.?), he told me once that siblings are the best partners, because they understand what your growing-up was like better than anybody. So I'm hoping you don't just write me off here. But tell me: Am I crazy? Does this all . . . fit? Or are these just random pieces? Am I grasping at straws here? I don't want to be, but . . .

And don't worry, I'm not gonna *do* anything with the damn knife. I'm just . . . holding it. For safekeeping.

Well. Alright. I spose it's time to sign off. I have better shit to do than beating my head against this wall.

But I do actually want to add one more piece before I log off tonight. It's maybe the most important one. The most convincing, I think. It's not about Renfield. It's not about weird creatures or giants or anything like that.

It's about us:

Did Grandma ever tell you her house had a slab of Renfield wood in the attic? It did. You could see the stain across the top of a board in the annex, a few yards away from the trapdoor. I only went up there once, when I was ten. That was after she told me everything about Lawrence Renfield. She was the one who first told me about the murders, the giant, the blood. We were alone at her place that night. I don't remember where you were. If I was ten, you would have been nine, so you were . . . wherever you were when you were nine. Anyway, Grandma told me, "Only people looking for trouble bought wood from the barn." And when I asked her what she meant by that, she said it was because the house was history, but the barn was a curse.

"There's a curse all over the county," she said. "People find it under the stairs, in their closets. My friend Nancy was redoing her bedroom, pulled off the old wallpaper, and there was a big stain right *there* over her bed. She'd been living there for *years* and never knew. She said she almost considered selling right there and then. Said if it was cursed wood, it probably explained her migraines and nightmares."

We were sitting by her fireplace in that big living room she had, up in the Mill. That cottage with one floor and the little loft she used as her office. I was sitting on the living room floor on that huge rug, and Grandma was in that great green armchair in the corner. I'd asked her to tell me a scary story before bed because it was October. But I hadn't expected Lawrence Renfield. She spoke to me for almost an hour over the rim of a mug of decaf coffee (of course—that fuckin coffee). Her eyes looked like they were on fire. I was riveted to the floor, my legs crisscrossed, drained of blood, all numb. There was wind outside, and I wish I could say something spooky like *it rattled the windowpanes* or *it howled*. Something predictable. I feel like, at the time, that might have made me feel better? Something recognizable, from *Scooby-Doo* or whatever? But it was worse than that. The wind was silent. You could just see the trees churning in the dark outside.

Grandma kept going: "My friend Susan bought a sewing table at a garage sale. Fine condition, not a scratch. But there was curse smeared all over one of the legs. Dark, too. Must have come from the giant's hair. Or its eyes. And the very next day, her husband divorced her. Swear to God." She drank. She smiled at me as she swallowed. "There are people who have history in their homes, and they go through their whole lives with nothing but a spooky conversation piece. But people with barnwood always seem to draw trouble. Migraines and divorces are only part of it."

I hated how she smiled when she said that. Like it was exciting. Like this was just a story, and not some very real thing. I hated the way she called it *history*. She said there was *history* in every house. *History* spread throughout our entire town, and all the towns around it. Even in her attic. It was like she was proud.

Her eyes kept dancing around over my head, like she was checking in with someone behind me. Do you remember Grandma's eyes? It's been a while since she passed, but I wonder, if I saw those eyes again, would I describe them as "sharp but distant," the same words the *Lillian Journal* used to describe Lawrence's before he died?

She asked if I wanted to see the stain in her attic, but I shook my head. I wasn't ready yet.

"Well," she said. "Then it's time for bed, Rachel."

As I rose from the rug, I remember having the impression that I didn't want to know what Grandma had been looking at when she'd been looking past me. I glanced back fast at the room as I left it, and

I swear someone was there, in the corner. Firelight moved in giant shapes along the wall. *Giant* shapes.

I had nightmares for weeks about someone stealing our door just like somebody stole the Renfields', then coming inside and stealing me. And after that night, the two or three times I left the county and came back, my throat would tighten as I passed that sign: WELCOME TO HISTORIC RENFIELD COUNTY.

A month later, when we were visiting Grandma for Thanksgiving, I got curious. You were downstairs eating some snacks, watching tv (as always), and Mom and Grandma were arguing in the kitchen (as always), so I snuck up into the attic to see the stain. I'd thought about it a lot, and I was ready to see this shit.

The attic ceiling was low. I had to walk hunchbacked through what seemed like miles of cobwebs, all clinging to my skin, before I reached the annex. When I found it, I had a hard time seeing the stain because the little flashlight I'd brought was shaking too hard in my hand, the light bouncing in these wild, knifing arcs. I could see my breath steaming in the light, misting my view of an ancient, foot-wide ripple of dried Renfield.

It was scary as hell. I looked at it for maybe ten seconds before I felt something crawling over my bones. Like a rat scrabbling around the pole of my spine. Looking for something. Digging. Somehow, I *knew* that if it found what it was looking for, something bad would happen to me. I'd get a divorce or a migraine, even though I wasn't really sure what those were yet. I just knew they were Bad. So I made myself look away from the stain, and the feeling drained out of me, like I'd peed my pants.

I ran to the trapdoor. When I got back down into the house, I checked myself for the cobwebs I'd felt clinging to me. But there was nothing there. Nothing at all on my clothes. Something *else* had been sticking to me up there, whispering over my skin in the dark.

I had a bad taste in my mouth for the rest of the day, kind of gritty and milky. That night, I brushed my teeth until all my gums bled. And even then, I had a dream that someone was whispering to me secrets about my spine I never wanted to know. When I woke up, I'd forgotten what those secrets were. But the voice, like ice and gravel, I remember to this day.

About a year later, Mom told me, "I used to go up there at night with my friends. We'd light a candle and ask May or Adelaide if they were with us. One night, we heard a baby crying somewhere behind the wall. We all heard it, all five of us. Swear to God."

We were sitting in Grandma's kitchen. Actually, you were there! Remember? It was summer? Grandma was making coffee. Decaf, of course, always the fucking decaf. She looked over at Mom and said, "You didn't hear a baby crying." She scoffed. "Come on."

"Why is that so unbelievable?" Mom asked her.

"First of all, you were a *very* imaginative kid. And secondly, the baby wasn't *on* that board."

"How do you know that?"

Grandma gave her this tired, uninterested sigh. "Because, honey, that board came from the barn. That's *Robert* on there."

I'd been running my finger down a black strip of stain on the table. I'd thought it was coffee, but when she said that, I yanked my hand back fast.

"You said the barnwood was cursed," I said.

"Well," she said, pouring herself a mug of steaming coffee. "Of course they warned me when I bought the place. But I figured there wasn't any harm in having it in the attic. Nobody goes up there and *touches* it. *In* the house would have been a different thing altogether. You know, Rachel, my friend Helen . . ."

I got up calmly and washed my hands five times in the bathroom, until the skin was pink and raw. I'd touched that stain on her table a lot, and I wasn't sure anymore where her distinction lay between *history* and *curse.*

I couldn't stop thinking about that barnwood like a puzzle. What piece of the picture was in her attic? The shoulder? The leg? The hair? If you got all the barnwood together again, could you remake Lawrence's giant? What would happen? Would it . . . say something to you?

Not that I'd want that.

I mean . . . I could ask it questions, maybe. You know? Maybe it would . . .

Well, never mind.

When I came back from the bathroom, my hands throbbing, Mom was asking, "Why do you always do that? Shoot me down. Tell me I'm a liar."

Grandma calmly sipped her coffee. She cocked her head and smiled sweetly, chuckling. "*Aren't* you? Come on. You didn't have *that* many friends. Who would you have been in the attic with? You've always had a flair for drama . . ."

I don't think Mom said anything back to that. I think she just absorbed it. I sort of remember her face turning red. I remember her crying angrily on the drive home. Just these quiet, bitter tears as she drove, shaking her head. I asked if she was okay, and she laughed. "Yeah, sweetie. Thank you. Sometimes I just hate your grandma so fucking much." She sniffed. "Don't say fuck."

Once, she tried to explain to me that she loved Grandma, but that Grandma had "a lot of things going on." That's why she drank all that decaf. She loved coffee, but she couldn't have caffeine anymore, because even *that* set her off sometimes, made her be really terrible, yell, disappear, spend a lot of money, shit like that. I get that now. Obviously, back then, I had no idea what the fuck Mom was talking about. But looking *back*, it all makes sense. I mean,

I've done the same shit, haven't I? Gone off? A bunch of times. And I'm sorry. But that's *history* now, isn't it?

Ha.

Anyway, I don't think Mom would have talked about that with you. About Grandma, I mean. Stuff like that is mostly passed down through women. I don't mean that in a dick-ish way, I'm just saying. I think she wanted to protect you, but she was always open about her shit with me. She talked about her depression and everything else like she had something lurking inside of her. Like it wasn't a chemical thing, or something she could keep mostly in check, but a dark mark on her soul. Like something had squirmed its way into her and settled around the base of her spine. She even called it a stain. A stain on her bones.

I think about that a lot.

I wanted so bad to hold her, so much of the time. I know you did, too. But she was always too tired, always somewhere else. And when you'd ask her for things, it was like you were annoying her. So you learned to leave her alone. Then she'd get pissed you weren't talking to her, and it'd be this weird cycle . . . I hated it. And I wish I could say I hated *her*, but that's bullshit. I miss her. I miss Grandma, too. It seems so long ago that Grandma died, but I guess she only drifted off, like, five years ago now? Jesus. That was just after I graduated from Edenville. You'd just moved to the city, just met Becca. You guys hadn't even started dating yet.

Man. Time. Feels like eight hundred years ago we were spending Christmas Eve in Grandma's loft. All cozy in our little sleeping bags.

We couldn't sleep because we were trying to see if Santa would come. And then it occurred to me:

"Tom?"

"Rachel?"

There was a lot of snow outside, and no clouds. The moon

bounced off all the white, throwing huge shadows across the ceiling. More than enough light to see the outline of your face. Blinking at me in the dim. I was eight, and you were seven. You were my best friend.

"Grandma doesn't have a chimney," I pointed out.

It took a second for the significance of this to sink in. Then you asked, "So . . . where's Santa gonna come in?"

"Through the trapdoor?" I said.

You looked up at the trapdoor, covered in the shadows of branches outside. Even though neither of us knew yet about the attic stain looming over us, we must have felt it because you said, "I don't know if I like that."

"Me neither."

You turned onto your back and stared upward. I followed your lead. And we stayed like that for hours. I remember the sun started to come, and I could see your eyes. You have eyes like clouds, did I ever tell you that? The darker they are, the more likely they are to rain. It's something I love about you. I love that I can see how dark you feel. How scared you were, imagining Santa crawling through that trapdoor.

Whatever. Santa never came.

Mom bought the set of knives at a flea market in the Mill. She texted me a picture (we'd been on tenuous good terms again, after not talking for a while), and she asked if I thought they were nice. If I wanted them. They came with a slip of paper that claimed they were carved from certified Renfield barnwood. She thought maybe I'd think that was cool, but I was pissed because it felt like she was saying I should cook more. Like, "Here's some nice knives, don't you want to take better care of yourself?" It wouldn't have been the first hint she'd dropped about my weight and fast food. Like, I *teach* all day. I'm too tired to cook, and I'm not making an *insane* amount of money, so . . . So I asked her why she spent so much money on things she didn't need. I was also pissed because I'd *just* asked her if I could borrow some money. I'd spent too much on random bullshit and I needed help with rent, which is *expensive* in Bent these days (Bent rent haha), and she said she couldn't help, I needed to be more responsible, so this felt like a doubly personal attack, even though I know it wasn't. I know that. But things got heated. Instead of explaining any of that shit about rent and my own self-care like an adult, I went on this tangent about stained wood, and the next thing we knew, she was asking why I was such an ungrateful, backward, superstitious daughter. Honestly, that's how our arguments always went, so I fell into the flow pretty easily, asking her why she always refused to help me even when I was drowning, and she was telling me that she hadn't been depressed before she had me, and I was asking her why she had me, then, and she was telling me she wished she hadn't, and I said *I* wished she hadn't and I didn't wanna talk to her anymore. And then three minutes later: "Goodbye then."

This was all over text. When people tell me it's not my fault, that's always the first thing that comes to mind: Yeah, fine. But it was all over *text*.

The very next night, her neighbors found her body.

Did I tell you the neighbors were the only ones there to clean up her blood? They felt, for some reason, responsible for her house. And I started drinking the *second* I heard Mom was dead. Of course I did. Anyway, the police or whoever didn't want to do it, and I was in no condition to drive, so the two elderly women who lived next to Mom cleaned up her blood by themselves. At the wake, I told them they hadn't needed to do that, I could have gotten there. They said it really couldn't have waited, and I wasn't answering my phone. They could smell Mom from their own homes. When they went in, her place was already filled with flies. The neighbors said the flies gorged themselves so much that if you managed to smash one, it'd pop bright red. They said she drained herself out onto the kitchen floor, pooling into the little hall and the foyer . . .

Fuck.

So . . . there it is. All my pieces of history and all the stuff about Mom I hadn't told you yet. I hope you understand and appreciate all this. The *history* of it all. How it keeps me up at night.

Look, Otto Mason Jr. probably had his own reasons to hang himself. Those poisoned peas might have been a coincidence. Maybe whatever fucks with our survival instinct is our own blood, not the blood of the county.

But can I say that for *sure*? Can I say that about Mom? Or is there some other madness there? Something that draws us in, makes us taste it, drives us so crazy we become someone else. A cannibal, a child-eater, a monster. Someone who berates their own daughter for being born.

Anything is possible, isn't it? Aren't these stories evidence of that?

That's my point with all this. Everything has roots. A history teacher told me that once. Even if those roots are so small you can't see them, they're there. Even if they're a single tiny stain in a big house. *History* infects everything.

I just can't stand the thought that maybe it *is* my fault, or that some people just go nuts. The stain is an easier thing. A scapegoat. Some way I can believe things don't just *happen*. People can't just . . . *be* the way they are. It's much easier to believe there's some crazy blood curse looming over all of us, rather than a thousand random little things.

I asked a friend of mine from the *Lillian Journal* about this at Mom's wake. She's usually pretty good with Renfield shit. A healthy skeptic, always game to talk history. In fact, she helped me dig up a lot of the old files I used for this report. So I thought she might have something constructive to say here. But she just said, "Oh man, I think about that all the time. When I broke my leg, was it just because I was running down the stairs like a dumbass? Or was it the stairs *themselves*? When my old boss Bill lost both of his eyes in that accident, *was* it an accident? Or something, you know, spooky? I drive myself crazy with that shit."

And suddenly her hand was on my shoulder. "Who knows, Rach? You can't torture yourself over it."

"Right," I said, sliding away from her.

The wake was winding down at that point. You were already holed up in your old room, watching tv with Becca. So I took a bottle of wine outside and sat on Mom's old wooden stoop. I stared out at the woods beyond her backyard. It was cloudy, and humid. My skin felt like it was expanding. Melting. I watched the trees sway in a silent wind. I watched a blue jay swoop down, grab a twig from the ground, and flap its way back up to a small nest buried in the branches of an oak. I watched it jostle and shake that twig into place. I could almost see the details of the nest from where I sat, or I imagined I could. I imagined I saw all the twigs and bits of paper and an old swath of plastic mesh. I thought about all the trees those twigs came from. Spread apart, then joined together in this one little home. I thought about the plastic mesh and the kind of fruit it'd held. And I wished that nest would fall. I wished it would topple over onto the ground, so I could run over and smash it with the bottle until everything was shards.

I drank, and drank, and I threw the empty bottle into the woods. I thought about burning it all—the entire county and all its *history*—to the goddamn ground.

I know. It could all be bullshit. Maybe I've wasted my time proving some point that doesn't exist. Maybe ole Lawrence *was* just nuts, and everybody else (me) is just paranoid. Maybe it doesn't even matter. Maybe the bottom line is just: There's a *lot* of scary-ass shit out there. Who even knows how much. And I want you to know you're not alone in it.

I know we've drifted. I know. I was lonely and scared, and I felt stupid admitting that. But I want to do a better job now of being there for you. For both of us. It's stupid to *choose* to be alone. I bet five bucks, if everybody just said, "Hey, I feel lonely, I feel scared," instead of doing all this fear-bullshit people do, everybody'd realize that everybody *else* feels pretty poor, too. And then maybe we'd all stop . . . sliding away.

So this is me reaching out. I'm lonely, Tom. I feel shitty. I'm sorry. Let's be lonely together again. Together in this weird-ass world. Please? You're not alone, Tom. I know that's hard to hear, but it's true. Nobody's alone.

Anyway, I hope you're okay. I hope you read all of this. I hope you understand. And I really, *really* hope you write back. Please?

I love you, Tom. Really, I do. And I want to show you that I *am* here for you. That you don't have to slide away into all the . . . the *muck* of the world.

In fact . . . I have a little proposition for you. If that's cool.

That thought I mentioned earlier, about all the pieces of Renfield wood like puzzle pieces? Like what would happen if you put the barn wall back together again? Well, having Mom's stained knife made me think. I've got this, and I've got that big slab I know where to find, in that dude's living room up in Lillian. That's two pieces. Then there's Grandma's house attic. I can probably talk my way in there, if the current owners are cool. And a professor of mine at E.C. had a bit of Renfield oak in his desk, I know. There's a bar in the Falls that has another big slab, and the Edenville Library ladies have a few records here and there that seem suggestive.

That's what I call a solid fucking start.

So I'm gonna do it, Tom. I'm gonna dig deeper. I know I've sailed a little close to the sun here a couple times, but I'm gonna find all this wood, and I'm gonna rebuild Renfield's giant. I'm gonna get it to talk to me, the way it talked to Lawrence and Detective Walt Harren almost a century ago. I'm gonna find out what it wants from us, from me, from Mom. I can almost hear it through the knife. Almost. If I press the blade into my ear hard enough to make myself bleed, I can *almost* make out the words. So imagine if I had the *entire. Fucking. Wall.*

I know you probably still don't believe in all this. But if you see any Renfield wood, *tell* me about it. Please? Tell me where to find it. Tell me who to kill, who to eat, to get my hands on it, and I fuckin will. Because I am tired of this bullshit, Tom. Tired of not knowing.

So really, yes, I had an ulterior motive in writing this. Sorry. But what else is new. You can *help* me here, Tom! In fact, you *have* to, or I'll never speak to you again. That's a joke, a joke. But please do tell me about any wood you know of. Please. Especially the barnwood. Especially the eyes.

I'm gonna visit that doctor in Lillian again. Then down to the Falls to see my buddy Andrew. He'll have some ideas for sure. I know, this is a mediocre idea at best, but I'm going, so don't even start. Might as well go tonight. I'm up, I'm at em. Risky? Yes. But I'm okay with that. It's *worth* the fuckin risk. It helps me feel *alive*.

Look, I'll have my phone on me if you want to call. I hope you do. I hope you come home so we can do this together. I mean, don't you want to know? I want to find out, together, what's out there. And maybe, together, we can avoid Mom's mistakes. Grandma's mistakes. This entire *county's* mistakes. Maybe together we can listen to these stories, really *listen* to all the madness of the blood, the giant, and the damned. Maybe we can ask the giant directly, *why*. Maybe we can actually learn something. And maybe, somehow, together, we can make *ourselves*—something better.

Love, your sister,
Rachel Durwood

ACKNOWLEDGMENTS

This is the little book that could. *Edenville* opened a lot of doors, and I didn't know I could even write a novel until that book, so I'm very grateful for it. But I love *Poorly Made* with all my heart. *The Poorly Made is* all my heart.

I began this book in earnest in the summer of 2018, but the ideas had been brewing for some time before then. "Wag" was my first-ever publication in January 2017, in *Dark Moon Digest*. I wrote it in January 2016, after driving by a bathtub on the side of the road somewhere outside Hillsdale, New York. Seeing this large ceramic tub waiting by the road, without context, made me realize just how beautifully bizarre the Hudson Valley is. I've lived here for twenty years now, but I never get tired of the balance between night and day, serenity and eeriness, that this valley holds. At a reading recently in Highland, I joked that the Hudson Valley is a very spooky place, "as anyone driving home tonight knows." That got a good laugh, because they *do* know. The roads get twistier here after dark. The trees close in. In the daytime, it's all *oo-ahh*, fall colors, Hudson River, craft breweries, pretty pretty. But there are hidden things lurking in these woods. And from the start, from that very first image of the roadside tub, Renfield County has, to me, been about sharing that spooky magic with everyone else.

After "Wag," "Detour" is the second-oldest child in this bunch. In 2016, I was driving back and forth from Poughkeepsie to Rhinebeck once a week, sometimes more, for a playwriting group I was a part of. We met at the Liberty House, which is sadly no more. But Route 9 became the inspiration for County Road 7 on those drives, and I *did* get stuck on a labyrinthine detour one night that I thought might be my doom. After that came the first season of *Stranger Things*, when Eleven comes out of the woods and approaches a diner from its back door. I wondered what else might crawl out of the woods into our open back doors, and that became the basis for "Cats." I was drafting it during a trip I took in early 2017, riding the Amtrak all around the perimeter of the United States. "Red X" was born from that trip as well, from a conversation I had with a guy who worked clean-up after Hurricane Katrina. He told me he'd been in charge of pulling bodies out of flooded homes. He would float the bodies outside, spray them with a giant pink X so the helicopter could see them, and then wait as they were airlifted away. How that anecdote became *this* story, exactly, I don't remember. But I'd say this is a good example of the truth being worse than fiction. I'd rather meet an alien than have to wait around with the waterlogged dead. "Ellie" began as an intellectual exercise: Could I write an entire story in which every sentence began the same way? Well, I didn't *quite* make it, but it was fun to try. "Southbound G" is an extrapolation of an old man I saw absolutely *noshing* on chicken bones one night in Brooklyn. I assume he was up to no good. "Allison's Face" was born from the image in *Texas Chainsaw Massacre II* when Leatherface holds a freshly carved face up to the light, and Stephen Graham Jones's story "Solve for X," in which the protagonist ends up helping the "antagonist." "Glitch" started as a story about human incubators, in which Tom's beeping hand indicated he was ready to hatch. Then I went through a horrendous breakup, and the story shifted accordingly. It's one of the stories I'm most proud of in this collection. And I actually don't remember where "Cousin" came from. I guess it just . . . slipped in.

So Renfield grew and grew, and by the time I began my MFA at Goddard College in the summer of 2017, I had many of these stories mapped out already. "Hector Brim" was the first story I submitted for review during my degree, and actually the first story I ever wrote as a "serious writer," back in 2015 when I was studying abroad at Oxford (shout-out St. Catherine's) and just starting to pay attention to what it meant to be a writer. Brim is based on a tour guide I met that spring at the concentration camp in Terezín, outside Prague. He shouted his entire tour at us, and carried in one hand the largest, heaviest-looking messenger bag I've ever seen. I was amazed at the tangible weight of the anger he carried in that bag.

John McManus saw an early draft of "Brim" and helped me realize that I had a much stronger voice than I had thought. John, thank you for your years of graceful encouragement and advice. Sherri L. Smith helped me understand where my characters were coming from and how I might make them more human. Sherri, thank you so much for keeping me grounded. Michael Klein met the very first iteration of "The Stain" with high praise. I told him I'd just heard about the Lawson Family Murders on *My Favorite Murder* (shout-out, fellow murderinos) and I was fascinated by all the weird details in that case. How the neighbors buried sheets of frozen blood in the yard. How Charlie Lawson seemed normal until a few months before he killed his whole family. How they opened up the house after the murders and people pocketed souvenirs from the property, including the raisins off Mrs. Lawson's final cake, resting in the kitchen . . . There are many more odd details from that case that didn't quite make it into this world, so I highly recommend checking it out if you're intrigued by the real-life origins of the Renfield murders. *Deadly Secrets: The Lawson Family Murder* is a nice bite-size retelling of the case in podcast form.

John, Sherri, and Michael were all wonderful advisors during my time at Goddard, and I am ever grateful to them for helping shape this landscape. If you're looking for a low-residency MFA, look no further than the Creative Writing program at Goddard College. The moment I stepped foot on campus, I knew that place would change my life in the best possible way.

Thank you to all the amazing people I met there, some of whom read *endless* drafts of this monster with me, especially Ben Hennesy, Jamie Sheffield, Aimee Delong, Ron Estrada, G. D. Brown, Amy S. Cutler, Diana Rush, Dennis Rush, Campbell Copland, Dylan Boyer, Aurora Hurd, Sarah Weiler, Sofia Molimbi, Smith Elder, Patrice Gerideau, Susannah Melone, Miriam Tobin, Lisa Chambers, Smitty Abel Smith, and above all: Jennifer Skura Boutell. Thank you so much, Jen, for all the late nights. You held my hand through this book and *you* made it possible. Thanks, Gus. And sorry to anyone I forgot!!

So, after graduating from Goddard in summer 2019, I took about six months to tighten this collection up even further (in other words, I was working on "one final story" that actually turned into what is now a trunk novel, lol oops), and I began querying it around to agents. I spent a year sending this around during the pandemic. Apparently, it's very hard to debut with a collection! People want novels! But God bless Claire Freaking Harris for pulling this out of the slush. She saw promise in this world, and I can never thank her enough for that. Claire got me that first meeting with Vedika Khanna, in which I explained the vast conspiracy theories I had about this whole world. Vedika guided me toward starting Ren-field's story with *Edenville*, but *this* is the book that gave rise to

Edenville. This is the book that kept me going through some very turbulent, difficult years. I often say that Renfield County is a literal depression upon the earth, and this is why. It was the symbolic place I poured myself into, for many lonely nights. So thank you, *Poorly Made*, for being there.

Alright, enough of the sappy stuff. Let's do some rapid-fire thank-yous:

Claire Harris, thank you for helping bring this book into the world! I am so grateful to you and everyone else at P.S. Literary. You all are incredibly kind and warm and fun and smart. How do you do it??

Ariana Sinclair, thank you for smoothing out the wrinkles in this one *again*. I was so excited to work with you on another book after *Edenville* and look what we did! I couldn't ask for a better editor or teammate. Go Crows!

Vedika Khanna, thank you for taking a chance on this! I am eternally in your debt, and I think of you often, wishing you well.

Jesse Rogala, thank you for always sitting with me and talking about writing and life. You taught me to see the world as a beautiful, accessible place, and I will always love you for that. Wilderdudes for life!

Ashley Pecorelli, thank you for all the drinks at Two Saints and other city adventures while I was developing this. ZBZ 4 life!

Thank you, Alec Frankel and Debbie Deuble Hill at Independent Artists Group, for embracing this collection.

Thank you to all my fellow writers and heroes who read *Edenville* and helped spread the good word about Renfield County: Chris Panatier, Todd Keisling, Richard Thomas, Stephanie Feldman, Lucy A. Snyder (my fellow Goddardite!), Eric LaRocca, Clay McLeod Chapman, P.L. McMillan, Kristi DeMeester (also thank you for all the Scent From Hell candles, I know I gush about them a lot, but they're truly my fave), Tim Waggoner, Jim Chambers, Gemma Amor, and of course R.L. Stine.

Thank you to the wonderful editors who published some of these stories before: Lori Michelle & Max Booth III, Tyler Berd & the Scummy crew, and Erik Secker. Thank you, Ellen Datlow, for reprinting "Ellie" in *Year's Best*. That was a dream come true.

Thank you, once again, to the entire William Morrow team: Leah Carlson-Stanisic for your beautiful designs and MAP!! Ana Deboo for your remarkably careful eye. Amanda Hong for being a total badass. And of course, Kaitlin Harri and Kelly Cronin: I am *so* lucky to be working with you. I couldn't ask for a better marketer and publicist.

Thanks to all the Titan team for handling the UK side of things: Sophie Robinson, Daniel Carpenter, George Sandison, Bahar Kutluk, and Miss Nat Mack for her gorgeous *Edenville* cover.

And oh my god, y'all, my fucking *mom*. Mom, thank you for sheltering me and for pushing me to soar. You are the guiding light of my time on this earth. Thank you for helping me feel whole, and never alone. I love you frafr.

ABOUT THE AUTHOR

Sam Rebelein holds a BA in English and Education from Vassar College, and an MFA in creative writing from Goddard College, with a focus on memoir and short fiction. His work has appeared in a number of speculative fiction publications, including *PseudoPod*, *Bourbon Penn*, *Planet Scumm*, *The Deadlands*, *Press Pause Press*, Ellen Datlow's *Best Horror of the Year*, and elsewhere. His first novel, *Edenville*, was nominated for a Bram Stoker Award. For more about Sam (and pictures of his dog), follow him on Instagram @rebelsam94. He lives in Poughkeepsie, New York.

Discover more from
SAM REBELEIN

An unsettling, immersive, and wildly entertaining debut novel from "a major new talent!" (R.L. Stine), for fans of Paul Tremblay and Stephen Graham Jones.

"[A] delightfully gooey blend of gothic, cosmic, folk and body horror churned by a sharp-bladed critique of academia."

—Lucy A. Snyder,
Bram Stoker Award–winning author of *Sister, Maiden, Monster*